MW01193764

NIGHT WATCHER

DAPHNE WOOLSONCROFT

GRAND
CENTRAL

New York   Boston

Cover design by Alexander Lozano. Cover photos by Getty Images and Shutterstock. Cover copyright © 2025 by Hachette Book Group, Inc.

Grand Central Publishing
Hachette Book Group
1290 Avenue of the Americas, New York, NY 10104
grandcentralpublishing.com
@grandcentralpub

First Edition: July 2025

Grand Central Publishing is a division of Hachette Book Group, Inc. The Grand Central Publishing name and logo is a registered trademark of Hachette Book Group, Inc.

The publisher is not responsible for websites (or their content) that are not owned by the publisher.

The Hachette Speakers Bureau provides a wide range of authors for speaking events. To find out more, go to hachettespeakersbureau.com or email HachetteSpeakers@hbgusa.com.

Grand Central Publishing books may be purchased in bulk for business, educational, or promotional use. For information, please contact your local bookseller or the Hachette Book Group Special Markets Department at special.markets@hbgusa.com.

Print book interior design by Taylor Navis

Library of Congress Cataloging-in-Publication Data
   Names: Woolsoncroft, Daphne author
   Title: Night watcher / Daphne Woolsoncroft.
   Description: First edition. | New York : Grand Central Publishing, 2025.
   Identifiers: LCCN 2025002257 | ISBN 9781538770900 hardcover | ISBN 9781538770924 ebook
   Subjects: LCGFT: Thrillers (Fiction) | Novels
   Classification: LCC PS3623.O7257 N54 2025 | DDC 813/.6—dc23/eng/20250221
   LC record available at https://lccn.loc.gov/2025002257

ISBNs: 9781538770900 (hardcover), 9781538770924 (ebook)

Printed in the United States of America

LSC-C

Printing 1, 2025

For those who have looked evil in the face.
And anyone who has lost a loved one to a monster.

"I have a perfect cure for a sore throat: cut it."

—Alfred Hitchcock

Drawn by

NOLA
AGE 8

1

HIM

The creak, the squeak, from in the night,
Is quite enough to cause a fright.
But when you see his wielding knife,
It's far too late, he'll take your life.
He lurks from deep beyond the gray,
He thrives as loose among the prey.
Like a fox, to his hen,
This "He" is called the Hiding Man.

His first victim's stifled scream echoes in his ears as he composes each line, acting as background noise to his typing. Mere hours ago, while he drew his blade across her throat, her lips pressed against his gloved hand, the woman wrestled for mercy. Mercy, compassion, pity that would never come. It now forms as an unforgettable memory in his mind, one he has been replaying repeatedly since its recent genesis.

In clean gloves, he tugs the poem from his aged typewriter and settles it delicately into a manila document mailer.

His breath is heavy against the mask, with only thin slivers of air available through the mouth slit he cut out himself. But wearing it completes his transition like new skin, letting him embody the man of his choosing—his making. He's finding it loathsome to remove the newly created mask from his head, nearly wishing it would melt into his flesh and become his authentic face.

With his nondominant hand, he scribbles the Portland Police Department's address on the front of the mailer and thinks still of the screams, and the sirens approaching the dead woman's house, and the pigs finding his slaughtered hen. A tight smile forms beneath the fabric.

He knows this is only the beginning.

He's just getting started.

2

NOLA

Twenty Years Later

I play with the silver rings on my right hand while a raspy-voiced woman from Massachusetts spews a horror story she claims occurred just yesterday. Sliding them on and off my index and middle fingers, I let my mind wander to a different place. I don't know where it takes me, but I follow for half a minute or so. When I realize I've faded, I adjust in my seat and undertake my usual role of Attentive Radio Show Host.

During certain stories, I slip away into my own head, often wondering how many of the tales I'm told are elaborately crafted in hopes of fooling me on live radio. To my knowledge, this has happened several times, leaving me to scramble for a clever response. Most stories we're told feel authentic, the person's tone showcasing fear and realism. But I guess it depends on your beliefs.

Having heard stories like these my whole life, I automatically believe in it all. Spirits, aliens, even the boogeyman. It's hard enough to accept that we're all alive with skeletons and feelings and problems, spinning faster than we can comprehend on a giant sphere. Seeing doesn't have to be believing.

So far, the woman on the line—Maggie—has told me that she visited a lake outside of Boston with her granddaughter and decided to cut their rowing trip short after the previously sunny skies turned silver and considerably wet.

As they were rowing back to shore, her eleven-year-old granddaughter turned around and saw what appeared to be a woman on the other side of the lake, standing at the shore, very still. And for some ungodly reason, the caller then decided to paddle closer to the unknown figure. She noticed that the woman hadn't moved an inch as she approached, but worse, that her mouth was gaped open and black, just like her eyes.

Some phrases of warning she should consider moving forward: "curiosity killed the cat" and the ever-simple "mind your business." I don't tell her this.

As the caller hurriedly plunged her paddle into the frigid water below, the creature woman, clad in a long white dress, dropped to the ground and scratched at the dirt like a wild animal.

The caller's fear is visceral, almost tangible; her story is somehow leaning away from hokey, especially when she explains that she wants to send us the photos her granddaughter took.

"We've heard stories about women in white, but this one is definitely unique," I tell the microphone.

"Neither of us can stop thinking about her eyes. They were the blackest I've ever seen," the caller says. "I'm telling you. She wasn't human."

I share a look with Harvey through the big window that divides the studio from the control room. He takes over, saying, "Well, let us know if anything else happens, Maggie. And for anyone out there listening, we'd love to know if you've seen something similar in the Boston area. Thanks for dialing in with this one."

He ends the call, and we go back and forth on air, discussing her story along with the terrifyingly real creature-woman we can see in the photos Maggie just sent us via email—which are better than most images we receive. After a night of supposed UFO sightings in the Midwest and a short ghost story from an unknown woman, I welcome this lady-on-the-lake tale.

"All right, Night Watchers. I'm Nola Strate, and this has been *Night Watch*. Until tomorrow night, from Telegraph One and KXOR, stay safe out there."

I pull my headphones off and massage the tips of my ears.

I'd think my ears would be used to these things after four nights a week, three hours per show, and five years of hosting. Instead, my body lightly rejects the technological advancement that is padded headphones.

"That was a great show," Harvey calls from the control room, his voice muffled by the glass barrier between us. I can see the iridescent sheen of his teeth from here as a smile crosses his mouth, his lightly stubbled jawline tightening.

I stare into his blue, sunken eyes a little too long before responding.

"I still can't get over the photos Maggie sent. I'm just going to be imagining her following me down to the bar. All by myself," I say with a hint of sarcasm, pulling the door open and snatching my bag from a cubby.

"If you wait a few minutes, I'll walk down with you. That, or face the wrath of Lake Lady." He pulls off his headphones and runs his hand through ear-length, chocolate hair, sweeping a tousled lock off his forehead.

"She can face the wrath of my need for some fresh air. If she dares," I say, desperate to get out of the studio.

Our routine includes walking to our favorite bar and drinking something that will warm our bodies after hours of chilling stories. Though, sometimes, I walk alone while Harvey wraps up and posts tonight's show to all the podcasting platforms. Usually that's my editor Josiah's job, but he took the night off for his daughter's dance recital.

Kids. Dancing. Important life stuff.

"I'll keep your seat warm," I shout on my way out the door.

I trudge down the dimly lit staircase that snakes to the KXOR building's main entrance. It's a quiet spot with many nighttime studio vacancies, as most of the company's shows spotlight in the daytime hours. That only adds to the unsettling feeling I get whenever I leave this place by myself after recording.

Old, battered brick walls.

A big, creaky door that slams loud enough to wake the entire neighborhood.

A forever-flickering streetlight located just overhead.

I close one eye in anticipation of the door slam, and it still makes me jump, quickening my pace to the bar.

Despite my general fears, I was drawn to paranormal stories like mother's milk growing up. My father launched the radio show when I was three years old—twenty years before he passed it on to me—and tales of Bigfoot and Bloody Mary replaced those of *The Cat in the Hat* and *Charlotte's Web*. I slept with a stuffed Sasquatch every night until I was fourteen, when he'd become too tattered, like the

Yeti doll I received when I was born. The Yeti doll whose teat I'm told I embarrassingly tried to suck as an infant.

Like I said, mother's milk.

The sound of my feet slipping on the wet cement sidewalk creates a soundtrack for the entire street, with no one else in sight. It's eerie. Petrichor, creepers hiding in bushes, monsters lurking under potholes. I think I hear the familiar crunch of branches across the street in a crowd of trees. The imagination runs wild. Then, a squirrel skitters out with a massive acorn hanging out of its cheek. A relieved grin cracks across my face, but I quicken my step anyway.

As soon as I turn at the next block, the city of Portland comes to life, putting me even more at ease. Pairs of people stumbling out of bustling establishments; groups, chatter, loud music in their wake. An uncharacteristically lively Thursday autumn evening.

While I stroll on autopilot, I look at my phone to see a text from thirty minutes ago.

Can't sleep so I tuned in! I love getting to hear your voice when I'm missing you.

I smile to myself and shoot my mom a text back.

Aw. Miss you too. You still awake?

Within seconds, I have an incoming call from her.

"Jeez. What is it? Three a.m. there?" I ask when I press Answer.

"Don't remind me," she says with a lighthearted groan. "I can never sleep when Bryan's gone. But he'll be back from his fishing trip in Portland tomorrow. Maine, of course."

I don't know her husband of two years well, nor his adult children whose residences are sprinkled mostly across upstate New York—where my mom and Bryan also live. Although they've come to visit me sparingly since she relocated, I've never returned the gesture. Not because I haven't wanted to. I've just found traveling arduous in recent years, being tied to the studio's physical location much of each week.

"Well, I don't want to keep you up. I'm just walking to the Noble Fir to wait for Harvey," I say, the bar being an old favorite of hers. I pass a particularly loud pub, causing me to raise my voice. "But I want to finally come visit you guys soon."

"You just missed all the fall foliage, but winter will be beautiful." She suddenly changes her tone to one that's slightly mischievous. "And speaking of Harvey. You could bring him with you."

I look around to ensure he's not within earshot, knowing he isn't. "And why would I want to bring my producer and coworker to visit my mother?" I ask.

She guffaws. "Is *that* all he is to you?"

Harvey and I have been buddies since before I started hosting *Night Watch*, back when he was an assistant producer and my dad was still running the show. I considered him an attractive, slightly-older-than-me thing who worked for my dad. He had a cool job and dressed like Kurt Cobain and was always nice to me when I came into the studio. He's still all those things, but now, we work together.

I gently scoff. "I can't date someone I work with."

"But he's handsome. And he likes you. A mother knows these things."

"I think it's time you get back to bed, you crazy lady." Realizing that I had stopped walking, I continue the four-block jaunt down to the Noble Fir.

"Okay, okay. Well, hey. How about you come over here in a couple weeks for Thanksgiving? Or are you spending it with your dad and what's-her-name?"

This is my mom's way of getting the name of my dad's current girlfriend out of me, even though he doesn't have one. I don't know exactly why my parents divorced when I was fifteen, but I often get the feeling she's still recovering from it in her own way.

"It would be just Dad," I reply. "But I'd love to come see you. Let's talk about it more this weekend when it's not the middle of the night."

"Remember, Bryan and I are heading off on our anniversary cabin trip on Saturday, so I won't have cell service until Monday or Tuesday. I'll try to check in if I can, but don't be worried if I don't pick up. Or if I don't call you during the witching hour."

I confirm the exact location of her trip for safety, and we exchange *I Love You*s and hang up. As I do, my phone buzzes with a local news notification about a car accident on the highway that's parallel to where I am now. It's an update to a developing story from a few hours ago.

It reads:

FIERY CAR CRASH ON I-5 NEAR DOWNTOWN PORTLAND, FATAL INJURIES

Always keeping up-to-date on local news, I scan the article for more. "At around 8 p.m., a vehicle carrying two people from Southeast Portland collided with a semitruck heading northbound as they swerved lanes, according to the Oregon State Police. Jolene Moor, 39, and her son, 12, died at the scene of the crash."

Those poor people.

While I'm lost in thought in the middle of the sidewalk, someone suddenly grabs me from behind. I let out a yelp that sounds more like it would come out of a Chihuahua than a woman. Before I even have time to turn my head and protest, I hear Harvey laughing, putting his hands up to surrender.

"You *ass*," I say through gritted teeth, feeling a bit embarrassed. "That was fast."

"Someone's a little on edge," Harvey remarks. "You saw Lake Lady, didn't you?"

"Yeah. She looks exactly like you."

The Noble Fir is slow tonight, even for a Thursday. The bulbous, midcentury modern lights above create a soothing ambiance, as does the rest of the futuristic log cabin–inspired design. The wooden walls and ceiling make it cozy, and the panel of windows facing the busy street keep it feeling communal.

Harvey and I sit at the glossy cedar bar, him enjoying a beer and me a dirty martini.

"How would your dad feel—" He pauses. "—about making a return for the twenty-five-year-anniversary episode next month?" Harvey finishes slowly before taking another sip.

"I think he'll take any excuse to talk about his writing career and market whatever book he's announcing this weekend."

I don't bury my feelings.

"Well, I think it would be good for download numbers."

"You told me last month that download numbers have been going up a ton lately," I say matter-of-factly.

"Well, yeah, it's still 'spooky season,'" he says with air quotes.

The tinge of snark comes from my relationship with my dad. He's always been the buried-with-work, I'm-too-busy-and-important-for-you type. Even for his one and only child: me. I grew up listening to him on *Night Watch*, using that time to get to know him. I would pretend he was telling me stories in my room, and it was just us two as he lulled me to sleep. Maybe that was why I grew so comfortable with the uncomfortable. Or maybe it's because I've lived through a horror movie.

I shake that last thought from my head quicker than it arrived.

"What's he been working on lately anyway?" Harvey asks.

"Should I drive up the hill and get him so you can hang out with him instead?" I chuckle.

"Whatever," he says, lightly swatting his hand. "It's not my fault you have the coolest dad in the world."

I'm used to people doting on my dad, and part of me understands it. When he asked me to take over the show as he prepared to retire early, I realized how amazing his work was once I was sitting in his seat—even though he could be crass on air, often poking fun of people's stories if they gave him information that sounded fake. But that was part of why so many people loved him. I didn't get it before, as his attempts at being the funny lead translated into egomaniacal babble to me. Though it also gave him a stark realness that people seemed to find exciting.

On air, he was everyone's favorite. But at home, he was absent. And I haven't fully let it go, despite his attempts at making up for it in recent years.

"He's been writing another book, but he hasn't told me what it's about yet," I tell Harvey.

I tip the rest of the martini in my mouth and flag our bartender Alejandro for another, then anxiously chew on the toothpick that hosted two bleu cheese olives minutes ago. Before I can get his attention, a young woman leans on the bar and asks Alejandro for a Lonely Island Lost in the Middle of a Foggy Sea. It's not often that you hear a cocktail with ten words in its name. By the look on his face, Alejandro is just as mystified as I am.

The girl follows his bewildered look up with, "You can just leave out the cold brew if you guys don't have that. I hear coffee liqueur works, too."

Now I really want to know what this drink is.

Harvey interrupts my eavesdropping. "I'm getting a deep inkling that you want to change the subject, so I'll change it for you," he says. "Let's do karaoke."

I let out a laugh and turn around to see the empty stage.

Thursdays are open-mic nights. Since we've been here tonight, only one man has graced the stage with a sad tune about his dead dog. And now that it's close to one, the bar is beginning to shut down the festivities and prepare for closing about an hour from now.

"What?" I say, popping a smoked almond in my mouth. "It's open-mic night, not karaoke night."

Harvey grabs Alejandro's attention as he attempts to make the long-named cocktail. "If I grab a karaoke version of a song from You-Tube, can I plug my phone in?"

Alejandro sighs so deep he gives himself an underbite. "I want to say no so bad, dude," he says with a straight face. "But I guess you can."

Harvey looks at me with pleasure. "It's you, me, and Oasis, baby."

He says that as if it's our weekly tradition, when in reality, we have never done karaoke together. I don't think I've ever done it, period. But the bar is near empty, so I consider it.

I can't say no to this man. "Fine. But I want a shot first."

"Yes!" Harvey says with satisfaction. "What of?"

"Gin? Is that weird?"

"Uh, extremely," Harvey says. "Alejandro! A shot of gin for my friend, the psycho."

Alejandro pauses and stares. "God, you guys are weird."

Harvey joins me, and we both shake our heads in disgust as the clear liquor slips down our throats. He lets out a whooping cheer before taking my hand and pulling me to the stage behind him.

His fingers are soft and nice to hold. But his grip is confident. I don't want to let go.

Before I know it, we're side by side onstage, and I have about ten seconds to guess from the drums alone that he picked "Live Forever." I end up missing the first few words and get a handful of cheers for messing up. But with so few people in-house, it's a humorously disappointing display of appreciation.

There's not a chance my face isn't tomato red from shame, but I give it my all, belting notes and singing to the ceiling, laughing between verses. Harvey does almost too well at mimicking Liam Gallagher's beloved nasality.

As the outro approaches, I meet eyes with Harvey and we repeat "Gonna live forever" into each other with all the heart in the room, and everything feels beautiful and like it's moving in slow motion. For now.

3

JACK

hick Strate returns to the billiards table holding two freshly
opened bottles of beer, the liquid so cold against the humid air
of the dive bar that water vapor is lightly wafting out of them.

"Come on, Chick. I told Tammy I'd be back at a reasonable
hour," Detective Jack De Lacey says, lifting from his pool stance.

Jack's wife, Tammy, has had years to adjust to Jack's after-shift
billiards games with his longtime friend Chick, a weekly ritual they
seldom miss. But tonight's game is running into family dinner time,
something Tammy isn't quite as understanding about.

"Just have one more with me. We have to finish this game anyway," Chick says, removing his denim jacket.

Jack sighs, stroking his stubbled chin. "All right, all right. Can
you grow out of being a bad influence already?"

"Since when am I a bad influence?" Chick asks playfully, taking a
hefty swig of his beer. "You know, if I'm not mistaken, just a couple

weeks ago I agreed to give Ethan some creative writing tips. I'm such an asshole."

"Well, he's been getting into football now, anyway. And he's pretty good. Tammy and I are going to his game at the high school tomorrow night."

"I'm always around if he changes his mind," Chick offers, missing his shot on the billiards table. He cradles the sleek cue in his hands, leaning his black-jeaned hip against the table and motioning for Jack to take his turn.

The dimly lit dive is buzzing with conversation and live music offerings from a local folk band. As Jack surveys the remaining two solid balls on the emerald surface, a burly man drops a quarter on the table's wooden edge.

Chick nods at the man and returns his focus to Jack. "How's work been?"

Jack leans down and tries his shot, missing the solid ball he was aiming for. "You know." He shrugs. "Crime's been going up. City's getting more dangerous." He quickly corrects himself. "Well, it has been for a while. I guess it's just been a different kind of homicide. More shootings, stuff like that."

As Chick drills a striped ball into a pocket across the table, cheering under his breath, Jack adds, "I don't understand why you still live in this city now that you aren't tied to the studio. And with Nola all grown up."

Chick shrugs. "Where else would I be? Living out in companionless seclusion in some nowhere town doesn't interest me. Where's the fun in that?" He banks another shot.

"Sounds nice to me. Safe. Peaceful."

"Peace doesn't exist," Chick says. He pockets his last stripe, eyeing the eight ball.

"You'd think I'd be the one subscribed to complete existentialism with all the shit I've seen," Jack says, drinking down his beer. He sits on the stool behind him.

"Speaking of," Chick starts, "I'm announcing the book this weekend. Just in case you'd need to know for work. For whatever reason."

Jack pauses, a frozen stare taking over his face. "We're really going to talk about that case right now?" He wipes a palm of condensation against his white T-shirt.

"It was just a heads-up," Chick says, returning his gaze to the table.

This is a subject Jack tries to avoid whenever possible. The two-decade taunt of the worst kind of unfinished business never sits well with him. For more than a decade, the case has been unofficially closed. But every year or so, a victim's family member will reach out to Jack, asking for any updates, none of which he's ever able to report. He's a living, breathing disappointment.

Jack moves the lip of the bottle against his mouth, and a pale stinging emerges in his eyes as they remain locked on the blurred hardwood floor. Returning to life, he asks, "How'd Nola take it?"

"I still haven't told her what the book is about," Chick says, head leveled with the table. His eyes remain focused on the desired ball.

"Seriously?"

"It was a long time ago. She's fine. We moved on from it. Just like you and I did from our—" Chick pauses. "—misunderstanding. It's in the past."

"Then how come you haven't told her yet?" Jack asks, guzzling the rest of his icy drink.

Chick leans down, aims for a corner pocket, and sinks the eight ball. "I win."

4

NOLA

The muted sun violently streaming through my curtain wakes me up earlier than I prefer. I immediately wince and grab my forehead, and all the gin I drank last night floods into memory.

Only one more shift until the weekend, my brain reminds me; tonight being my last show in the studio until Tuesday evening.

I roll over to get my face out of the direct stream of light from the overcast sky outside and try to fall back to sleep on the cold pillow next to mine. It's plush and fluffy, begging me to lie into it for hours with my duvet wrapped around me as I slumber diagonally.

This is the side of the bed that—in my despondency—belongs to nobody. Undented, ever empty. Cold, how I like it.

I hug the pillow harder and nearly pop a vein in my temple. My head has a heartbeat and my stomach acts like it hasn't seen food in weeks.

I roll back over to my side and reach for the little white bottle of ibuprofen, pour a few liquid gels into my mouth, and drink them down with water from my nightstand. Far too exhausted and hurting to crawl out of bed quite yet, I grab my phone from the charger and scroll through it as a distraction.

With one eye open, I search through my notifications. One in particular catches my eye. The Northwest Protect app has an alert from twenty-seven minutes ago that reads: *There is a Person at your Front Door.*

It's always eerie to read because of the way it's worded, but considering it was broad daylight when this Person approached my house, I assume they weren't here to rob me but, instead, drop off a package or some mail.

I click on the notification to watch the recorded video and am surprised to see that it's Harvey, walking down the stone pathway to my front door with a large, pink box. Without ringing the doorbell—surely assuming I was still asleep—he opened the box to showcase an array of colorful donuts to the camera, closed it, set it on my doormat, and sent me a wave before promptly turning around and leaving.

Despite feeling soul-sucked from the liquor, I can't help but grin at this gesture.

The app also informs me that at 3:15 a.m., my side door camera went out and didn't come back on until 3:37 a.m.

My neighborhood is the safest in the city, but we still get porch pirates and houseless people wandering around every so often. Those aren't the sole reasons that I have security cameras. It's mostly because of the paranoia my job instills in me, as if I believe shadow men or aliens are going to come to my house in the night. I don't, but I prefer being safe and informed.

I lock my phone, slide into the slippers at my bedside, and clomp down the stairs to the front door. It's a pathetic, steady movement with squinted eyes to avoid the blazing lights from the curtainless windows in my house's stairwell. I reach the door and drag the box inside while crouched on the floor like a goblin.

A note is scrawled on top of the box that reads HAPPY HANGOVER! SEE YOU TONIGHT in Sharpie.

I snap a photo of the box and text it to Harvey along with the word "Lifesaver" before heading into the kitchen with my unexpected breakfast.

Pulling myself to the French press, I somehow find the strength to grind coffee beans and boil water. The house is quiet, filled with nothing but the sounds of a sloshing kettle and the rumbling water in its belly.

In the last two minutes, any remaining sun has escaped behind the gloom, painting a foggy scene over Portland. The view is rich with near-black clouds and dark green Douglas fir trees, wrapping around the city like I live in a snow globe. The existing rainfall outside makes for a barren street, hosting only an Amazon delivery truck and parked cars. From the window, I glimpse scenes of neighbors in their houses below: a crew of teenagers scarfing breakfast before school, a man chain-smoking at his desk, people walking past windows, others talking to a hidden person across the room. It's a perspective I've enjoyed for more than a year now, living in the solitude of my pretend castle on the sloping hillside looking down at the city, the gaping river, and the famed mountains, not yet forming even basic relationships with my neighbors. It's part of my ever-difficult quest to find like-minded creatives in a neighborhood of generational wealth.

While the kettle begins to whistle, I head for the balcony to ensure my side outdoor camera is in working order after its middle-of-the-night failure. But as I cross the room, my mind is instantly filled with dread when I spot something strange, distracting me from my mission.

As I approach the balcony door, my eyes catch a glimmer on the floor. The daylight seeping through the door's glass pane reflects off a spot of water on the hardwood, just in front of the indoor floor mat. It's a single left boot print, as if someone began to step into my house before realizing they had water on their shoes, and then stepped back to wipe them off on the grippy mat.

My heart drops when I shift my gaze up and notice the balcony door behind it is unlocked. I think about last night, seeking a memory that will explain this away. I remember parking in the garage and walking up to the balcony through the side gate—as I often do in the rain when I don't want my car to sit out on the street by my front door. It was most definitely pouring when I got home, creating a logical conclusion for the boot print: It's my own.

I was exhausted and drunk when I stumbled in, stunting much of my memory.

But as much as I try to make sense of it, fear lingers. The kettle is now screaming—like a warning. All my senses tell me that I should turn around, like someone must be standing behind me. I rotate on my heel as my vision blurs from the movement. When I steady myself and peer around the rest of the room, I don't see anyone. The room is empty.

I hustle to the kettle and shut off the burner as I try to make sense of the print.

When I return to it, I see that it's mostly dry—as though it's been there for hours. Could it be, say, seven hours old, when I was last on the deck as the rain came down? It's so foreign for me to forget to lock the door. My paranoia ensures I'm meticulous about it. It makes the whole situation that much more unsettling.

I stand on the mat barefoot and align my left foot with the print. It certainly looks bigger than my foot, but is it bigger than my boot print? I can't be sure right now. Unease stops me from ascending to my bedroom for the pair I wore last night.

I don't see any other footprints or indication that someone was in my home. And if there was, I'm sure I'd recognize it.

As I creep around my house looking for the boogeyman, the space feels like a vicious maze. I don't find anyone under my bed, nor in my guest room, the office, or the creepy electrical room that I try never to go into.

And although I'm put at ease that no one's hiding away, I can't help but wonder if someone had been here.

After a heavy afternoon of emails and thinking about the now fully dried boot print, I sit in my open-concept dining room for a dinner break, looking forward to getting out of the house and into the studio tonight.

The rain lets up for the first time all day as the sun says its final goodbyes beyond Mount Hood, penetrating the nearby clouds as it does and creating a beautifully monochrome twilight. I salute its departure from my wooden dining table and shovel spaghetti into my mouth, licking remnants of marinara from the edges of my lips. I sprinkle more parmesan atop what's left and take another bite as I watch the sky darken and streetlamps pop on in rapid succession across the city below. There are only two that populate my street, and they cast a friendly glow on the asphalt.

I push my chair back and walk over to my kitchen sink, painting the white porcelain pink with tomato sauce as I rinse the bowl. My mind is blank, my eyes still fixed outside as I return to the table to finish drinking my apple kombucha.

And then something moves in my peripherals. I cast my gaze at one of the streetlamps, expecting to see a familiar neighbor cross under the radiance and head into their house.

Next to a white utility van, silhouetted from the light above, is a figure, but they're not heading anywhere. Because it's so dark, I can't tell which direction they're facing, or what they're looking at; they're just standing still a few feet in front of the streetlamp. On any other day, though consistently aware of my surroundings, I probably wouldn't be giving this visual a second thought. But with the unresolved boot print still lingering in my mind, I can't be too cautious.

Since my house sits on a hillside, the ground floor is technically on the second floor. From up here, in the shadows of my own home, I don't immediately think I'm catching the person's eye. I wonder for a moment if it's my best friend Amoli, who should be stopping by for tea any minute now.

But I don't know why Amoli would be standing there, not moving, not on her phone, not doing anything at all. The person below doesn't appear to be talking to anyone, or stretching before walking up the sloping street that wraps around my house. They're completely still. Maybe their dog is up in the bush doing its business, and they're simply waiting for it to finish up while they stare into space and think back on their day.

I stride out to my balcony to assess the situation from the edge of my deck. Neighborhood watch: party of one. I lean against the cold iron railing and take a deep breath, then coolly look around and land my eyes on the streetlamp as I exhale, covering the figure in frosty air. They're still standing there, in the very same position.

The wind sweeps the hair from my neck, causing goosebumps to rise on my collarbone. Trying to act casual, like I'm not out here to spy, I look at the bridge that connects one side of Portland to the other, reflecting on how every tiny car I can see holds people—going somewhere, doing something. I feel much less alone thinking of all the little humans down there, feeling every emotion there is to feel, all at once. There are lights of every color scattered as far as I can see, until the only thing I can make out is silhouetted mountains—black against a darker shade of black.

I look back to my left, hoping to catch the sound of a big dog rustling against some leaves, marking its territory and finally returning to its owner by the van. But I don't. And when I look back at the person, they seem to have gotten closer to me, disguised in even more darkness than before, still totally unrecognizable. I play the Non-Final Girl in a Horror Movie, putting on my strongest voice to say, "Excuse me, can I help you?"

For a few seconds, they don't move, as if they didn't hear me. Like my words bounced off the frigid air in front of me and flew right back into my mouth. I wait a few more beats before deciding to speak again, but as I'm about to say "Hello?" and only get out the "H—," the person slowly picks up their hand and waves. It's a painfully unhurried motion—almost robotic. I wouldn't be surprised if their joints made pitchy, squeaking sounds as though they were corroded. Based on the curve of their palm, I can now determine that they are facing me, motioning at me.

Normal people don't stand on the street, camouflaged by nightfall, and stare at other people—whether they know them or not. Especially once they've been caught. When you're caught, you're supposed to awkwardly chuckle and move on, knowing you were doing something off-putting. But this person isn't doing that.

They're taking ownership of the fact that they've been seen watching me.

Against such a regular week, this occurrence combined with the boot print is enough to send me into a mini spiral. My life is fairly uneventful; never have I felt particularly unsafe in my home. But suddenly, I regret living alone in the large house looming behind me. Amoli can't get here soon enough.

What is going on today? I ask myself.

Purely because I don't know what else to do, I lightly wave back, wanting so badly to make this a common neighborhood confrontation. But as soon as I do, they lower their own hand swiftly and cock their head in a way that makes all the spaghetti I just ate frantically churn in my stomach. Then, slowly but with purpose, they start walking up the hilly street toward me.

"Hello!" I hear behind me at the same time the balcony door clicks shut. It's Amoli, my beautiful friend, pinning jet-black curls behind her ear with a smile.

I let out a yelp and grip my own chest. Before I greet her, I whip my head back to see if the person is still stalking up the hill. But they've vanished.

"I didn't mean to scare you," Amoli says with a laugh as she pulls me in for a hug. "Didn't you hear me ringing the doorbell like ten times? I called you, too." She shakes her phone.

I pull my phone out of my pocket to see numerous front door notifications and two missed calls.

"No. Sorry." I quickly change the subject. "Were you just down on the street?" I ask, knowing it couldn't have been her unless she suddenly gained the power of teleportation. "Down *there*?" I emphasize, pointing to where I spotted the person seconds ago.

"No, I parked up top by the front door." She pauses in concern. "Is everything okay?"

I lean over the railing to look under the balcony at the garage, and then move to the left side of the house to check the sloping road. But no one is on the street.

"Should I be worried right now?" Amoli continues, halfway between unsettled and sarcastic.

"Yeah," I whisper. "I mean no." Clearing my throat, I add, "I've just been freaking myself out today. Thanks for coming by." I squeeze her shoulder. "It's freezing out here. I'll put on the kettle."

Amoli joins me inside, where I promptly lock the balcony door before skittering over to the front door to do the same.

Getting more concerned looks from Amoli now, I act like nothing is bothering me. If I rant about the person outside, or the boot print, it'll all become real. I opt out of letting these silly—albeit strange—occurrences take over my night, prepared instead to have a friendly chat with my closest friend before I need to leave for work.

I snatch two Earl Grey sachets from the cupboard above the stove and boil some water, asking Amoli about her day and making affable conversation like everything is fine. Like I'm not secretly worried that someone has been stalking my house.

5

NOLA

I persuaded Amoli to stay with me until I had to leave for work so we'd get into our cars at the same time and there wouldn't be even a nanosecond where I was in my house alone with my thoughts. And alone with whatever it is I saw down on the street waving at me.

That still, transfixed figure. Taking an undetermined interest in me, in my house. Motionless until I asked if I could help them.

Why did I ask that? Why did I wave back?

As though I were inviting them in. Welcoming them, in some way.

Because right after I returned the gesture, they started trekking toward me. What would have happened if Amoli hadn't shown up when she did? Were they even coming over to me? Am I severely overreacting?

As we said our goodbyes, I pictured the figure standing outside my garage on the street. I imagined them waiting for me all that time we chatted over tea, itching for the moment I'd arrive at my car alone. The thought creeped into my head between sips and exaggerated laughter. Whenever I could, I'd stand up and pace just so I could look out the window to see if the figure was down there. To see if they were still watching me. But the streets remained occupied by nothing but the fresh blanket of drizzling rain. Maybe it was all in my head.

I'm relieved when I arrive at work to see Harvey and the team already inside, giving me a welcome distraction from whatever I may think is going on at my house.

I run up the big, dark steps leading to the office and studio so fast that when I spring through the door, I'm out of breath.

Harvey gives me a shocked look from his desk, located next to mine. Pulling out his earbuds, he says, "Whoa! Lake Lady chasing you?"

I laugh, too hard, even though that was yesterday's joke. My nerves are bursting out of me, making me sound like a maniacal lunatic. My agitated laughter begins to rub off on Harvey, who begins to chuckle.

"You're early. Not that I'm complaining," he adds.

"I was just feeling antsy at home. Needed to get out," I say as I cross the room and plop into my rolling chair.

Harvey doesn't look away.

"Can I help you?" I ask.

"You're the one who came in here acting weird. Just making sure you're okay." His smile is unwavering.

I clear my throat and wave my hand at his laptop. "Back to work. Nothing to see here."

There's a big window that takes up an entire wall in the office, giving lots of natural light during the day and a beautiful view at night, showcasing people walking to and from restaurants and bars on the busy street three stories down. With brick walls, the office theme could be described as "industrial boho," I guess. The walls are covered with large paintings, while the furniture and décor consist of potted monsteras, Persian rugs, and tufted leather sofas. The kind of place you'd think would have an office dog and an espresso machine.

"What's up? You can talk to me," Harvey says, still prying.

Unlike with my other friends, talking to Harvey always feels uncomplicated. I didn't want to bring any of this up with anyone, but getting his advice could help.

"I think I'm being followed," I say nonchalantly while taking off my coat and hanging it on the hook by the door.

"To work?" he asks. "Like by a listener?"

"No, nothing like that," I say quickly. "Well, actually, I really don't know."

It hadn't occurred to me that it could be a listener of the show. Someone who's obsessed with *Night Watch* and was able to find me online—as disturbing and unwelcome as it is. I shudder thinking about how people's home addresses, phone numbers, and other intimate details like birthdays and personal connections can be found on certain websites.

"What even happened?" Harvey asks.

I pull my phone out of my pocket and Google "Nola Strate address." I audibly gasp when I see that the first link correctly displays it.

"Do you think someone could have looked me up and found my house?" I ask, showing Harvey my screen.

"You should definitely have that record removed."

"On it," I say, following the instructions on the page.

"And what is even going on? What do you mean someone's following you?"

I explain this morning's partially wet footprint. The unlocked balcony door. My brief camera outage. The person waving at me on the street less than two hours ago. I detail to Harvey that I don't know where they went after marching up the hill, that they couldn't have walked up and around my house without me spotting them, or them coming up on my now-working cameras. That they couldn't have gone in the other direction without me catching a fading glimpse. The person was at the intersection of two streets laid out perfectly in front of me. With my sprawling view, I would have seen which way they traveled. But then, what am I saying about them? That they vanished into thin air? None of it makes sense.

"I'm not trying to gaslight you because I believe everything you're saying. But does a small part of you think these could be coincidences? Or are you worried about your safety here?"

He thinks you're crazy, idiot.

Leaping to the conclusion that a listener—or someone—is stalking me is a far cry from a few weird things happening around me. Physically, I'm perfectly all right. No one has hurt me. No one has tried to hurt me.

"Forget I said anything. I'm totally out of line," I say with a smile, pulling my fingers down my face.

Harvey takes a beat. "You have a spooky job. You live alone in that big house. I don't blame you for being scared. But I'm always here for you if something happens," he says with a grin. "Even if you're making it all up."

UFO sightings in Arizona. A haunted hotel in Colorado. Someone in an anonymous location who thinks the FBI is sending doppelgängers into their life. A whole lot more. Friday night is our busiest for call-ins, and as I speak to people about their experiences, Harvey is already vetting the next call. From behind the dividing glass, he'll ask the callers questions like: What are the basic grounds of what you're calling about? Where are you located? He pushes through the stories that sound the most promising, and we hope for the best.

I finish up a call with an Idahoan about their affair with a Ouija board and take the next and likely final call for the evening, depending on how long it lasts. Some calls are quick, with the person on the other end giving brief details and nothing else. Harvey always flashes me an apologetic look when this happens because they're certainly not preferred. But it can be tough to tell how it's going to play out when he only gets a primary idea of the story from the caller before sending it through to me.

"Felicity from right here in Portland, Oregon, welcome to *Night Watch*," Harvey says into the microphone with his radio voice. Since we get calls from all over the country, I'm surprised this one is coming from our literal neck of the woods. They rarely do.

At first, all I can hear is panting. Heavy, breathless heaving. A woman's whimper.

I shoot a look at Harvey, wondering if this is a prank call, and he raises his arms up in confusion. Before I can speak, Harvey repeats himself into the microphone, wondering if she didn't hear him push her through. That's happened before. It's always harmless. But something about this feels different. "Hey, Felicity? You're live with *Night Watch*."

In. Out. In. Out. Hushed, rigid breathing. It sounds like a very scared individual trying to keep quiet. Or a very rude person trying to mess with us. It's impossible to tell.

"Can you hear us, Felicity? This is Nola. Tell us what's goin' on," I suggest kindly.

The breaths get louder. Harvey swipes a flat hand across his neck to indicate he is going to cut the call and switch to another. Before he does, he begins to announce his plans and is stopped.

"We're going—" is all he can make out before he's abruptly interrupted by the woman on the other end.

"Hello? Is anyone there?" the woman whispers.

"Yes, can you hear us? You're live on the air," I chime.

Harvey looks a bit panicked. As producer, the responsibility falls on him to make sure there aren't any big moments of silence, any pranks, any audio issues. I can see him struggling with this, and even though the woman is now—sort of—speaking, he's quickly trying to figure out what to do.

"I think there's a ghost in my house. Right now."

Most callers discuss things that happened yesterday, or last week, or last month, or last year. At soonest, earlier that day. Rarely the same *moment*. And because of that, I'm void of response. I feel mute. I'm caught off guard. But I do my best to draw information out of her.

"What do you see?" I ask.

Still, her voice is low. "I can't believe I'm on live radio again."

Again?

She continues. "Oh god, I'm so sorry. One second. I need to go lock my bedroom door." Following this is denser breathwork, the sound of a twisting knob, something dropping, and the prehistoric moan of weighted furniture being pushed.

With everything any one person knows about ghosts, or spirits, basic knowledge would include no fleshy body, no physical restrictions. So why is she locking doors and moving furniture around?

Harvey fills the silence. "It sounds like our caller is figuring some things out. Again, we're on with Felicity from Portland, Oregon—which is actually where our studio is. So, our guess is she isn't too far away. Felicity says she thinks there's a ghost in her house, so let's hear more about that. Felicity?"

She keeps her tone hushed, only marginally louder than her previous whisper. "Okay, I've moved to my closet where I feel more comfortable speaking. There's a dresser in front of my bedroom door, so that should keep him out."

Him?

"What makes you think this is a ghost? Can you tell us what happened?" I ask.

I want to say this bluntly and rudely because at this point I am officially bothered by this call. It's as though she's forgotten she dialed in to us, and not the other way around. I try to mask my emotions with a respectful tone until I know what's going on.

"Okay, okay. Two nights ago, I started to notice things going missing from my house. Like, first it was keys. I keep them on the hook by my front door every night. But yesterday morning, they were in my laundry room. Then last night, I found them in my bread box, i-in my kitchen," she says. "And it's not just the keys being moved. It's the doors. The past two nights, they've slammed a couple of times and woken me up. And I know it wasn't my cat because she sleeps in my room with me."

"Do you live alone?" I ask.

"Yes. I've lived in the same house for five years, always by myself. But that's not all." More gasped breathing. "I've been feeling like someone's been watching me for weeks now. I can't explain it—it's just this feeling I have. Without getting into too much detail about myself, I'm a mental health professional. There's something called the psychic staring effect. It's still being studied, but it's essentially the phenomenon in which that feeling of being watched is sensed by humans via extrasensory means. And I—" She cuts herself off.

I hear the chime of wire hangers crashing together, proving that she's still in her closet. I look over at Josiah and he has a full-blown what-the-hell face on. I mirror his confusion.

"My apologies. I'm extremely anxious right now," she admits. "Okay. So anyway. I think that's how I know I'm being watched—my body is sensing it. And tonight, I was getting ready to take a shower when I heard a door in my house close. And a few minutes ago, I went out to investigate and saw a shadow. So, I called you guys because you know best. And no one else has been in my house, so I started thinking about everything that's been going on. It's like something is trying to terrorize me, and it's gotta be a ghost. Someone from my past coming back to fool with me."

Admittedly, this call isn't unlike others we have gotten about ghosts. People usually tell us they hear things they shouldn't hear, see things they shouldn't see. Clanging dishes, doors opening and closing, unknown voices, shadowed figures, orbs. But the specifics of this call are off.

"Well, you said you've lived there for five years," I mention. "Have you had experiences like this before?"

I can tell this strikes a chord in her because she lets out a "humph" sound.

"N-not that I can remember. No. But ghosts just pop up sometimes, I mean, don't they?"

Despite what she may think, I'm no expert on the subject. I guess a house has to become haunted at some point, but for all these strange things to suddenly start happening out of nowhere seems odd.

I hear the creaking of a door, making me wonder if she's opened her closet to hide elsewhere. Choosing not to answer her question, I instead ask her another one. "What exactly did you—" is all I can get out.

Because then Felicity releases a bloodcurdling scream. One so piercing and alarming, it makes us all jump in our seats.

"What's going on? Are you oka—" I attempt.

"He's there! He's in the window! He's standing there, watching me!"

"It's outside your house?"

"He's outside my bedroom! Please help me!" Felicity shouts.

Harvey cuts in, voice raised. "Ma'am, we advise that you hang up and call the police. What you're seeing doesn't sound like a ghost. You need to dial 911 now because we can't help you."

I don't even know if she heard a word he said because her shrieks continued the entire time he spoke. We don't know where exactly in the city this woman lives; we don't know her last name, or even if her first name is real. We have no way to get her help if a person is really inside—or outside—her house.

I feel panicked now. I keep adjusting in my seat, chewing my thumbnail bare.

The woman begins wailing like she's in physical pain. Or she's so scared that it's making her hyperventilate. "He's got this ghastly face!" she yells. "It almost looks like a mask!"

My mouth dries up at this comment. No words come out. All I can do is listen.

"Felicity. Please hang up and dial 911," Harvey presses, not wanting to terminate the call himself.

"Please! His face is pure white—i-it looks like there's stitching around his eyes and mouth. That can't be real," she bellows. "What is that?"

A stitched mask? It can't be.

I suddenly feel faint, like I'm going to vomit and pass out simultaneously.

"Oh my god. He's gone. Where did he go?" she cries. There's loud banging on the other end followed by the sounds of movement. "Help m—"

Silence.

I am numb; traumatized at the thought of the call not being a prank.

I think of my own concerns of being watched, and my fear deepens.

This can't be happening. There's no way.

I jump when I hear a knock on the glass, which rips me out of my trance. Harvey is signaling me to announce the end of the show, but I'm paralyzed.

He speaks in my place, his tone befuddled. "We hope Felicity is okay, and we're sorry for that disturbing call. Um. This has been *Night Watch*. Until next week, from Telegraph One and KXOR. Please stay safe out there."

Josiah halts recording.

"Nola, are you okay?" Harvey calls out from his chair.

"Dude, you should have ended the call sooner. What did we just hear? Can we even publish that to podcast apps?" Josiah says.

"I didn't know what else to do, man. How do we even know she wasn't messing with us?" Harvey defends. "Nola!"

All I can do is blink, mouth agape. My whole world is imploding in front of me as I process what I heard. I think I just witnessed a woman's final moments.

Mask. White face. Stitched eyes. Stitched mouth.

The Hiding Man is back. And he's watching me, too. Just like he'd warned me he would.

6

Twenty Years Earlier

Nola and Mia are having a dance party. It's almost past Nola's bedtime, but that's why Mia is unquestionably her favorite babysitter. She's cool. She goes to college, she wears tops that show her midriff, and she lets Nola listen to songs like "Almost" by Bowling for Soup, which includes lyrics about sluts and getting drunk at school; things her mother would find vulgar and inappropriate.

If Chick and Donna found out, they might make those other babysitters come back, and force Mia to go away. So, Nola keeps it their little secret.

Mia is an impressive dancer, and she helps Nola make up different routines that they spend hours memorizing before crashing to the floor in exhaustion and laughter. And that's precisely what they're doing on this December night. Most of the blinds are open in the living room, with the stereo blasting next to the TV. The Strate home has a timeless, midcentury modern theme with a sleek, black leather sofa, a slate fireplace, and stylish pops of color throughout. As Mia and Nola lie on their backs—where the coffee table usually resides—and catch their breath, Nola asks a curious question.

"What's your boyfriend like?"

Mia laughs. "I've told you about him before."

"But I like when we talk about boys."

They roll over on their stomachs and face each other, Nola with her head in her hands and her feet flying back and forth through the air in anticipation. The rug beneath them is warm from all the friction and feels soft enough to sleep against. But Nola is wide awake.

"Well. He's super hot," Mia says, snickering. "He's a little bit older. But those are the guys you want because girls mature quicker than boys. And the last thing you want is an immature little boy, you know?"

Nola blinks. "I want a boyfriend. I think," she mutters.

"When you're twenty-one, you'll have one, too. But for now, you're too good for a stupid boyfriend."

Nola can't help but smile at Mia's words, excited to grow up and become just as glamorous.

"What do you guys do together?"

"Well," Mia breathes. "He takes me to nice dinners, or sometimes we drive to the coast and stay in a hotel on the water. He's very romantic."

Mia glances up at the clock on the wall of the living room. "Shit." She smacks her mouth as if to shove the word back in, remembering she's next to an eight-year-old. They both giggle. "It's getting late. We need to get you showered and into bed before your parents get back."

As Nola clumsily runs up the stairs, Mia pauses and looks out the window as if she heard something. She roots her stance for a few seconds, listening. When she doesn't hear anything else, she follows Nola to the second floor's hall bathroom and stands outside the door while Nola washes her hair and body with soap.

"Are you really scrubbing in there?" Mia asks after a couple of minutes pass.

At first, she's met with silence. Nothing but trickling water.

Mia knocks using the back of her index finger. "Nola? Answer me."

She presses her ear to the door. The rushing water is unchanging. There are no sounds that would indicate Nola is wringing out her hair or moving around. The consistent flow of water sends a worried chill up Mia's spine.

"I'm coming in," Mia announces.

As she slowly pushes the door open, a cloud of warm, humid steam hits her face. She tries to open the door fully, but something is blocking it. She can only open it halfway before stepping in.

"Boo!" Nola shouts from behind the door. She's robed, but the water is still running.

"You little—" Mia stops herself from using whatever word was coming next and shuts the water off. "I'm gonna get you!" she yells. She chases Nola into her bedroom, mimicking a predatory animal and creating claws with her hands.

"Okay, okay, I surrender!" Nola says in a giggling fit.

Mia dries Nola's hair, brushes it, and tucks her into her powder-pink, ruffled sheets. Then she curls a hair behind Nola's ear and wishes her good night. As she crosses the room toward the door, Nola stops her.

"Hold your horses. You need to do your checks, remember?"

Mia turns around and smiles mischievously. "I wouldn't be scared of what's in the closet or under your bed right now. It's when I get you back for scaring me that you should be worried about," she says with a wink. As she crouches on the floor to peer under Nola's twin-sized bed, she adds, "Cause I'm gonna get you back! Or will I?"

After opening the closet and pushing past hangers of clothes, Mia announces, "All clear, kiddo."

Nola's eyes shoot open when she hears a loud *clunk*. She can tell by the distance that it came from downstairs—probably the kitchen. Her room is dark, sans the twinkling nightlight plugged in by her closet door. Nola despises waking up in the night, unable to tear her eyes away from the closet. Surely one of these evenings, something will smell her fear and pop out of it.

Nola checks the clock next to her bedside to see that it's 11:04 p.m. Mia tucked her in only thirty minutes ago, but her mom and dad aren't set to arrive home until midnight. She slithers out of bed, tiptoes over to her door, and cracks it open enough to fit her head through. It sounds like Mia is talking to someone downstairs.

She catches what seems to be the end of a sentence: "—wake Nola up. Hold on, let me check," she hears Mia say.

Wondering who she's talking to and why her name came up, she pauses in the doorway to listen for more but hears footsteps approach the base of the stairs. Nola snaps her head back inside and waits to see if Mia's going to come in and check on her. She's not worried about getting in trouble with Mia; she wants to eavesdrop on her conversation.

As Nola hears the footsteps getting farther away, she knows Mia has returned to her spot in the living room or kitchen. Sneaking back out as quietly as she can, she peeks her head around the corner and listens with intent.

"—last few times I've been over here I just get this creepy feeling," Mia admits, troubled. There's a long pause where no one speaks, so Nola figures she's talking on the phone. Knowing her parents aren't going to be back for around an hour, she slips into her parents' bedroom across the hall, quietly makes her way to their bed, and gently takes a seat. She reaches for the cordless phone on her mom's nightstand and presses On, then Mute.

"—because of her *dad*, it's when me and Nola are alone," Mia's voice says into her ear.

"Girl. You're alone in a house that isn't yours, at night, with no one except a little girl. No shit you're freaked out." This comment came from a woman, someone Nola doesn't recognize. Presumably a friend of Mia's.

"No. You know how many families I babysit for. It just feels different here. Or at least lately. I didn't used to feel like this."

"So, stop working for that family? And I'm telling you this because I'm your friend, but maybe you should get a regular job. Babysitting is so high school."

"Okay, ouch," Mia says.

"I'm sorry. I'm trying to help you reach your potential. It's time to move on, girl."

"I don't want to do that to Nola," Mia sighs. "But maybe you're right."

Nola is hurt and confused by what she's hearing. She has no idea why Mia would be scared to be in her house and why she's thinking about leaving her. She's tempted to hit the Mute button again and say all this into the phone, but Mia says something abruptly.

"I gotta go. I think her parents are home."

"Good. Now go home and *relax*," her friend suggests. "Watch the new episode of *Lost* from last Wednesday already. Love you."

Nola's eyes widen as she looks at the clock again, remembering she's in her parents' room and not in bed as they will expect.

As it's only 11:07, Nola guesses their party must have ended early. She delicately drops the phone back on its base and lunges for the door. In no time, she's back in bed, trying to calm her breathing for when her mom inevitably pops in to check if she's asleep. But as Nola lies in silence waiting to hear her parents' voices, she instead hears Mia's. She can't tell if it was a laugh or a yelp. It was almost like a squeal, if she had to describe it. Whether in excitement or dismay, Nola is unable to decipher. Is she still on the phone? Did her boyfriend come over? Maybe Nola's parents aren't back after all.

Then, Mia squeals even louder. This time, Nola can tell it's not good. It was loud enough to be heard from upstairs, but it was muffled. Something bad is happening downstairs—she can sense it.

Nola runs once again to her bedroom door, sticking her head into the hallway to catch any other incoming noises. There's clanging, more muffling.

Mia is in danger.

Nola's mind races with what to do. Since she doesn't know what's going on, she hesitates to call the police. What if it really is just Mia and her boyfriend goofing around downstairs and then the cops show up? Mia would get in trouble for having him over, and Nola would get in trouble for doing something so drastic. Wouldn't she? Her parents taught her how to dial 911 and said if anything ever happened, to dial that number before calling her mom or dad. Is this the right time to do that?

A full-on scream shatters the night. It was high-pitched and fleeting, like she was halted in the middle of it. Desperate to help, Nola descends the stairs one by one, not wanting to draw attention to herself. The plush carpet mutes her movements, but she takes it easy, one by one. Nola pushes her head forward to look through the living room, where it's now silent, with no one in view. She peers around the corner to check the kitchen.

That's when she sees the most horrific sight she's ever witnessed. A sight she may never be able to get out of her head. Mia is on the kitchen floor, lying motionless on her stomach, with her chin propped against the sparkling tile floors. It's easy to see even from the stairs that much of the blood in Mia's body has spilled out of her neck and produced a scarlet pool beneath her. Her eyes, open ever so slightly, look down at the floor only inches away. From what Nola can see, the nightmarish puddle is growing.

Nola loses all sense of reality, convinced she's in the worst nightmare she's ever had. Tears well up in her eyes rapidly, obscuring everything around her. She wants to cry out for her babysitter, but she's holding her mouth closed, afraid whatever happened to Mia will now happen to her. Her mind is racing, attempting to figure out what occurred over the last few minutes. She thinks about the phone call between Mia and her friend, when Mia said she was scared.

Was she afraid of the person who did this to her? Nola wonders.

Nola collapses on the staircase, gripping the handrail with tears streaming down her face as she silently sobs into her fingers. That's when she hears another sound come from the kitchen. Footsteps. It can't be Mia, and she knows that.

Nola crawls up the stairs backward, afraid to turn her back to the monster who stole Mia from her. When she reaches the top, she stands up. And before she can turn to run, someone comes into view. She can do nothing but stare back in utter terror.

The man at the bottom of the stairs looks wounded. Nola can't quite figure his face out. It's pure white. Something about it doesn't look human. His mouth isn't like a real mouth. It's not

43

open but instead sits in a subtle, flattened smirk, void of emotion. It's lipless, thin, and has stitches around the opening. As she studies his face, she realizes his eye holes are sewn, too. She sees the space within the holes where his pupils rest. That's what ignites the realization that this is a mask. There's no hair on top, just pure white and bald all around. No ears, but the mask includes two small nose holes that are also stitched around the openings. His mask looks homemade. Almost as if he took a colorless rubber balaclava and threaded the holes with black string. He's wearing a black turtleneck shirt, which Nola can only imagine is what keeps the mask tucked in and stops any movement that would expose his real skin. Lying on top of this shirt is an equally black coat, which feeds into the dark gloves covering his hands.

This stranger—this terrifying stranger—is standing at the bottom of Nola's staircase, peering up at her. She knows she needs to get back into her parents' room and use their phone, but time seems to be moving in slow motion; her mind and body aren't operating as quickly as she needs them to.

Seconds after this person appeared at the bottom of the staircase, Nola is on the move. She trips on the carpet, but it only launches her farther into her parents' bedroom. She tumbles in and slams the door behind her, then locks it. She knows the lock won't keep him out if he really wants to get in, but there is nothing nearby that she is strong enough to push against it.

A TV stand, a dresser, the bed. All too heavy. She tries for the nearby dresser anyway but fails. She pushes with all her might, yet it doesn't budge. All she can do is hope that the lock keeps that man out.

Nola reaches for the phone and begins dialing, pressing the wrong keys due to her trembling hands. While she tries to dial correctly, she notices that there aren't any noises coming from the other side of the door. No banging, no stomping, no speaking. *Is he gone?* Maybe she wasn't his intended target.

She is finally able to press 9-1-1 in a row and the line begins ringing in her ear as she tries not to drop the phone.

Knock, knock, knock.

Three knocks beat slowly on the other side of the bedroom door as if he wants to have a simple conversation and not slit her throat like he did Mia's. There isn't a chance she's going to open it.

It takes four painstaking rings before a dispatcher answers the call. "911, what is the address of your emergency?"

"There's a man in my house! He killed my babysitter!" Nola bawls into the receiver. She knows that if the man is on the other side of the door, he can hear every word she says. But she wants him to know she's calling for help. His minutes are numbered.

"Sweetie, what is your address? I'll send help right away," she replies.

"Um, I don't know, I can't think. He's here," Nola cries. "He's outside my door. My parents aren't home." Nola wonders if the man is still standing there, and if she's just ratted herself out, exposing how vulnerable she is, openly admitting that it's just him and her inside the house. "Please come now!"

In a moment of clarity, Nola is able to supply the address that she and her mother practiced years before. The operator tells her to stay on the line, and to stay put until the police have entered her home. By now, Nola is convinced that the man is gone. But she knows she can't open the door until she hears the sirens outside, when a cloud of refuge will be put over her head. Or so she thinks.

7

NOLA

I don't like to say his name. Not out loud. Not in my head. It sounds fanciful. It puts this real monster into a space that could be made to feel fun or contrived. I'm sure that's what he wanted from the start. To reinvent himself as the pure evil he was born to be, with a new name to show for it.

If only all serial killers could have foolish media-given pseudonyms like the Weepy-Voiced Killer or the Doodler. They deserve to be publicly shamed, not glorified.

Although I've tried for so many years to stow this all behind me, when I do need to reference that *thing*—which, luckily, is incredibly infrequently—I just say "Him." Before anyone really knew what he looked like, when he was just a silent phantom in the night, he was referred to publicly as "the Hiding Man"—or so I read on the internet years after Mia's murder. Victims usually had some sort of idea that they were being watched, followed, stalked; they just didn't know if someone was behind it or if they were working themselves up and imagining it. And that was what made his existence so frightening. He's good at making people feel like they're crazy.

But being under the impression that someone is watching you isn't a definitive sign. Were you just being paranoid because of what you heard on the news about a stalking murderer in your area? Or is he really after *you*, right now? You wouldn't know for sure until it was too late. Until he was pressed up against your back with a knife to your larynx.

Harvey drops his headphones on the table and rushes into the recording room, shaking my shoulders. I probably look insane to him because he has no idea what I'm thinking in this moment. He's blissfully unaware of what I went through nearly twenty years ago.

"What happened? Are you okay?" I hear Harvey ask. It sounds distant, even though he's standing directly over me. Even the grip of his fingers on my bicep feels removed.

After a few more seconds, I meet his gaze. "I need to go. I'm sorry." There's an underlying layer of guilt in my words, knowing that I can't properly relay more information to him about what's going on in my head. Not now, at least.

I sprint out of the studio and wince harder than ever at the slam of the building's main door but continue to run at full speed to my car. Left and right, I'm dodging moving vehicles, nearly tripping on the sidewalk when I reach it.

Knowing what I know now, believing He *is* back, there are two majorly conflicting feelings rising inside me. First, that I'm probably in the clear right now because he is over at that lady Felicity's house.

Not like you even know where she lives!

Second, even though I don't think he's here on Manse Avenue with me now, I can't help but sense that he is somehow. Having never learned his true identity, I am stymied that he has been able to remain anonymous, despite committing so many senseless crimes. For all I know, he can be in two places at once.

Either way, I don't let my guard down. I run like hell until I get to my car, only stopping briefly to check underneath it and in the backseat before springing inside and speeding off. The last thing I need is to be worried that someone is hiding behind my driver's seat at a time like this. Or that someone is lying beneath my Jeep with a razor, ready to slice my ankles.

Seriously, it's happened to people.

I contemplate calling my mom, even though it's after 3 a.m. in New York. She's one of the only people in my life who could understand how staggering this development is. And she'd want to know every detail. Despite the hour, this is an emergency, so I try her anyway but get her voicemail after a few rings.

"Dammit!" I shout into the void that is my empty car.

I decide not to leave a frantic voicemail and worry her before her anniversary trip tomorrow.

Instead, I hang up and continue driving out of the city, as Felicity's screams play over and over in my head.

As a night owl, my dad should still be awake. Although I want to explain everything in person, I call his phone to announce my arrival, but it just rings, and rings, and rings like my mom's did. As I shakily hang up, I closely escape clipping a parked car with the right side of my bumper. Dropping my phone on the seat and putting both hands on my wheel, I take deep breaths to avoid total hyperventilation.

How can he have come back? Where has he been all this time? Is it the same person, or a copycat?

Questions flash through my mind as I crack into the options. But without more information, without concrete knowledge that what I believe is the truth, I can't possibly speculate.

The sky is particularly dark tonight with the moon covered by clouds, unable to grace me with its guiding light. Not that I'd be able to see it on the road to my dad's house, which is perfectly and eerily swallowed by trees. My foot is pinned to the gas pedal as my body sways side to side with the curve of the forested road beneath me. My dad's house is a little higher in the hill than mine in the adjoining neighborhood, showing off similar views—and not just of the city, like mine, but the woods, too.

I wind through the trees alone, no other cars on the road. No oncoming traffic ahead of me, no vehicles coming up behind me. All I can see is the four-hundred-some feet in front of me that my high beams are illuminating. When I'm about half a mile from my dad's house, a set of headlights become visible a ways behind my car. I can't help but glance at the rearview to check their progress, noticing how fast they're driving. I'm already surpassing the speed limit—they must be doubling it. My heart picks up speed as my wheels do. I lock eyes with the road. When I finally look up again, the car is barreling toward me.

I approach my dad's street and take a sudden, jerking right turn up the hill. The vehicle races past, unfaltering. As I climb the road and approach his house, I note that his car isn't in the driveway and mentally weigh the probability of him even being home.

It's 12:07 a.m. It *is* a Friday night, but I can't imagine where else he'd be. I fling my car into park, lock it, and run to the front door as I flip through my keychain for the key that will let me inside. We each have a key to the other's house—for safety—though we never have to use them. Tonight might be the first time this key has touched a lock.

As I thrust it into the hole, I whip my head back and scan the street. *Empty.*

After I push my way through the crimson front door of his contemporary home, I slam it behind me and lock it, then lean against it with a sigh, as though someone out to get me is on the other side.

"Dad?" I shout. My voice echoes off the heights of his soaring ceilings.

I grab the railing to his floating staircase in the entryway and call for him again, projecting my voice upstairs. I drop my purse on the entry table and walk into the living room, fearing the wall of windows into the forest for the first time. I step closer and peek out at the trees but can only see a mixture of their jagged outlines and my own reflection.

I make my presence known early, continuously calling his name as I walk down the hallway of the second floor after failing to find him on the ground level. I knock on his bedroom door and continue to say "Dad?" before opening it.

The lights are on, and the bed is made. No dad.

I jog downstairs, slump into the sofa, and call him again on my cell phone.

My heart drops to my toes when the kitchen lets out the blaring bell of a phone ringing. I jump to my feet and spin around as I search for any signs of life, wondering if my dad has been here the whole time. But then I notice his phone, face down, its gray case blending into the glossy concrete countertops. This explains why I didn't see it when I walked through the kitchen upon my arrival.

"Dad? Are you here?" I shout.

Still nothing.

I hang up my phone and pick up his, seeing my multiple missed calls and other notifications dating back four hours. I grab the largest knife from the magnetic holder on the wall and make my way into the garage: the one room I have yet to check, besides the bathrooms and closets. Making my way toward the front entryway again, I put one hand on the matte knob while holding the massive knife in the other. Wasting no time, I twist the knob and kick the door open with my foot, only to be met with pure darkness. Terrified of what could be waiting, I reach my empty hand in and flip the light switch on as fast as I can.

My dad's car isn't in here, either, though his storage boxes and instruments don't leave much room for it anyway.

No dad. No car. No monsters.

Where is he?

I close the garage door, cross the living room, and make my way out to the balcony, taking in the sound of cooing owls and scampering wildlife. If I closed my eyes for a moment—which I don't dare do—it would be a tranquil orchestra. You can't even hear the city to the left of all these Douglas firs. Purely the sounds of nature. A glass of bourbon from my dad's whiskey collection is calling my name from inside, begging to be consumed on one of the balcony's Adirondack chairs with their million-dollar view.

Not now, bourbon.

I return to the sofa and think about what to do. Even though I don't know where my dad is or what's going on, I feel safer here than I do at my own house right now. I don't want to go to the police— not until I'm clear on what happened—so I turn on the TV to keep me company and grasp the knife in my lap as I wait for my dad to come home.

"Nola?"

My eyelids abruptly unfasten to the image of my dad standing over me with a knife in his hand. I groggily scream and try to bounce off the sofa, but my limbs are too tired from sleep.

"Honey, calm down! What's gotten into you?" my dad demands.

"Why are you holding a knife?" I yell.

"Because it was in your lap! You were sleeping in *my* house with a knife. I didn't want you to wake up and stab yourself or something," my dad replies in agitation. "It's almost one a.m. Are you all right?"

Wide awake now, I blurt, "He's back. The Hiding Man is back!" Just saying his name out loud hurts my stomach.

He takes a long pause, processing what I've said.

"I came here to tell you that. But you weren't home, and I was too scared to leave," I add.

He seems taken aback. "What strange timing," he says calmly. "Did you hear about it on the news?"

"What's that supposed to mean?" I ask, unsure if he's referring to what I said about Him or about coming over.

He shakes his first comment out of his head and starts chuckling. "What I mean is: How do you know he's 'back'?" he asks, using air quotes. His tone is coming up on mocking. "What station is reporting this?" He drops the knife on the coffee table and grabs the remote.

"I don't think it's on the news." I watch him flip across all major stations and come up empty. "We got this really weird call on the show."

I tell him about what Felicity said and explain why I think someone might be watching me.

My dad sits down on the sofa next to me. "I'm sure whatever happened to that woman will be in the news tomorrow if it's anything serious. It might be good publicity for the show," he adds lightheartedly.

My mouth drops open at his bluntness.

"And until we know more, let's take it easy here, honey. The police think that guy is long dead."

"You mean they *assume* he's dead," I correct him. "They have no evidence of who he even is. Or what happened to him after he went dark."

This is information I have overheard in sprinklings of news about Him over time, as I've never brought myself to search his name online. Only Mia's when I was a tween.

I let out a sigh, not wanting to argue. And because I hope to God he's right.

I'm exhausted. All I want is to fall into his shoulder and receive that fatherly comfort I longed for as a child. When I do, almost to my surprise he hugs me back affectionately, and we just sit like this for a while, uninterested in letting go. It's a long-overdue gesture that brings a soft smile to my face. Suddenly, I feel safe.

When I pull away, I ask, "Where have you even been? Why did you leave your phone here?"

"Oh, um." He squeezes the bridge of his nose. "Well, Clarence and I got some drinks after going over the reading and book announcement for tomorrow night. I left my phone on the counter by accident." He changes the subject. "Why don't you stay here tonight? I can make you a special breakfast when you wake up, huh? It would worry me to send you home after the day you've had. You need a good night's sleep."

I pout at the suggestion, softened by his newfound impulse to be the protective, doting dad. Dazed, I nod my head in agreement and settle into the guest room upstairs. As I attempt to shelter under the thick, cold comforter, I can't help but refresh local news bulletins on my phone. My dad said it would make the news tomorrow if it was anything serious. But maybe it's *so* serious that it'll make the news tonight. We're coming on two hours since it happened, so, surely, word of a gruesome murder would have circulated to news stations by now. Although, with each refresh of the page, the same mundane stories stay in their slots. When I remember it's the middle of the night, I plug my smartphone into the charger and flip onto my back.

My dad's right about my needing a good night's sleep, but I can't get that awful December night out of my brain. My mind is on fire with memories of the night Mia died. The night I met Him. And the stark uncertainty that immediately followed.

8

Twenty Years Earlier

The 911 dispatcher remains cool and undisturbed despite the alarming details that Nola is spewing into the receiver. Nola wonders if she's ever heard a call quite like this one, if talking a little girl down from an encounter with a killer is in her repertoire.

The woman on the phone keeps hitting Nola with questions so that she can glean as much information as she can in case anything happens. To Nola's dismay, each one pertains to the horrors to which she's just witnessed. In a time when she so desperately prefers to be distracted, she must relive, and relive, and relive again.

"What happened to your babysitter?"

"What is her name?"

"Who did this to her?"

"What did he look like?"

"Did you get a good look at his face?"

Nola does her best to answer each one, but she's finding it harder and harder to speak about it. Especially when she's asked about his face.

"An officer just got off the phone with your mom. She's on her way to the house right now."

"Where's my dad? And are they almost here?" Nola asks, crouched on the floor next to a nightstand. She's clenching her fist hard enough to leave crescent marks in her palm. Her fear is so ferocious that the pain hardly fazes her.

"I'm sure your dad's just fine. And soon, sweetheart. Just like the police. All you have to do is keep talking to me until they show up. Everything is going to be okay."

"Promise?" Nola asks quickly.

There's a moment of hesitation on the other line. Nola notices it. "Yes. I promise," the dispatcher finally offers.

But before Nola can say "Okay," all the lights in the house go out. The phone goes silent. Not even her own breath can be heard through the receiver.

The piercing ring of total silence fills her ears, but so do the sounds of her heartbeat and jagged breaths as she slowly shifts positions to sit against the wall behind her.

Nola tries to whisper into the phone to explain that she is now sitting in a pitch-black room, more scared for her life than she was before. But the dispatcher is gone. There isn't even a dial tone.

She closes her eyes and hugs her knees, rocking back and forth and needing nothing but to be rescued. Knowing she's sitting in darkness, her brain showcases the scariest things she can think of inside her head. But the one image that's at the forefront of her mind is the harrowing face she saw at the bottom of her staircase. The image is pasted across her mind like a collage she'd make at her bedroom desk, typically full of magazine cutouts of all her favorite boy bands. But this one is the same terrifying face, over and over again. That, and the image of Mia's dead body lying in the kitchen.

As the minutes pass and the lights remain off, she grows desperate to get out of the house. But she can't bring herself to move. She almost wonders if she died, and if this is Hell. The idea makes her break down into silent tears, utterly traumatized by the agony of her reality.

Nola slowly rises from the floor and turns around to open the curtains. Leaving her back vulnerable against the dark room, she steadily pulls them open and peeks out before exposing herself completely. The view below shows small glimpses of the house next door, which is mostly covered by trees. There's no way she could get a neighbor's attention from here. Taking a deep breath, Nola thinks hard about what to do next, realizing she hasn't heard any sounds coming from inside or outside the house since she called 911. Dashing to her neighbors can't be any worse than sitting in this blackness, could it? She'll get to the front door via muscle memory alone, knowing she won't be able to see anything.

Nola starts to turn toward the door before freezing again, pondering if the scary man is waiting for her.

Is he still outside the door? she wonders.

"No," she whispers out loud to herself, shaking her head. She begins to think of happy things, like her mom always told her to do if she's sad or afraid. With the power of as many positive memories she can think of, she jumps to her feet.

Three, two, one. Go.

Nola sprints through her parents' bedroom, then across the hall, and then down the stairs. Holding the railing so she doesn't trip, she tries to push through the fear of seeing the man in the mask lurking at the bottom like he had been before. She's so focused on whether or not he's going to be there that she doesn't even hear the sirens approaching her house. Since the last time she was downstairs, someone closed all the curtains, allowing only the smallest flash of red and blue lights to appear through a gap. Multiple police officers slam through the front door, pulling out flashlights and brightening the room, causing Nola to scream from the sudden noise.

While Nola is charging through the living room to get outside, one of the officer's lights flashes across Mia's body in the kitchen next to Nola, exposing her to that awful sight once again. One of them grabs her as she stops to see something new to the scene. Something that most definitely wasn't there when she saw Mia's body before.

Written in large letters on the tile next to her are the words:
I'LL BE WATCHING

It's written messily in red, and even Nola knows that it has to be Mia's blood. Just like she knows the message is intended for her. Although it's painful, she takes a farewell glance at Mia. The twenty-one-year-old babysitter remains in the same position, her eyes still fixed on the floor. Nola realizes this will be the last time she'll get to see this young woman who became the closest thing she had to a sister.

When the police officer notices Nola is staring at the words on the floor, he yanks her outside to get her assessed by paramedics.

The sirens are deafening now, and Nola can't help but look at the streets, on the roof, all around her—confident that the man in the mask is still lingering, doing exactly what he promised he'd do: watch her. But even the streets are vacant, despite all the commotion that's made its way to their neighborhood in the last sixty seconds. But since the Strates' home is situated on the sharp curve of a street and most houses around it are fixed on a hill, it alludes to a particular type of privacy.

An ambulance comes to a screeching halt in front of the Strate home at the same time Nola's mother, Donna, arrives.

"Honey! What happened?" she screams, running to Nola. "Are you okay? Where's Mia?"

Bombarded with the same questions the 911 dispatcher asked her, she can't bring herself to answer them. All Nola can muster is "Mia's dead."

Thirty minutes after Donna and the police showed up, Nola's father, Chick, finally arrives at their house.

Just two hours earlier, they'd been making their rounds with Chick's associates at the party. "Rockin' Around the Christmas Tree" was echoing against the walls as they sipped too-sweet holiday cocktails and found themselves on the dance floor; until an out-of-town colleague flagged Chick from across the room, beckoning him. With that, Chick was gone.

When an unfamiliar number popped up on Donna's cell phone more than thirty minutes later as she caught up with an old friend, she answered, originally wondering if something had happened to Chick. But she couldn't have imagined the news she received. And everything felt instantly worse when she couldn't get ahold of Chick. He'd left the party for what was supposed to be a quick trip to the studio in their car, leaving Donna to get a ride from her friend.

And here he is, well over an hour after he'd abandoned her at *his* holiday work party. Suddenly back in the swing of things, sprinting out of his car without so much as a glance in her direction, Chick races over to Nola, but Donna stops him.

"What do you think you're doing? Where have you been?" Donna asks in distress. "Our daughter was almost killed."

"Please let me see her," Chick says, pushing past Donna.

She grabs his arm and tugs him back into conversation. "But *where* were you?"

"I told you before I left the party. I had to run to the office. I didn't see your calls until fifteen minutes ago because I was working," he retorts. "I got here as fast as I could. What happened? Where the hell is the babysitter?"

Donna breaks into a silent sob, shielding her face with her hands.

"Is she—" Chick looks over as Mia is being taken out of his house in a body bag, one paramedic on each end of the stretcher. "Jesus Christ," he whispers.

"Hey, Chick. Donna," says Detective Jack De Lacey, one of Chick's closest friends.

They met when the Strates first moved to Oregon and Jack lived in the house next door in a neighborhood across town—back when he was just a patrol officer and before he was married to Tammy.

Detective De Lacey is shaking his head in disbelief. "This is the fifth one in three months," he mutters, eyes fixated on the stretcher that holds Mia's corpse. "I'm sure you guys have caught wind of it on the news lately. This is his first attack in your neighborhood."

"I've heard about the murders, of course," Chick says sternly. "But how do you know the same killer was here tonight?"

Detective De Lacey sighs. "There's only one other person who's alive who has ever seen this guy—and her description matches Nola's to a T."

Chick runs to Nola's side, abandoning the conversation.

"What are we supposed to do about that message, Jack? Is that about our girl?" Donna asks.

"Well, for now, your house is a crime scene, and you can't go back in there anyway. We can grab some of your things but—as your friend—I don't think this is a safe place for Nola to be until we catch this guy."

"Are you close? Do you have any suspects?" Donna presses, adjusting her blond updo.

Detective De Lacey lowers his voice and looks around. "He's not leaving prints. And we're not getting any hits on any of the samples we're running. There doesn't even seem to be a motive or connection between the victims. They're all over the city."

"What about the weapon? Did you find it?" Donna asks desperately, knowing Jack can't give her most of the answers she's seeking. She presses for them regardless.

"I can't release that information right now. But so far, it appears the same weapon has been used in each murder. Between this and the fact that everyone was being stalked before they were killed—we feel strongly it's the same guy."

Donna looks over to Nola, accompanied by Chick. He's clutching her small body, staring at the ground.

"I'm sure you guys will understand, but I'll need to question both of you—and Nola, again. Properly. We're also going to talk to all your neighbors and the people in Mia's life. We *will* find this guy."

Donna is hesitant to believe him, particularly now that she is grasping just how little the police know about the mysterious man who wreaked havoc upon her home tonight.

9

NOLA

My dad flips a third pancake onto my plate before placing it in front of me next to a glass bottle of maple syrup. He plops a handful of blueberries on top and throws a dish towel over his shoulder in pride—even though these came from a box mix. It feels clichéd to make pancakes on a Saturday morning, but since I'm here, my dad seems to be attempting a quasi-grand gesture. Well, and he was out of eggs. It was this or yogurt.

This is the exact type of dad I wanted growing up. The dad who wakes up early on the weekend to make breakfast for his family. Who asks about your day and your life at the table. The dad who takes time. Since he used to work late nights, he'd sleep in, and my mom would have already made me waffles or a cheesy omelet before he woke. Oftentimes, we felt like a family of two. When Dad would eventually come down to the kitchen of our old house, I'd still be waiting for him at the breakfast table like a loyal puppy dog, hoping he'd sit with me while I doodled or read a book. I never had such luck, as he'd flash us a wave on his way out to meet business associates for coffee, and I wouldn't see him again until much later in the day. After that night, he became more protective of my well-being. But even that didn't last.

The bitterness still lingers in me, but I'm working on it. It's hard to let go of being made to feel small and insignificant by one of the only people who really matters to you—especially during such formative years. But after a partial retirement five years ago when he passed *Night Watch* on to me, I think he experienced a period of reflection where he was able to shift his attitude a bit for the better. He tried to be more present in my life, since work was no longer taking up his days. It's not been a perfect relationship, but I can see it continuing to improve in time.

I smile my thanks for the breakfast and, in my seat at the counter, take a big bite of fluffy sweetness.

When I came downstairs to the smell of browned butter, my dad had the local news turned on, already anticipating my inquiries. The biggest headline of the morning was: POWER DOWN FOR THOUSANDS AS STORM SWEEPS THROUGH PACIFIC NORTHWEST. I shivered at the headline and flickered back to that night—as if it hasn't been on my mind since last night anyway. With a lethal fear of the dark ever since, I still fall asleep with the TV on to this day.

"Nothing yet," my dad said when I descended the staircase. He had a look of sympathy. "Now sit down. It's a beautifully gloomy day out there, and I'm makin' pancakes!"

When I take my second bite, he slides an espresso my way with a packet of raw sugar and a tiny spoon. While I stir, still in a sleepy, anxious daze, I sense him watching me. He knows I can't get it out of my head. He grabs my hand and squeezes it.

"I can't begin to imagine how hard these years have been on you after what you saw." He takes a breath. "It isn't fair. No one, no child, should have witnessed that. But until we know more about this phone call you guys got, let's just try to forget about this."

I look up at him.

"I know, I know. Easier said than done. But let's try."

He's right. Until I see a news report confirming this woman *was* murdered and the call wasn't some callous hoax, I need to loosen up. My name was never released into the media because I was very much a minor when Mia died, so I don't know how He would even know who I was to be able to come back and find me. But in the age of the internet—and when you're dealing with a person known for stalking—it's certainly possible.

The odds of falling into the grips of the same serial killer twice feel astronomically low. No way my odds would be that unlucky. With that realization, I wonder then how this Felicity woman could have known who I really was to be able to make such a rotten joke on my show. To lie about the mask—that specific mask—she'd have to know I was there when Mia died; that I saw him with my own eyes. But how?

I stuff these thoughts down with another bite of pancake and decide to move forward. It's unhealthy to dredge this up again.

I want to say, *Yes, Dad, it's been hard.* And *You have no idea what it was like to be in our house that night.* But I don't feel like having a family therapy session this morning. We've been so good at bottling our trauma up all these years. Why start healing now?

"You're right," I say, staring at my fork. "Thanks for letting me stay the night. And sorry for just barging in here. And scaring you with that knife."

"Are you kidding? You're always welcome," he says, taking a bite of his own pancakes while he stands on the other side of the counter. I think this is the first time I've seen him eat breakfast.

"So. Do you still want to come to my book reading tonight? It's probably going to be pretty boring, but you're more than welcome to join," he says, mouth full. "But maybe you don't want to hear about paranormal stuff and murders on your night off. Especially today." He scrunches his face.

His tone has me wondering if he doesn't want me to come. Perhaps he's just being thoughtful, trying not to make me feel bad for skipping out in case it's what I would prefer. As he guessed, I don't particularly want to hear about such topics tonight, but I do want to support him. Plus, there's going to be an open bar; and even when you can afford your own drinks, free ones taste better.

"No, I'd love to come. If that's okay."

He blows air out of his lips and squints his eyes. "Of course."

We finish eating our breakfast and I retire to the sofa for a while, not entirely ready to go back to my own house. There's this persisting doubt in me. I can't help but feel like I shouldn't go back there at all. I roll my eyes at the stupidity, knowing I have security cameras, locks, and my wits—sort of.

My dad and I keep our attention on the news for a while, lounging on opposite ends of the sofa before he runs off to meet his agent again. I settle deeper into the sofa and flip through the channels, anxious to see something new pop up on the news. There's nothing. I check my phone, seeing no relevant news there, either, but I do notice a couple missed calls from earlier this morning. I don't recognize the number and pass on listening to the voicemails for now, assuming they're spam. When I open my texts next, I see a few from Harvey checking in on me. I quickly respond, telling him I'm sorry for running out last night, and that I'm at my dad's. As I finish typing, the TV promises a breaking news story. I sit up, dropping my phone on the cushion next to me, heart thumping in suspense.

I slump back down when I see that said-breaking story is relating to local politics, not about a murder. I'm happy with this news. I don't *want* to be right. I want this to all be some massive misunderstanding, the product of a delusional imagination caused by psychological damage. It's only natural that I feel this much tension surrounding the topic. Because after that horrible night, I never stopped wondering if He was someone I already knew, and if I would ever be safe again.

It's the afternoon and I'm finally driving back home after nearly twenty hours of avoidance. I'm half expecting my front door to be busted open or something cryptic to be scrawled on my driveway. Thinking back to after Mia died, and how I never returned to my childhood home, I hope I don't have to do it all over again. The police were in and out of there for a while after that night, gathering evidence with the hope that it would lead them to one particular identity. An identity they had tried to pinpoint for months.

With the grim message that was left beside Mia's body, my parents refused to live in that house another day, knowing the killer could come back for me. They all but entered me into Witness Protection. We moved to a different neighborhood across town, and, as I tried my best to forget about it all, my parents stopped watching the news when I was around. My mom stopped reading the morning paper at breakfast. This didn't stop me from turning on our local TV station when they weren't in the room, wanting to learn any sprinkling of information out of fear. But when I was a kid, I also wanted to pretend like it didn't happen, and that worked for me. I processed the event as much as I could with a child psychologist and wiped my hands of it all. Like it was nothing more than a night terror.

My parents did what they thought was best: flee. Well, sort of. We didn't move out of the city or the state. Knowing police still hadn't caught the guy when we moved into our new house, I imagined they would want to get as much distance from the tragedy—and the man behind it—as they could. But we didn't go far.

The decision revolved mostly around my dad's work—which made my mom feel guilty. All I know is my dad didn't have the ability to take the show on the road, and other people's jobs depended on the show staying in the area. Since our names weren't released to the media, no one even knew my dad and his family were affected by the serial killer who plagued the region for months. Nor did anyone from my school or any of my friends know what I'd witnessed. Our neighbors knew a story that wasn't completely true, but they didn't go telling people after my parents spoke with them and requested that they keep quiet, just like everyone else did. So, we stayed in the same county and lived life like nothing had happened that night. And everything was fine. For twenty whole years.

10

NOLA

I pull up to my house, squinting my eyes, preparing for horrors. But nothing looks suspicious at first glance. While parked in my driveway by the front door, I check the Northwest Protect app for any notifications from the past day. I haven't noticed anything pop up at strange hours, but I need to make sure.

I glimpse at my door and the windows on this side of the house. It's a picturesque cottage from all sides, with faux shutters and cream paint. In part, I sit and admire the house I don't want to leave—or be forced out of by a potential stalker. But mostly, I scan for any changes or anything suspicious. All the lights remain off, but the blinds on my kitchen window are pulled up.

Did I close them before I left with Amoli?

When I study the app, I see that there's been a few side door detections since I left last night.

A chill runs down my spine, as I wonder if someone was at my house in the night hours.

Seeing that the timestamps are from this morning and afternoon, I loosen. Both recordings are from assumed neighbors on walks. The front door has one alert, and it's from the postman dropping off some letters earlier today. I breathe a sigh of relief knowing nothing nefarious slithered in, and, with a puffed chest, exit my car and head toward the front door.

Felicity's howls still echo in my head, acting as the base of my terror.

Upon entering my house, I do a full check of the ground floor. No boot prints. No unlocked doors. And again, no monsters.

I ponder if the trauma of what I endured as a child has come back to bite me, hard, and that's all any of this is. I'm paranoid and sensitive and that's normal.

After making my way upstairs, I look at my phone, tempted to call my mom again but well aware she wouldn't be able to answer in the isolated woods of Vermont. She texted me back earlier to ask if I had dialed her by accident last night, considering how late it was. Feeling the need to lie—for now—I agreed with her assumption, telling her that I hope she has a relaxing time on her anniversary cabin trip.

"The police think that guy is long-dead," my dad had said last night. And I think I believe him. A killer doesn't usually return and pick up from where he left off after nearly two decades. Has it happened across history? Surely. But I'm no expert on the subject, so that answer remains a curious mystery.

I run upstairs, still a bit on edge, and find myself in my bedroom, searching for an outfit to wear for the evening. All I need is an ordinary night out with my dad to set things right.

Suddenly looking forward to the event, I blow out my wavy bed-head, slip into a tasteful black jumpsuit, and call a car to take me down to Powell's Books.

There's around three hundred people mingling in small clusters inside the bookstore; some sipping wine, others popping hors d'oeuvres in their mouths. Not your typical book signing, but my dad wouldn't have it any other way. I grab myself a caprese skewer and head to the bar, the cherry tomato bursting under my teeth and oozing sweetness along my tongue. I beeline to the bartender and grab a cup of Cabernet Sauvignon, taking it with me to find a spot in the back while trying not to spill on the sleek concrete floors.

We're in a place called the Pearl Room, where all the surrounding books are based on physics, art, architecture. It's located on the third floor right across from the Rare Book Room, which is enclosed with, well, rare books.

Scanning the room to find my dad's fans and colleagues, I suddenly wish I asked Harvey or Amoli to tag along. Unknown guys and gals fill the space, gripping books, flipping pages—some annotated and swollen with yellow highlighter and sticky notes, others crisp and unbroken. Bookless and unchaperoned, I stand out.

I wonder now if anyone recognizes me, since the exact type of person who listens to my show is in this room. If anyone does, they're not staring at me or making it known quite yet. I hope it stays that way, at least until I've moved on to my second drink.

There are a handful of people in the room that I've known for years through my dad—some who are in my industry—but I'll save hellos for later. The event's about to start.

A man I don't know offers me his seat, since they're all taken by now. I politely decline and lean against a bookshelf instead, desperately hoping they're secured in the floor and not going to domino.

I'm taking a sip of wine when an employee approaches the podium and welcomes the room. "Hello, everyone!" a buoyant, forty-something woman in eyeglasses and an adorably unfashionable scarf says with punch. "Today we have a very special local guest who has made the things that go bump in the night his business. You'll know him from creating and hosting the popular late-night radio show *Night Watch*, and more recently, for writing nonfiction books like *Midnight on Cape Dreary* and what he's reading from tonight: *Possessed Pacific*. Please join me in welcoming Chick Strate."

The room erupts in a passionate but hushed ovation. I hold my plastic cup of wine with clenched teeth and join their applause.

My dad walks in through the room's main door in an attempted grand entrance and takes the podium. "Thank you, everyone, for coming. It's been a few years since I've done one of these, but it's good to be back!" More applause. "I also have a special announcement tonight about my next book. But first, I'd like to read a few excerpts from my newly released collection of paranormal stories, *Possessed Pacific*, which is about hauntings and lore from our near and dear Pacific Northwest."

He picks up his hardcover copy and opens to a section that he's preselected, then reads a few different stories.

I look around the room. Roughly half of the attendees already have his book in their laps, awaiting his signature. The others will probably buy a copy and have it signed, too.

The book is essentially an anthology of short—and supposedly true—stories from around this part of the United States. After passing *Night Watch* on to me, he became somewhat of an investigative journalist, traveling to different areas and researching hauntings. *Possessed Pacific*—which I've already read—includes plenty of seaside folklore: haunted lighthouses along the West Coast, sea creatures, small-town legends. The Northwest is home to densely forested landscape, so there's also a healthy dose of hair-raising woodland tales.

My dad dances among the topics, sharing short sections of various stories across the book in a somewhat gruff voice. The audience is eating his every word.

After reading for a while, he opens the room to some questions. The audience cuts in with inquiries like "How do you choose your book topics?" and "What's your favorite haunted place to visit?"

Then someone asks something that makes me want to sink into the crevices of the bookcase against my back. "Why did you leave *Night Watch* and what made you choose your daughter as the new host?"

I can't tell by her tone if she's pleased by my takeover or unhappy with the decision. Even though it's been nearly five years since it happened.

"After twenty years of late nights in the studio—although I loved it—I was ready for a change. And my tremendous daughter Nola—who's here tonight," he says, pointing at me, "was interested in moving into a radio career. And she proved to be the perfect person to take my place."

I send a quick wave to the audience, who are mostly looking my way. Finding my cup empty, I take this time to quietly walk over to the bar for a top-off.

I find my way back to the spot against the bookcase just as my dad closes the questioning. Holding a foam board poster in hand, he is about to reveal the cover for his new book. His face shows a sense of excitement, but there's some underlying uneasiness that would be obvious to any eye in the room.

He remained ambiguous about the topic of this new book, even to me. Not like we see each other often enough for me to scrape for details, but he has kept all discussions on the subject short. "It's just another nonfiction," he'd said months ago.

He turns the poster around and places it on a stand next to the podium. My brow instantly furrows at the sight of the cover.

"My new book, which will be my first work in the true crime genre, will be out this summer. It's called *Living Shadows: How a Serial Killer Called the Hiding Man Terrified a Nation.*"

My thoughts whip from wondering if I'm mentioned in this book to why he didn't tell me privately before announcing it like this. But I shouldn't be surprised at his selfish actions at this point.

I focus on the words "Terrified a Nation" on the oversized image, which seems comically sensational. I don't think anyone outside of our rain-drenched bubble knew what we were dealing with. And if they did, I don't think it was nearly as big a story as other murders across the country that happened in the surrounding years.

I reflect on our small-hours conversation in his living room—how strange he was acting. How his first response to me telling him I believed that He was back was "What strange timing." Now I know what he meant. But something about it feels fishy.

The room is showcasing various reactions: Most are excited, some look confused—likely about his expedition into a connected yet mostly dissimilar topic. But nothing is scarier than the truth. Which is why I've fought to keep my own from the light. Yet here it is, about to be aired like dirty laundry.

"I know this is both a fragile and captivating subject for many of us here—particularly for those who lived in the area in 2004 and

2005." He makes eye contact with me. "But I felt it was my duty to help serve justice to those who lost their lives or their loved ones to this abominable brute and tell their stories for the first time—since there are countless rumors and speculations across the internet. This is a space where I could tell the truth, from what I learned after years of research."

Years?

"What made you choose the Hiding Man as your subject?" a man in the audience asks suddenly.

"Well. It had a profound effect on me at the time. I had moved here from California with my family just a few years earlier. And the fact that he was never unmasked has always felt unjust to me. But I dive into some personal details in the book to expand on this idea and why I think he seemed to disappear the way he did."

The man who asked the question seems pleased with this answer as he responds with an approving nod.

"I'd love to take some more questions and get a moment with each of you now. For anyone who would like to chat or get their book signed, we have a table set up right over here." He gestures to his left. "So, come on down and bring your books. But if you don't have a copy, they're available for purchase right here at Powell's. Thank you!"

People quickly pop up from their seats and form lines like sardines in a briny tin. They can't get to him fast enough.

I glance up at the shop's exposed ceiling with fluorescent light bars scattered across it, suddenly feeling queasy and helpless, like I did in 2004 after Mia died, desperately wanting this all to go away.

After we moved into our new house back on Christmas Eve, my parents tried to hypercorrect my childhood. My dad started showing up for a while. My mom started taking me on girls' trips, as if a ten-year-old ever needs a spa day. Our new house was on a beautiful lake outside of the city, far enough away from the horrific events but close enough for my dad to have a short commute to work. In a small, nature-surrounded community that had never seen a murder, it seemed like the perfect place to fix me.

I down a merciful glug of wine as the crowd chats excitedly about this stupid new book and continues lining up to get their copies of *Possessed Pacific* signed. I rest the back of my head against book spines on the shelf behind me, already feeling emotionally exhausted.

As I lean against the bookshelf, with no one to vent to, I face the same door my dad used to make his initial entrance. My eyes graze the open doorway, and what I see thwacks my spine straight.

Standing on the staircase is a person I recognize instantly. A person I haven't seen in twenty years. He's slightly hidden by the otherwise empty stairs, but I can tell he's sporting the same white stitched mask with an emotionless grin, dressed in the same dark clothes. And he's looking into this room, where he was spoken about only seconds ago.

For a moment, there isn't fear. But that's because I'm two wines deep and in a room full of people. And if everyone else sees him, too, I won't feel crazy anymore.

I also wonder if this is some type of publicity stunt. Did my dad hire a man to wear his outfit and mask to take photos with people who are supporting his new book? No. That would be far too insensitive, even for my dad.

I stare right at him, half believing that I'm imagining him. But as I watch, unable to move, he does something that makes every hair on my body rise and sends a twitching chill through me. From the low light of the stairwell, He cranks his head ever so slightly and raises his hand into a curve. They're the same two motions I watched the silhouetted figure under my streetlight make last night before Amoli arrived.

It was Him. Outside my house. And now He's here.

This floor is mostly reserved for the book signing, though anyone can walk in and out as they please—yet no one is. As is his trademark, he seems to have gone undetected again. Except by me.

I frantically look around the room to see if anyone else is taking notice, but the patrons are too fixated on getting in line to meet my dad instead of watching their backs. I look at my dad, hoping he spots me so I can point to the doorway, and we can catch this jackass. But he doesn't sense my urgency. And when I look back at the stairs, He's gone.

11

NOLA

I'm on my fourth glass of wine, which will make approximately a bottle's worth. I'm anxious to speak with my dad, seconds away from making brusque statements across the room at him—or worse, unloading on a stranger. But I'm an affectionate drunk. And that's why most of my anger—and fear, for that matter—has dissipated by this point. I'm not letting him off easy, though.

After I saw Him disappear from the stairwell, I ran down to follow, and then all around the damn store like a child frantically looking for their mother down the aisles of a grocery store. But what would I have done if I'd caught up to Him? I've had nightmares where I'm just about to be killed, just about to be attacked, on the brink of death. And then I wake up. What happens when the anticipation dies? Would He really kill me in the middle of a bookstore?

In those minutes that I fast-walked through the abundance of rooms that make up Powell's Books, my rage was palpable. Any one of the people who looked up from their books knew I was on a frantic mission. Though no one would guess I was looking for a masked maniac—maybe my cheating boyfriend or my own child—but not that.

Somehow, he disappeared, vanished like the ghost He seems to be.

I know I saw Him standing there.

If it weren't for the wine, I would have stayed put and shriveled into the eight-year-old version of myself that hid from Him during our first meeting. This time, I went after Him in what turned out to be a grandiose embarrassment.

Where did He go?

I took the elevator back upstairs to the Pearl Room and regretted it as soon as the stainless steel doors closed. It could have been a part of his master plan: trapping me in a confined space where no one could save me. He'd materialize in the elevator once I hopped on, press the Stop button, and kill me by the slice of a knife like everyone before me. As the elevator landed at the Pearl Room, it would mimic that scene from Kubrick's film adaptation of King's *The Shining*, except with far less blood. And my lifeless body would send everyone running for the alternative exit.

In a surprising change of script, none of it happened.

There's still time, the dark voice in my head warns me.

"Bitch," I grumble.

I returned to the same spot as before, stewing in my disgrace, visibly defeated.

The line to see my dad is less swollen now, as fans have gotten their books signed and promptly exited downstairs. I doubt He'll be back with the current traffic, but I continue to scan my surroundings just in case I'm wrong.

"Nola, darling! How are you?" a familiar voice says from my right.

I'm startled from my strained trance and am met with an old friend of my parents named Sandra.

I forcibly paste a smile on my face and lie through my teeth. "I'm good, how are you?"

"Excellent. And so proud of your dad. And you, of course." Sandra is beaming with excitement. Why is she beaming with excitement at a time like this? "Your dad has told me about how well the show has been going. I try to tune in when I can. You are *good*."

I open my mouth, ready to make an excuse to leave. But she continues.

"And aren't you just so happy for your dad? Look at all these people here to see him. And that new book? Spooky stuff," she says, shaking her perky chest and feigning goosebumps. "I don't know how he does it."

Before I can respond, I look just past her head and see a man staring at me from the corner. As soon as we lock eyes, he looks away, like he's been caught doing something he shouldn't be doing. I keep my stare, hoping to catch him looking back, and he does very briefly, trying to play a game of cat and mouse. I refuse to be the mouse.

The man across the room is handsome, and almost looks out of place—as if book signings aren't his style. He appears to be in his fifties and isn't holding a book, standing in line, or talking to anyone. It's as though his only agenda is to watch. I wonder why he's here.

"Anyway, how are things going?"

I'm suddenly snapped back to the conversation. "It was nice seeing you, but I actually need to go check in with my dad. Make sure he has everything he needs."

"Of course. How thoughtful. Hope to see you around," Sandra says, giving my elbow a squeeze.

I look over at my dad, who is steadily sipping red wine and smiling for photo ops. Making my way over to him—feeling a bit wobbly on my feet—I stop and lean against a post to steady myself.

"Had a few too many?"

My dad's agent is standing in front of me, making me aware of how flushed my face feels.

I sneer at him as jokingly as I can, but with my rising anxiety, I'm finding it difficult to jest as we usually do. "Nice to see you too, Clarence. How many have *you* had?"

"Not enough. Your father's fans are a—" He pauses. "—peculiar bunch. Which means yours must be, too." He scrunches his nose.

His accent sits somewhere between Queen's English and Transatlantic, and he looks the part. His silver hair is perfectly combed and coiffed, his salmon suit is crisp, and he even has a white handkerchief stuffed neatly into his chest pocket. It's like his job is to perpetually make everyone else feel underdressed.

Clarence and I have a playful relationship. He's one of the only people in my dad's life who knows everything there is to know about everything. Including what He did. Though, as Clarence lives between London and New York City, I rarely see him.

"Who's that guy?" I ask, looking at my mouse. I lock eyes with him again as I say it, so he knows I'm talking about him.

"How should I know?" Clarence replies. "One of your strange fans, I'd assume." He makes a face in his direction as if to say, *Move along.*

To our surprise, the man walks out of the room and descends the stairs.

"Your power," I say to Clarence with mocking praise. But I straighten my face quickly and grip the post behind me. "So, how long have you known? About the new book."

"You say that like you didn't know." I stare back and he drops his smile. "He didn't tell you?"

"I found out when everyone else in this room did."

"How evil of your father. Well, I've read it. He doesn't mention you or any inkling of a connection, I'll tell you that much. Is it in poor taste? Possibly. But even that detective friend of his didn't try to stop him."

Jack knows about this, too?

I wonder then if Jack has any inside information that he could share on the call I received on the show last night. Thinking about it now, I should have reached out to him directly instead of waiting for things to get worse, so I'd know for sure if I was right. I consider drunk-dialing him but decide to save our call for the morning. I'll tell him everything I know, everything I've seen over the past two days. He'll be able to help, I'm sure of it.

"Did my dad hire some kind of impersonator to this event? Of the killer, like, in his mask and outfit?" I ask Clarence, still feeling unsure about what I saw.

"Now why would he do something like that? I said he was evil but he's not stupid."

"I thought I saw him." I point. "Over there."

"This is all taking quite the toll on you. Let's get you some water."

I want to object, but I probably do need some. We walk over to the bar, where I'm poured a large cup of water. I down the whole thing.

"I'm gonna go find the restroom," I say.

I send him a wave and begin looking for it. I think I remember passing it when I was on the hunt for Him, so I descend the stairs again—this time at a more relaxed pace—and peek around the second floor's Purple and Red rooms. Neither room is painted its color, and neither is really an enclosed room, either. But both are filled with readers perusing books on travel, history, religion, and health—among other themes.

Despite its likely obvious location, I don't find the restroom right away, so I flag down a kind employee with a pixie cut, who gestures toward the bathroom and supplies me with the code to get into it: 4386.

I stumble across the second floor and press those four numbers into the door's metal keypad, its 4, 3, 8, and 6 buttons significantly more worn than the rest. Inside, it's unnervingly quiet and dim. No music, no running sink, no people. I use the toilet and then take a moment to look at my phone and mindlessly scroll before getting up.

The first thing I see is a news notification. Expecting it to be yet another weather report, I begin to skim past it. But then I see a word that draws my attention: "murdered." I start from the beginning and see that the full headline reads:

WOMAN MURDERED IN PORTLAND HOME, SUSPECT AT LARGE

12

JACK

There are around a hundred murders in this city each year, give or take. Most are a result of gun violence, whether during a burglary or group dispute, or in other cases, the repercussions of drug dealing and addiction. Stabbings, poisonings, and blunt trauma are significantly less frequent, making murder by premeditated homicidal violence—particularly against an arbitrary victim—unique. So, when Detective Jack De Lacey was informed of the murder of a woman in her own home, killed with a slice to her neck by an unknown assailant, he was intrigued yet horrified. In his twenty years as an investigator, he's seen more than his fair share of domestic violence murders, assaults within the houseless community, and robberies gone wrong. He's also seen a reasonable amount of one-off homicide cases cross his desk. But as soon as he arrives at the scene of this murder, he knows something feels different about it. Yet all at the same time, it feels familiar.

Early this Saturday morning, Jack was called to the site of a savage crime scene. The victim, Felicity Morton, had been dead for at least seven hours, and her cause of death was the gaping wound in her neck caused by a knife. Death by blood loss. Death by homicidal violence. The woman was found lying in the entryway of her closet, face down, as if she'd been attacked from behind. The house she was discovered in, her own, was quiet and mostly tidy, but her bedroom was a mess, with furniture haphazardly moved around the room. Her cell phone lay next to her body, inches away from her hand.

Jack's shift wasn't supposed to start until noon. He had been greatly anticipating the opportunity to enjoy a slow weekend morning after a late Friday evening at his son's football game. This shift would allow him to quiet his usual alarm and stumble out of bed in his boxers much later than his customary 8:00. Before he'd even open his eyes, the house would smell of cinnamon rolls straight out of the oven: Tammy's specialty. Instead, the harsh vibrations of his cell phone against the nightstand wake him up at 7:53, roughly an hour before his wife's internal clock would ring. Wanting at least one of them to benefit from the Saturday, Jack hurries into the bathroom, sits on the closed toilet seat, and whispers into his phone. Although his voice doesn't rise above a breath, a cavernous sigh escapes upon hearing the purpose of the call.

Even with the basic facts given to him during those fifty-eight seconds, Jack knows he'll be in for the long haul, trying to piece together a truly difficult puzzle for the first time in a long time.

Jack stares into the bathroom mirror, already anticipating the crumbling of his home life that another lengthy murder investigation could cause. Still attempting not to wake his wife, he tidies his short hair and dresses in his standard attire—a two-piece suit—before handwriting a note and placing it on Tammy's night-stand. It reads: HEADING INTO WORK EARLY. CALL YOU WHEN I CAN. I LOVE YOU, J.

Dumping coffee into his insulated mug, he throws on a wind-breaker and checks on his sleeping teenage son, Ethan, before slip-ping out the door and making the seventeen-minute drive to the crime scene.

Jack was originally planning to head straight to the office and let the forensic technicians do their jobs, but he needs to see the scene for himself and interview the person who found the victim. He starts observing his surroundings a few streets from the scene, thinking of ways out of the neighborhood and looking for surveillance cameras outside businesses and houses. Already knowing the victim lived on a safe and quiet street, Jack ponders the motive behind this woman's slaying.

As he turns onto her street, he admires the tree-lined curbs and quirky houses, longing to know what the sidewalks have seen in the previous ten hours. Three houses down from the victim's is a short row of shops before more homes fill the blocks leading to the hillside. One is a recently closed French restaurant, then an unfussy coffeehouse, and finally, a clothing boutique. They're all small spaces with minimal foot traffic, which could have explained the restaurant closing. Jack can guess the coffee shop and clothing store weren't open late the previous night, but he makes a mental note to stop in after he wraps at the scene. Across from the shops is a small park, its grass lawn emptied of people due to the weather.

Jack parks in front of the victim's house behind a police cruiser and immediately notices that her home sits at the top of a fifteen-step staircase off the sidewalk, like a few of the other homes on her street due to the short hill. This would make it much trickier for neighbors to see or hear anything, especially since there are two large trees spotted with red leaves rooted in the sidewalk, shielding much of the house. Her 4,500-square-foot plot of land is barricaded by cypress trees, and her yard consists of a small firepit and a shed, which is open and being examined.

The responding officer is Austin Torrance, a responsible and congenial man whom Jack has worked with for years. He greets Jack at the bottom of the steps.

"Hey, man," he breathes. "It's a brutal one."

"What have you got?" Jack asks, lightly sipping his still-piping-hot coffee.

"Victim is forty-one-year-old Felicity Morton. She was found on the first level of the home on her bedroom's closet floor with what looks like a single slash to her neck and no apparent defensive wounds—but we'll wait for the autopsy. Doesn't appear that the body was moved, but her cat stepped in the mess and trailed blood across the house."

"Jesus." Jack bites his cheek. "What else?"

"There are just two entrances to the home—front door and back door. No signs of forced entry and all the windows are locked."

Jack wonders if the victim knew her killer. Did she let him in? Or did she fail to lock one or both of her doors before he arrived?

Officer Torrance continues, "It appears she lives alone. Oh, and her phone was found next to her body, so it's possible she was trying to contact someone when she died. Or maybe it was just next to her. I don't know. But look into it."

"Who found her?"

"Her friend, this morning. A woman named Gale Thompson.

The victim didn't show up to their usual Saturday hike, so Mrs. Thompson came by to check on her and saw her lying in a pool of her own blood through the front window. Problem is she has a key, so she let herself in through the front door without checking if it was locked or not. And then she let two other people in before I arrived."

Jack knows the importance of keeping the integrity of the forensics at a crime scene, unfortunately having learned the hard way at the scene of his first murder so many years ago. Officer Torrance's comment makes him sigh deeply through his nose.

"Christ. Who?"

"One was another friend and the other was a neighbor. Uh…" Officer Torrance flips through his notepad. He gives Jack the names of the two other witnesses so Jack can gather their statements.

"All right. I'm on it. Thanks, Austin."

Jack gently kicks pink leaves at his feet and peers around the rest of the road below. From up at the house, there's a sense of privacy. Neighbors' homes are shielded by trees, with the road far enough removed to feel tucked away. Despite its short distance to Downtown, he also notes how charming the street is. It's a quaint spot where the residents would likely chime, *Nothing bad ever happens here.*

Jack approaches his first witness: Gale Thompson. While walking toward her, he notices that some of the blinds in the house are drawn. He questions if the victim's friend pulled them up herself or if they were already open.

"Mrs. Thompson? I'm Detective Jack De Lacey. I'm very sorry about what you had to see this morning. I'd love to get your statement so we can find the person who did this to Ms. Morton."

Gale stands up from the bench outside Felicity's home, wiping a tear from her chin. "Hello, Detective. Thank you." Gale explains everything that Officer Torrance already briefed him on, giving Jack the opportunity to ask about the other witnesses.

"So, they came into the house with you. Why was that? And did you touch anything at all? The blinds, the furniture, the body?"

"There was so much blood, but I wanted to make sure she was really gone, and I couldn't do it. I'm one of those people that just can't stand the sight of blood," she says, her voice shaking. "So, I called Jenny, the other friend we were supposed to hike with. And while I was waiting for her—and the police—to show up, a neighbor passed and offered to help. Thinking back now, that probably wasn't wise, but I didn't know what the hell to do. And no, none of us touched anything other than the front door."

"How do you know Ms. Morton? Are you coworkers?"

"No, we met years ago through a mutual friend and have been great friends ever since. I work at a school, so we both get to work with kids. That's something we always bonded over."

"What exactly did Ms. Morton do?"

"She's a child psychologist. Her patients adored her." Gale takes a deep breath. "I just can't imagine why someone would do this."

"Did she ever complain about patients? Or give the impression that any of them were dangerous?"

"Well, she worked with kids twelve and under—so I can't see them being responsible. But she wouldn't be able to tell me about their conversations anyway." She wipes her nose on her wrist. "Felicity was a pretty scared person, though. Despite how logical and steady-minded she was, she hated living alone. She didn't even want to sleep upstairs because she said it made her feel too vulnerable. Like if something happened, she wouldn't be able to get out of the house. But she never mentioned anything about being afraid of a specific person."

"Did she have a boyfriend? Even a fling or anything like that?"

"She'd been dating a guy named Connie for the past couple years, but they broke up last month. It seemed amicable."

Jack finishes taking Gale's statement before locating the other two witnesses. They don't have much to add, but all their stories line up. He can only hope that their traipsing through the crime scene won't screw up his chances of solving this murder.

Jack takes a big sip from his insulated mug as rain starts to fall from the sky, heavily. With that, he slips disposable shoe covers on his lace-up oxfords and carefully heads up the steps of the seafoam-colored farmhouse. The porch is picturesque, closed off with a white wooden gate, the light above the address number still switched on. Jack imagines a woman he doesn't even know relaxing in the corner chair, admiring the fruit trees by the shed; one plum, one apple.

As he enters, he notices Felicity's purse perched on a hutch. Inside it is her wallet, full of $72 in cash. Past the narrow, carpeted staircase is her bedroom and adjoining bathroom; jewelry rests untouched in a box on the cobalt-blue tiled counter. Jack peers into the bedroom next door to see Felicity's feet sticking out from the walk-in closet. There are numerous technicians working around her, finishing up and preparing to move her body. The blinds in both bedrooms are drawn. Jack wonders if she had been watched from outside before she'd been killed.

It doesn't appear to have been one of those robbery-gone-wrong situations but a premeditated murder. He hopes forensics can lift usable fingerprints. If the killer cut himself during the assault, they might find some of his blood.

Jack stares off in the distance, already anticipating the stacks upon stacks of paperwork he will need to fill out, among other crucial tasks—like keeping this out of the media until he can find out more about their suspect.

He exits the house and strolls to the coffee shop to see if they have any security cameras. Every piece of him is praying there won't be more victims.

13

NOLA

As I read the headline over again, I hear a sound coming from the stall next to me—a faint, abrupt shuffling that wasn't there when I entered. It was eerily hushed as I strode in. But now, something undiscernible is breaking it.

I frantically bend over and hold my hair back so it's not visible as I attempt to catch sight of someone's shoes. I thought I was alone in here, but I suddenly feel like He's on the other side of the black partition, ready to pop out and do something He's been wanting to do for too long: Kill me like He killed Mia, and Felicity just last night.

My head is spinning from the wine and the realization that the phone call I received last night was real; I *did* hear a woman's final moments. My gut clenches and my mouth fills with saliva as nausea pervades me. Her screams were so audible that it's as though they're now coming through the bathroom speakers. It only grows worse when I remember that I was briefly annoyed with her lack of details and speech on the phone. For much of the call, I thought she was playing a prank. How painfully wrong I was.

All I want to do now is shrink and flush myself down the toilet.

Scritch.

There's that sound again, coming from the stall next to mine. I can't tell if it's the pipes, the low fan, or a person.

I swallow hard and refuse to feel exposed in this rectangular box. I slowly peer under the one-foot gap beneath the stall. No feet. In my terrified state, I imagine Him huddled on the seat in a squatted position, ready to hop out and snatch me.

Scritch.

All at once, I leap up, unlock the door, dash across the restroom, pull the door open with force, and run out. Before I know it, I'm practically in the middle of the bookstore. People around me are quietly perusing books, and they give me disgruntled looks for running in such a peaceful setting. Everyone is looking *at* me, not *behind* me, but I turn my head without slowing down to see who is giving me chase.

No one followed me out of the restroom.

I catch my breath by completing short laps around the second floor, simultaneously keeping watch. Across the room is a couple sitting side by side on the floor, his right knee touching her left. Reading novels, separately. They both sport glasses, short haircuts, and black sweaters. They're huddled against each other as if to keep warm, or to keep close while they fall into their respective universes.

I'm tempted to grab a book off the nearest shelf and snuggle up between them, faking normalcy for as long as they'd have me. They look like they could keep me safe. If I followed my intrusive thoughts, I could anticipate exactly what they'd be thinking—likely too polite to say any of it out loud—wishing they had synchronized telepathy.

Who is this woman? he'd send to her brain.

Hell, if I know. Should we move? she'd reply.

How?

Despite their confusion, we would sit in unproblematic bliss for the rest of the night.

No such luck. The intrusive thoughts don't win.

I sigh and head toward the staircase, not the elevator. People flow up and down it alongside me, casting a short-lived safety net.

I finish climbing the stairs to the Pearl Room, where people are still in line to meet my dad. Considering there are still at least fifty people waiting, this is going to take a while. I grab what may or may not be my last glass of wine for the night and take a big sip, which causes my shoulders to quake. Spotting Clarence next to my dad's table, I wave him over to me.

"I need to talk to him. Can you have the line wait just two minutes?"

"Do you see how many people are over there?"

"Exactly. That's why I just need a minute with him. Please. It can't wait until this is over."

Clarence looks back at the line. "Okay. Two minutes. He'll talk to you in the Rare Books Room."

The Rare Books Room is within the Pearl Room, and it's devoid of people. I move in there and wait. Grazing the selections, I trace my fingers across a glass lamp and look at the books: inscribed editions of Patricia Highsmith's *The Talented Mr. Ripley* and Ernest Hemingway's *A Moveable Feast*. Other books, dating back hundreds of years, are locked in glass cases.

I hear Clarence announce that my dad is taking a brief break, but that he will be right back. Then, my dad walks into the Rare Books Room with a sympathetic look.

Before he can say anything, I ask, "Why didn't you tell me at breakfast? Is this why you acted like you didn't want me to come?"

He struggles to speak. "I messed up. But I had just been telling you to move on from this whole thing. And then I was supposed to spring this on you? I didn't know what to do."

"You didn't write the book in a day. Why didn't you tell me before?"

As I see him searching for an answer, I remember that this isn't even the most pressing matter. I pick up my phone and find that article again, putting it in front of him so he can read the big, bold letters. "Look."

"Is this supposed to match that call you guys got?"

"You said if it was serious, it would be on the news. Well, it is now." I shake my phone.

"And what does it say?" he asks.

"Just that police responded to a house in Northwest Portland this morning and they found a woman murdered."

"So, what is our clarification that this is the woman from the call? Does it include her name?"

It doesn't. It doesn't say her profession, her name, her address, nor her cause of death. Just the manner: Homicide.

"Look. Jack is probably working on it now. I'll call him in the morning about it and we'll get it figured out, okay?" He pulls me in for a hug. "I'm sorry. I didn't want to cause you stress."

I don't know what to say, so I remain silent. He fills the space and adds, "We can talk more about it later and I'll explain everything. But for now, I need to get back out there and get this finished so all these people can go home."

I nod with a sullen expression as he swaddles me in a hug and then leaves the room.

My face is hot and feels like I've been socked with a boxing glove. Whether it's from the wine or the tension, I'm unsure. But my dry, berry-soaked tongue insists on the former.

I call a car to take me home because I'm far too wasted to care about any of this anymore. I don't want to go home alone, but I'm still not sure if what I saw tonight is real. And if the murder in the paper is connected to Him and *Night Watch*.

I duck out of the Pearl Room as quickly as I can to avoid any more conversation and take the elevator to the ground floor of the bookstore. The doors open and, as I exit, I nearly collide with a man holding a copy of *Possessed Pacific*.

"My apologies. Are you all right?" the man asks, grabbing my elbow.

"Yeah, sorry. Are you looking for the book signing?"

"How could you tell?" he replies, waving his copy of my dad's book in the air. Dressed appropriately in a white T-shirt and black blazer, nothing about him is unnerving. But his lack of movement makes me wonder why he's trying to stop and talk to me instead of carrying on into the elevator, giving me nothing more than a passing comment.

"Lucky guess. Just go up to the third floor and it'll spit you right out into the signing," I suggest, motioning to the elevator.

"Thank you," he says with a wink and a suave air to him. "Have I missed much?"

My phone buzzes as it informs me that my rideshare driver is approaching the shop. I can't help but have a fraction of my worries alleviated when it tells me my driver is a woman.

"Um, kind of. He announced his new book. But he's still up

there, so he can sign that for you," I reply, walking away slowly to prove I'm not interested in holding this conversation.

"What's his new book about?"

I stop and turn around, still confused. "A serial killer, actually." I swallow. "The—the Hiding Man."

His expression lightens. "Fascinating," he says, locking eyes with me.

"Yeah. He can tell you all about it. Have a great night," I say as I walk away, not giving him the opportunity to add anything else.

As I exit Powell's and stand on the street corner waiting for my car, I shield my face as soft raindrops fall overhead. I snap my head left and right in helter-skelter fashion, willing my driver to pull up so I don't have to stand out here, defenseless. As she pulls around the corner and onto West Burnside Street, I call Harvey, hoping he'll let me vent and believe everything I say. But he isn't answering the phone.

14

NOLA

The blaring doorbell startles me awake. I'm spread on top of my duvet like melted butter, sporting an oversized T-shirt and sweatpants. I guess I was able to get dressed for bed last night but was powerless when it came to slipping under the covers. I army-crawl to my nightstand and gulp room-temperature water from a plastic bottle, collapsing back onto my pillow.

Five more minutes, my body pleads. *Or hours.*

The doorbell rings again, making me say "Okay, okay, hold on" to myself out loud, knowing the person can't hear me up here. I wipe mascara flecks from under my eyes and run my fingers through my hair to look somewhat presentable, suddenly realizing I don't even know who I'm fixing myself up for.

Who is looking for me at ten o'clock on a Sunday morning?

I check the front camera to ensure it's not a solicitor or other stranger and see Jack De Lacey's face leaning into the frame. I press the microphone button on the screen and groggily say, "Jack? What's up?" while I stumble to the bathroom to speed-brush my teeth.

He jumps when my voice comes through the other end, startled.

"Hey, Nola. Sorry to bug you on a Sunday. Can I come in? It's important."

I had planned on calling him at some point today anyway to explain everything that's going on, so his timing is convenient.

Although our busy schedules don't allow much quality time, I still consider Jack as somewhat of an uncle figure to me in the way that your dad's longtime best friend usually does. But not in the way that I'd seek out a close in-person relationship.

"Sure. Give me a minute. I'll be right down."

I brush my tangled hair and throw on some real clothes as quickly as I can, feeling a bit wobbly on my feet. When I open the front door, Jack's attire hints to this being business related. Considering he's in the business of crime, my hands clench up from anticipation. I hide my unease well.

"I'm glad you're here," I say, ushering him inside. "I've been wanting to call you."

He sighs. "I think I know why."

We move into the living room where I turn on the overhead lights and gas fireplace, then plop on a cushion of my sectional sofa that's diagonal to him. Jack settles in at the very edge of the sofa with his elbows on his knees and his hands clasped in front of him.

"You go first," I say, curious to know what's going on.

"You want to tell me about the phone call you received on Friday night?"

"How do you know about that?" I ask.

"We're working on accessing the woman's cell phone records, but we also received numerous calls on Friday night regarding that conversation. Some of your listeners were concerned about its nature. The station must have called you about it by now."

I play with my fingers and look down, remembering those missed calls from an unfamiliar number yesterday while I was at my dad's.

"We didn't know whether or not it was real. Sometimes we get prank calls. And we have no way of verifying who people really are. We only have the names and locations they give us. And their phone numbers."

"Did anyone try to call the woman back after the line dropped?"

Something about his tone makes me feel like I've done something wrong. And maybe I did. Maybe I could have done more during that phone call.

"I don't know. Maybe Harvey or my editor, Josiah, did. I left right afterward because I was scared." I look him straight in the eye, curious to see how far his conclusions have gone, wondering if we're on the same page about all of this. "So, that call really is connected," I say, more like a statement and less like a question, "to what I read about a woman being murdered last night."

Before he can answer, my gut wrenches. I feel like I'm going to be sick.

When I look up at him, he nods his head slightly in place of speaking, his tongue in his cheek.

"Did you hear what she described? Doesn't that sound familiar to you?" I press.

Jack licks his lips and runs fingers through his short chestnut hair. "I know what you're thinking. But there are still a lot of questions that need answers. It's too early to throw out baseless theories."

"Baseless?" I say a little too loud. "Jack. Didn't you hear how she described this guy?"

"I also heard her explain that she thought he was a *ghost*." He sighs. "Look. I hear what you're saying. But we don't even know if this woman was in her right mind. We don't know if she saw what she described to you."

I ignore him. "Does her cause of death match all the others?"

"You know I can't tell you that."

"Why is it so crazy to believe it's him? You never caught the guy!"

The room feels heavy and hot all of a sudden. I get up and switch off the fireplace, pacing back and forth.

"Let's not get hasty, Nola. I want to get to the bottom of this as much as you do. But I need your help. First, we need to remove that podcast episode or at least cut out the ending immediately. I'd like to talk to Harvey anyway. Can we get him to meet us at the studio?"

Harvey.

He never called me back last night. I check my call log and texts, but there's nothing. The last messages I have from him are from yesterday, when I confirmed that I was okay after leaving work so abruptly. I call him again, worried something happened.

After three rings, he picks up, mid-yawn. "Hey, Nol."

"Harvey. Are you okay?"

"Yeah, why wouldn't I be?"

Even through the wine haze that is last night, I specifically remember seeing Him in the stairwell of the bookstore. It feels like a dream now, but I know it wasn't. When Harvey wasn't answering my calls, my mind immediately assumed he was dead somewhere— the rational conclusion. With the unpredictable couple days I've had, anything is possible.

"You never called me back last night."

"My bad. I didn't even see your calls. What's up?"

I meet Jack down at the studio after changing clothes again. In the office upstairs, I hang my coat next to Jack's and join him at Harvey's desk. Harvey arrives just minutes later full of confusion. It's the first time he's seen me since I stormed out of the recording room on Friday night, but he greets me with a hug so big it's as if he hasn't seen me in years, not thirty-six hours.

"Can you tell me what's going on with you?" Harvey presses, keeping his voice low in an attempt at a private conversation.

"I'll explain later. I promise."

I do intend to tell him, just not with Jack here.

Harvey shifts to Jack and shakes his hand, and I remember this is probably only their second or third time meeting. Harvey powers on his desktop computer and pulls up the audio file from Friday night as well as the recording of the woman's call, including her phone number. Jack jots it down in a notepad.

"I tried calling her back after the call ended and it just rang through," Harvey explains. "I had a feeling it was real, but not enough to call the police. We get joke calls sometimes."

"Yeah, that's what Nola said, too."

We listen to part of the call again before Jack pauses it right as the woman starts to explain that she was locking her bedroom door, before she described the man in her window.

"What did she mean by 'again'?" Jack presses.

The exact line in question is, "I can't believe I'm on live radio again. Oh god, I'm so sorry." This came directly after I asked her what she saw.

Harvey claps his hands. "Okay. So, I've actually been thinking about this since I left the studio Friday night because I wondered the same thing. Then, I remembered that we got a call on Thursday night from a woman who wanted to keep her name and location anonymous, which people do from time to time. I'm pretty sure she had a ghost story. I haven't listened back yet, but are you interested?"

"Of course," Jack replies.

Now that Harvey mentions it, I think I know the exact call he's talking about. Our discussion was extremely brief, and it was before the call about the Lake Lady. Harvey locates it quickly and presses Play while he checks the call log for a phone number match.

"Hi there. Big fan. I wanted to ask you guys about ghosts, because I'm pretty sure there is one in my house," she said in a low and anxious tone. "I have never seen a spirit before or had any paranormal experiences, so I could use some advice." Then she started to babble. "I actually am quite a logical person, and I'm surprised at myself that I'm even calling in about this. And a little nervous to be live. But I don't know who else to turn to, and I've been a frequent listener of the show for a handful of years."

"I think we can help you with that. Tell us what's going on," I hear myself say.

The woman continues, now shaky voiced. "It's just that things have been going missing around the house. And I live alone an—" The call cuts off.

A few seconds later, Harvey chimed in. "Looks like we may have lost that caller. We'll wait to see if she calls back, but in the meantime, let's move on to our next caller. Here's Maggie from Massachusetts."

Harvey pauses the audio file. "She never called back."

"That sounds just like the woman in the Friday night call," Jack says.

It seems like he's trying to avoid using her name—Felicity—like he's unable to confirm or deny certain details and wants to keep what he knows hidden, even from us.

"Do the numbers match?" Jack asks.

Harvey scrolls until he finds it. "Yeah. It's the same number."

I don't know exactly what this proves other than the already known fact that this woman truly believed that the house she lived in for five years suddenly became haunted. But Jack appears intrigued by this development, which makes me question it deeper.

Jack crosses the office and puts his coat back on. "All right. I'm gonna need you to send me those files. And, please, take both calls out of the podcast episodes while we investigate this. But, guys, I know you have a lot of ideas and want to be involved in this, but try not to worry yourselves. Let me do my job. I'll be in touch."

After Jack leaves, Harvey and I sit in silence until we hear the building door slam downstairs. This jogs Harvey to speak. His eyes are locked on the screen, unblinking.

"I can't believe we were the last people someone talked to before they died. And we thought it was a fucking joke." He drops his head in his hands and then drags the skin of his face down with his fingers.

This feels like a good time to tell Harvey everything. We're already talking about Felicity's murder and the call and Jack's involvement.

But the thought of spewing it all is exhausting, and I'm more focused on what Jack's thinking than cluing Harvey in. How would he react, anyhow? Would he want to protect me, help me? Or would he be skeptical like he was when I told him I thought I was being followed? I don't want to find out. Not yet.

I wait a few seconds to reply, also feeling oppressed by the weight of the circumstances. "We didn't know. She should have called the police instead of us," I say gently.

Harvey looks at me. "But it wasn't her fault, either, you know? She seemed so confused."

"I know. I'm not trying to blame her. I'm just trying not to blame us."

"Yeah," he says sincerely, touching the tip of his shoe to mine.

My phone buzzes as a string of text messages come in. They're from Nicole, the sales director of Telegraph One. I'm initially curious as to why she's texting me on a Sunday, but considering we've known each other since my dad was still hosting *Night Watch*, and she's a workaholic, it's fitting.

Nola!

I was looped in regarding that call on the
Friday episode and am noticing the listener
impressions going up drastically. Faster than
they have been over the last few weeks.

Will stay on top of this. Could be big!

I show them to Harvey and he's clearly sharing the same conflicted feelings I am. Part excited about the possibility of getting more attention to the show, part horrified at the reason why.

Nicole probably doesn't even think that call was real. Or she's already made the connection herself and doesn't care. I simulate joy and thank her for the support in a quick text response.

"Well. Do you think the police have any leads on who did this to Felicity?" Harvey asks.

Jack was so quick to dismiss the idea that He is back. I consider the fact that Jack knows a lot more about the case than I do, as whatever information they've had on Him has never been publicly released to maintain the purity of the investigation. Surely, the last thing they wanted was a false confession. But as his only known survivor, I've seen something the police never have: Him. His face. Well, his mask. And now, I've seen it twice. And although I'm confident Jack won't believe me when I tell him what I witnessed last night, I have to warn him. I have to help.

"I don't know. But I'm gonna go find out."

15

JACK

A 5.3-inch gash across her neck indicates a single deep throat cut that severed her carotid arteries and breached both jugular veins. She sustained neither a sexual assault nor defensive wounds in the brutal attack against her and she succumbed to her injuries quickly." This is what Jack reads in forty-one-year-old Felicity Morton's autopsy report.

Jack De Lacey furrows his brows at the new information that crossed his desk only minutes ago. The terror Felicity was experiencing during her phone call into *Night Watch* was clear. She knew there was someone watching her, someone who had entered her home unwarranted. That was why she blocked her bedroom door with a dresser and sought refuge in her narrow, claustrophobia-inducing walk-in closet. So why were there no defensive wounds? And how was she slain so seamlessly with the single stroke of a knife? Jack imagines the killer must have struck from behind—leaving her vulnerable. But how was she caught by surprise after she knew enough to hide?

Her bedroom has three tall, single-hung windows, making it easy for the killer to enter from outside, had the windows been unlocked. When Jack walked through Felicity's bedroom yesterday, he noted they had been locked, and he didn't recognize signs that someone had moved through any of them. Forensics found no footprints; furthermore, spiderwebs on the outside of each were perfectly intact. This also indicates that Felicity didn't open her windows frequently. That left the bedroom door as the only possible entry point, allowing the killer to access her closet and slice her throat.

While on the scene, Jack checked the back of the dresser and both sides of her bedroom door. Neither had sustained damage, which told Jack that the killer had not forced their way into the bedroom.

The call to *Night Watch* had abruptly ended, leaving Jack to think Felicity's death probably occurred at that precise time. But that's not the only possibility. The call might have dropped due to the killer hanging up the phone, or Felicity might have done so by mistake. When the phone was bagged at the scene and taken into evidence, it was powered on. That rules out her phone dying and suggests that the killer—or Felicity herself—terminated the call. Knowing that she was still in her closet when the call ended makes Jack believe she hung up by mistake, as the room would have still been barricaded and there was no sign of forced entry into the bedroom.

Leaning back in his creaking desk chair and staring at the white popcorn ceiling above him, Jack recalls her claim that there was a ghost in her house. Based on these thoughts, the most realistically unrealistic solution is that that's exactly what the killer is: a ghost. Jack tosses the idea from his head and returns to logic. He knows

DAPHNE WOOLSONCROFT

there must be a reasonable explanation for this that has nothing to do with the paranormal.

It's possible that after Felicity hung up the phone, she moved the furniture off the bedroom door and fled from her room to another part of the house, perhaps so she could attempt escape. Jack thinks back to his conversation with Gale, about Felicity purposely occupying the downstairs bedroom so she wouldn't feel trapped upstairs. Since the killer appeared to be outside at the time the call dropped—Felicity had said the suspect was at her bedroom window, staring at her—it's likely she ran out of her room and to a different area before being chased back into her bedroom, where she was killed.

Jack takes a bite from a sub sandwich he picked up on his way into the office as Nola's words from this morning vibrate in his ears.

Did you hear what she described? Doesn't that sound familiar to you? Does her cause of death match all the others?

The responses he wanted to give her were *I did*, *Of course*, and *Yes*.

He wipes yellow mustard from his trimmed beard and tries to find a rational explanation for how Felicity's murder played out exactly like a killing by the Hiding Man. Like most murder investigations, his case had persons of interest, just none whose names were released to the public since they were never considered official suspects. They all had alibis for multiple nights of the killings, and although it was possible that the crimes weren't connected, Jack and the department felt strongly that they had to be. The cases shared too many similarities for them to have been committed by different people.

Then one day, the murders just stopped. A very similar MO was found to intersect a few murders in Washington State shortly afterward, and Jack investigated these as much as he could. Being

108

in a different state and jurisdiction led to many roadblocks, but he developed a relationship with the local sheriff's office and they exchanged notes. All the Washington murders occurred around the Tacoma area, meaning the Pierce County Sheriff's Office was put in charge of the slayings. And to Jack's dismay, they didn't uncover any solid suspects for those cases, either—nor a concrete connection to the Hiding Man, hence why the FBI never became involved. But the similarities were damning. The same sense of fear crossed all victims, there were no signs of self-defense, and each woman's life was taken by the honed slice of a knife across her throat. But then the murders stopped again.

According to various articles Jack found online from the likes of Oxygen and the *New York Times*, sometimes serial killers do simply stop for one reason or another. But after all these years, Jack didn't think that was the case. Maybe it was wishful thinking, but he wholeheartedly believed that the person responsible for the murders had died. Now, he's not so sure about that.

One of the people the department had theorized was behind the killings was a shock to Jack himself: his good friend Chick Strate. He worked hard to protect Chick's name—and Nola's, for that matter—trusting that he was incapable of committing such acts.

But then Chick dropped a bombshell on Jack. He confided that he had been casually dating Mia—the young woman who had been brutally murdered in his house. He had been cheating on his wife, Donna, with their daughter's babysitter.

This development severely muddied things up for Jack. Because for a brief time, he had to consider Chick—his own friend—a person of interest. He wouldn't be doing his job well if he didn't, and Chick had motive to murder Mia. Perhaps Donna was catching on to their affair, or Mia had threatened to tell her herself. It was awfully convenient timing for Chick to leave the Christmas party to go to the KXOR office, not to mention that it was 11:00 at night. Why would Chick need to be at his office so late? And during a holiday party where his wife was waiting? On top of that, he didn't arrive at the crime scene until nearly thirty minutes after Mia's murder occurred. It was all a bit too strange. So, he needed to find out if Chick really was at the office that night, or if he had snuck home to commit a gruesome act—before leaving a red herring in the form of a threat to his own daughter.

Chewing on another bite of his sandwich, Jack thinks back to his formal interview with Chick in December 2004.

"So, Chick. How long were you dating Mia? How serious was it?" Jack had pressed shortly after hitting Record on the tape player, feeling his blood boil not only at his friend's adultery, but at the tight spot Chick had put him in. He thought about Nola and Donna, who were unaware of Chick's wrongful actions.

"Since the summer. About five months," Chick said with a sigh, pinching the bridge of his nose. "Her car was in the shop one day when she was supposed to watch Nola, so I offered to pick her up and drop her off that night. We flirted. She seemed into me, impressed by me. What was I supposed to do?"

"Drop her off at home and leave the poor girl alone," Jack spouted sternly. "She was your kid's babysitter. What were you thinking?"

"Come on, man. She was twenty-one years old, Jack. She wasn't a child. Don't paint me as some sicko." Chick's legs were bouncing nervously, lightly vibrating the table. Jack took note.

"You've painted yourself that way. And you can't deny that this looks really bad for you." Jack sat back in his chair across the table and massaged his earlobe. "Tell me where you went when you left the Christmas party last night."

"I told you. I went to the office."

"Why did you go to the office at eleven o'clock at night, Chick?"

Chick leaned forward with a serious expression. "Do you seriously think I had something to do with Mia's murder?"

"I'm just trying to get the whole story here," Jack said with his hands up. "So, tell me. Why so late? Explain to me exactly what happened, and please be specific for the recording."

Chick sighed. "It was a KXOR party at the Bower." He looked at Jack, who was whipping his index finger in a spiral motion, urging him to explain further. Chick sighed again. "The Bower is a ballroom, I guess? In Southeast Portland. This was yesterday. So, um, Saturday, December 18? It was a holiday party for the radio station I work for. Many people flew in to attend it. And one of those people was Thomas Hensworth, who's a board operator at Telegraph One, which is our network." He huffed. "I wanted to show Thomas the studio, since he had never seen it. Show him how we run things. It was a short drive over the bridge anyway, so we just went."

"I spoke with Thomas this morning and he said you stayed longer than him. That he had to take a taxi to his hotel because you needed to—I think his exact words were 'hang back.' Why was that?"

"I thought I'd do some emailing while I was there, I guess."

"While your wife waited for you at a holiday party for *your* job?" Jack pressed.

"This is getting ridiculous. What is this?"

"Just answer the question, Mr. Strate. Please."

In the years they had known each other, never once had Jack called Chick "Mr. Strate." Chick began to wiggle in his seat.

"I was already there. I just wanted to do a couple things. Check my outbox, why don't you? You'll see the proof that I was working. I had nothing to do with Mia's death."

"And I never said you did. I'm just trying to get a clear picture of what the evening was like for you. This is standard protocol."

"Well, that's everything. As soon as I heard the voicemails from Donna, I sped over to our house. That's when I learned what had happened." Chick looked into Jack's eyes. "Trust me. I wish I had just stayed at the holiday party."

Jack slowly nodded. He believed his friend, yet he knew he had to press for more. He looked down at the piece of paper in front of him that listed basic details about the previous murders. "Can you confirm your whereabouts for the nights of September 19, October 9, November 14, and December 6 of this year, 2004?"

Chick blew air out of his lips. "Jack, I don't know that shit off the top of my head. I was probably working most of those nights."

Jack swallowed. "All of those evenings were your nights off the show. And those are the nights the other murders occurred."

Chick made a huffing noise in his throat, astonished.

Jack continued. "I'm not saying you were behind any of them. I'm just getting the record straight."

Jack was able to collect alibis from Chick for the nights in question, but most were loose and consisted of him being home with his wife and daughter. They were as far from airtight as they could get. But in his heart, Jack knew Chick couldn't be behind this, and he had no reason to be. Jack lightly interrogated him only for the record, so his supervisor could see that he did his due diligence. But there was no real evidence—or motive—regarding Chick's involvement, so he fell to the wayside.

Two more murders came in the months after Mia's—Jasmine Petri and Doniesha Wilks—and Jack couldn't find a connection between them and Chick.

He forgave Jack for thumbing him that day at the station, and Jack did everything he could to keep the Strates' names out of the media. To his knowledge, no one ever found out. And despite the Hiding Man quickly becoming an infamous serial killer in the area, once he stopped killing, people lost interest.

Jack rocks in his desk chair and once again picks up Felicity's autopsy report. From what he remembers, the details of all seven murders from the Hiding Man case are starkly similar: stalking, paranoia, the slitting of the victim's throat, a clean crime scene. The DNA tests that the Oregon State Crime Lab is working on—for the blood at the scene and other fibers and samples submitted, including seemingly foreign hair—might take weeks if not months to get back. But he needs answers before then. The time-sensitive pressure to catch this person is suffocating.

Jack is jogged from his thoughts when someone knocks on his office door.

"Come in," he shouts from his desk.

The department's secretary, Minnie, peeks in before closing the door behind her and tiptoeing over to Jack, sporting her voluminous red hair in its usual curls. Minnie has been the backbone of the division for over twenty years and helps Jack with virtually every case he works on, from keeping his favorite pens in stock, to sending him the criminal history of possible suspects, to assisting in report approvals. She's even good enough to come in on a Sunday morning and help him in the wake of a murder such as this.

Minnie keeps her voice low. "Nola Strate is here. She wants to talk to you about the case you're working on." She grimaces and resets her bright red glasses, knowing Jack can't talk to civilians about an active investigation.

Confused, Jack checks his watch to find that he left her at the studio only two hours ago. "She does? I was just with her this morning."

Minnie shrugs and adds, "She says it's important. Says she might be able to help?"

Jack gives in and takes his final bite of sandwich. "All right. Send her in. Thanks, Minnie."

He's uneasy, knowing she's going to pry into what he's working on and heave her exaggerated theories at him. But knowing she has a stake in this and is—in a way—involved, he decides to humor her. For all he knows, she may be able to help him after all.

Minnie leans against the door and ushers Nola inside. She nods at Jack and closes the door behind her.

"Everything okay? Did you remember something else?" Jack asks Nola, motioning to the visitor's chair so she'll sit down. She chooses to remain standing.

"I'm worried you're not taking this seriously enough. You can't honestly tell me this case doesn't feel familiar." She's clenching her fists at her sides, speaking with urgency, eyes filled with torment.

"Nola. You don't know what you're talking about, sweetie—"

"I've been in the same room with him," Nola interrupts loudly. "I've stood mere feet from his body. Can you say the same?"

Jack wonders if he ever has, unbeknownst to him. But he can't have Nola sparking fear that the Hiding Man is back until he knows more.

"We don't know if it's the same guy," Jack responds firmly. "Respectfully, there is a lot about that case that you don't know." He takes a breath and calms his tone. "What you experienced that night at that age is unacceptable. But it doesn't give you authority."

Jack almost feels bad letting these words leave his mouth; he doesn't want to hurt Nola's feelings or minimize her concerns. But this is sensitive territory, and he needs to stand his ground.

"I saw him again. Last night," Nola offers.

Jack cocks his head, stunned. "What do you mean? Where?"

"At my dad's book signing. I swear. He was standing in a stairwell."

Jack looks disappointed. "I want to believe you, I do. And I'm not saying I don't. But do you think your dad's book announcement could have manifested some bad memories?"

"I. Saw. Him."

"Did anyone else?"

Nola pauses, unsure of how to answer.

Jack whispers, "Sit down. I'll share something with you. But you have to promise me it doesn't leave this room. I could get in a lot of trouble."

With the same disturbed glare, Nola finally sits in the chair and leans forward with her forearms on the desk, fingers interlocked, awaiting information.

"The victim had an on-again-off-again boyfriend. We're still looking for him, but I will say this: He was only nineteen years old when the Hiding Man murders occurred. According to his records that we pulled this morning, he was living in Pennsylvania, going to school. But we found some weird texts in the victim's phone between her and him, and we haven't been able to get a hold of him. This could be nothing more than a domestic dispute."

Nola sits in silence, staring at his oak desk and saying nothing at first.

"I want to see the evidence boxes for the Hiding Man murders," she finally says, ignoring everything Jack said.

Jacks laughs and stares, awaiting a punchline. It becomes excruciatingly obvious—and quickly—that she isn't joking.

"You can't be serious, Nola. Did you hear nothing of what I just said?"

"Some of those files are mine. I have the right to look."

"No, you don't."

"Jack, come on. We're like family. If you believe this is a simple domestic dispute and the Hiding Man is dead somewhere, then surely, you'll have no problem putting me at ease by letting me take a look at the evidence." Nola's tone is lighter now, convincing. She even shoots him a soft, close-mouthed smile.

"How is looking at that stuff going to help anything?"

"Like you said. I experienced something unacceptable. Maybe reading through some things will help me. And get me on your side of the fence regarding Felicity's murder. Maybe this can help me understand the differences."

Technically, Nola could release the audio files of Felicity's calls or spread fear around the community about her ideas on the show. He needs to keep her worries at bay. But he has a bad feeling that looking at the details of the other murders will do the opposite: cement her belief that it's the same killer. Because unlike Nola, Jack knows the evidence is too similar for comfort.

"God, I can't believe I'm doing this," Jack sighs. "I will let you look at *your* file, under *my* supervision. And you cannot tell anyone that we're doing this."

"My lips are sealed," Nola says, quickly squeezing Jack's hand in appreciation.

Jack slips out of his office, leaving Nola seated inside, and passes Minnie's empty desk. Feeling rightfully culpable, he scans around the room to see if anyone will spot his movements, but Minnie is pouring herself an afternoon cup of coffee while another colleague gabs on the telephone, facing the opposite direction. Jack is allowed in the evidence room, more commonly referred to as the property room, but because he's agreeing to show Nola some paperwork from her own file, he doesn't want anyone to see him.

He presses his key card on the reader next to the evidence room's door, and it beeps green and unlocks the door. He scampers inside and closes the door. No one else is in the room with him. He repeats the case number in his head as he approaches the shelves full of bagged evidence and storage boxes, many of which are filled with marijuana from the 1980s and people's cell phones or personal belongings that were never picked up. Since there were seven murders, there are even more boxes assigned to this case, which should make the number 2004-0291 easier to spot. But when he stumbles upon the shelf where all the boxes should sit, side by side, he notices that two of them are missing. As he sifts through the ones that are there to ensure he didn't miscount long ago, he concludes that the box containing the notes, evidence, and documentation for Mia Parsons's murder—and subsequently the information given by Nola and her family from the time the murder occurred—are gone. As is the box of evidence pertaining to Jasmine Petri's murder, the one that was committed the month after Mia's.

Jack's heart drops, and he racks his mind for an answer as to what could have happened to them. He grazes his fingers across numerous boxes, reading the case numbers one by one to ensure his tired mind isn't misreading. But they're gone. Everything is strictly put back in the correct spot in this room and continually kept organized by the property officer. The files being gone makes virtually no sense. It's impossible. His colleagues would never be this careless with them, he's sure. And there's no one else in his department who would need to review them right now—especially since Jack is the lead on this case and his partner is out of town.

Jack exits the evidence room and makes his way back to his office, feeling guiltier than he did when he was on his way in there. Since Minnie is back at her desk, he decides to ask her if she knows anything about what's happened to the missing boxes.

"You haven't filled any requests to pull the Hiding Man evidence boxes, have you?"

"Woof," Minnie breathes. "That's a name I haven't heard in years. No, I haven't. Would you like me to?"

"No. But thank you," Jack says with a blank stare, still trying to figure it out.

As he opens the door into his office and sees Nola, it hits him. He last pulled those boxes two summers ago when Chick was working on his new book. He only let him review them under his supervision; just like he was about to do with Nola, he'd showed Chick Mia's box. Now he remembers that he pulled more than Mia's box; at least one or two others. The realization makes him sick at his lack of professional manner in a situation like this. And he was about to do it all over again for Nola simply because she asked to see them. He grasps now that he's been too lenient with critical information when it comes to his close friends. He's been working in this division far too long to let such antics continue, even for someone like Chick, or Nola. Jack never saw the boxes again after that day with Chick—though he remembers taking a lengthy call outside while Chick was looking them over at his desk.

Idiot, he tells himself.

Although it was a year and a half ago, Jack remembers that when he got back to his office, Chick had told him that he'd asked Minnie to put them back in the property room—and Jack just believed him.

Why would he keep them? And after all this time? Jack wonders, walking up to Nola.

"Where's the box?" Nola asks, puzzled.

Jack lets out a deep, chesty sigh. "I let your dad look at them a couple years ago. And I think he may have stolen them."

16

NOLA

H i. You've reached Chick. Sorry to have missed your call, but if you leave a message, I'll return it promptly."

This is the second time in a row I've gotten his voicemail. I make a third attempt as I drive away from the police station. I pray not to hear it again as I rack my brain for the reason my dad would have stolen those evidence boxes.

Seconds after I press his name on my phone, I hear, "Hi. You've rea—" and I hang up.

My dad, who is as well-versed in technology as I am, is usually easy to reach. The new version of him that hasn't picked up my calls these past few days is foreign to me. I don't dial him frequently, but when I do, he always answers.

As I drive over the Burnside Bridge toward home, I admire the rippled water seventy feet below, the hundred-year-old Italian Renaissance bridge towers, and the cruise ship I always see from my house just up the river. From this view in the daytime, although we're into November now, autumn is in full swing. The skyline is scattered with reds, yellows, oranges, and greens as far as the eye can see. And for just a moment, while I take in the beauty around me, I forget the drama, the dread. Everything is beautiful.

The moment ends as I'm flooded with more questions about my dad. I have half a mind to drive over to his house and demand an explanation. But instead, I continue home to do something I told myself I would never do. Something that has been tempting me for most of my life: google the Hiding Man. Since I can't sift through evidence boxes and look back at the details from the investigators' point of view, I can at least learn the basics from the internet when I get back to my laptop. Or at least I assume I can. Either I'll discover an array of disturbing, detailed articles, or a shockingly scarce supply of information.

Only one way to find out.

I know the basics of the case, like how there are numerous victims other than Mia, that he dropped off the radar months after her murder, and that the police never caught the guy behind it all. But I've always stopped myself from going down the rabbit hole, afraid of what I'd learn.

At this point, believing he may be back, I'm consumed with knowing what happened to the other victims, as some sort of self-preservation tactic. If he's really after me, I need to outsmart him. But I can't do that unless I know his game. Since the murders were never solved, I realize the media coverage will be missing information—details I had hoped to find in the evidence boxes.

Something about looking at photos of the message written in my childhood kitchen or even viewing a transcript of my interview with Jack after that night sounds as morbid as it does cathartic. Since it happened so long ago, and when I was just a kid, much of it feels like something I dreamed up. The actual events now feel faded and dim. I'm afraid to bring them to the surface, but part of me believes that if I do, I can destroy them. Like how the teenagers in *A Nightmare on Elm Street* had to take hold of the evil, deranged Freddy Krueger in their dreams, so they could pull him into the real world and end him once and for all. Maybe facing my nightmares will end in their abolishment, too.

I approach my house within fifteen minutes of leaving Jack's office in a flurry of emotions. Pulling into my driveway at the back of my house, I notice my next-door neighbor's car is in their driveway. I always take note because I've never seen the owners. It's like whoever lives in that house is invisible. I don't see them in the windows, bringing in their groceries, getting in and out of their car, pulling the trash cans to the curb—nothing. All I see are blinds suddenly open when they weren't before—and vice versa; candles appearing lit, and then, later, blown out; windows cranked open and then closed. But I never see any people. Though now, a black car sits in the driveway, proving someone is home.

I park my car and see that my mounted iron mailbox is overstuffed with packages and letters. After twisting my silver key in the front door, I grab the stack of mail and walk inside. I instinctively lock the door behind me and head for the dining table to drop my mail and continue with my plans. As the packages fall from my arms, a few of the letters I grabbed fumble onto the floor. I pick them up and flip through them, plopping them one by one on the table, expecting them all to be bills that I have on autopay.

Note to self: Go paperless.

But one of them sticks out among the others. It doesn't have that plastic window screen on it like its cohorts. There's no return address like them, either. The envelope is completely blank—and sans postage. It's one of those kraft mailers that can fit anything with the dimensions of a sheet of paper. I flip it over, fully expecting it to be open and empty, just a duplicate envelope that someone tossed by mistake along with a real letter, and it somehow got mixed into mine. But the mailer is secured shut. The sticky seal is pressed, and the metal clasp is folded down and fastened. As I pinch around the envelope, I feel something inside that's thicker than a single sheet of paper but thinner than a deck of documents.

What could this be?

Agitated, I take a seat at my dining table, slowly ripping open the manila envelope. Something tells me I should be doing this with gloves on, or at least tearing it open a little more neatly, but I don't own a letter opener and I'm perilously eager to see what's inside. When I finish ripping the seal, I bend the metal clasp upward and pull out a single piece of paper. It's protected, encased in plastic, and it reads "EVIDENCE" in large, bold letters at the top of one side. Included underneath is a case number, description, and other information that was only partly filled out. My stomach churns at the word "EVIDENCE," but I can't yet see what this is. Suddenly I'm touching it with the tips of my fingernails, holding it by the very corners. I flip the bag over and drop it on my dining table to be greeted with something I forgot I created.

Within the clear plastic evidence bag is a single piece of paper with a drawing I completed after Mia's murder. I used a black colored pencil to draw exactly what I saw that night standing at the bottom of the stairs, after I crept down to see if Mia's boyfriend was trying to play House with her while I soundly slept above their heads. Staring at the drawing brings the memory back so strongly, as if I've been yanked back in time. It's a detailed sketch of Him, showcasing the signature stitching that made up his mouth and nose, and the thread sewn around the holes over his eyes.

How did this get in my mailbox? I ask myself.

The fact that it's unmarked means it was dropped off personally by someone who wasn't my mail carrier, but shoved among the rest of the mail to blend in. I pull my phone out of my pocket only to find that the tumultuous weather has caused my cameras to go in and out all day—meaning my camera didn't even catch the mailman today. Nor whoever dropped this by for me to see.

Is this some kind of message?

My heart beats faster, adding this to my list of reasons to be afraid—even in my own home.

With it raining here over half of the year, this happens often enough that I've considered getting rid of the cameras altogether. The only way to get the cameras in working order again once they're down like this is to call the security company and, depending on how bad it is, have them fix it virtually or dispatch a technician to my house. Most of the time, they can do it over the phone. But this storm has been particularly nasty, so I say a small prayer that they don't have to send someone out. If that's the case, it could take days to get the cameras fixed. And at a time like this, I don't have days to spare.

I look up the number for Northwest Protect and dial, wanting to get this figured out as soon as humanly possible. After a short ringing, a female robot voice on the other end says, "We are experiencing longer than usual hold times due to numerous outages in your area. You are caller number sixty-four in the queue. Please hold for the next available representative."

I audibly gasp at the number of callers in front of me and hang up, making a mental note to try again later. It's a company that covers only Oregon and Washington, so I'm surprised at the number of callers. But with the recent storms, I should have expected as much. Checking the customer service hours on their website, I read that they close in less than an hour, since it's Sunday. I doubt everyone on hold right now will even be helped today.

Note to self #2: Call them again tomorrow.

The sooner I can get this fixed, the sooner I'll feel safe. And the more likely I'll catch whoever did this on camera if they try it again.

17

Twenty Years Earlier

Nola sits across a metal table from Jack in a room that's bright and bare. The chair beneath her is hard and cold, with a blaring single bulb above her head. Her parents sit on either side of her as an array of colored pencils lie across the table in all shades of the rainbow and then some. Jack spread them out just moments ago, directly after he asked her to draw the man she saw the night before.

Nola didn't stop crying the previous night, not until she fell numb to her feelings in the wee hours of the morning and stared blankly out the window of her hotel room, unable to sleep. She traced the dark horizon and conceived stories about the cars driving around far past what anyone's bedtime should be. A fraction of her wanted to return to her beloved childhood home and hide under the covers with her mom and dad in close reach. But she knew she could never feel safe in there again; instead, like a prisoner of a man whose name she didn't know. Looking back at her sleeping parents, she wondered how long the hotel room would be their home.

Her parents secured them a cushy room across town and six floors up, looking down on everything and everyone so that Nola would feel protected. The room is modern and clean, with sheets she would usually be ecstatic to sink into, as if she were on an adventure in a new place; like the trips she and her parents had taken to Disneyland, Hawaii, and London. Although staying in the hotel feels luxurious, it's nothing like the vacations in her memory. She's in her own city, after all, so it just feels alien not to be in her house.

They booked a king suite, with one bed for the three of them so Donna and Chick could stay close to Nola. She slept in between them where she couldn't possibly fall into harm's way again. But as they slept on either side of her, Nola studied the sparkling city lights through the sheer curtain for a while, awaiting daylight. This wasn't an adventure, this wasn't fun. This, too, was Hell.

On their way to the police station earlier this afternoon, neither of her parents said a word about what happened. They didn't mention Mia, or ask Nola what she had seen, or question if she was okay. It was almost as though they were trying to pretend it hadn't occurred only hours before, or at all. Nola didn't dare bring it up on her own, wanting to avoid the subject as much as possible.

As her father drove under the speed limit, seemingly in a daze of his own, he had said, "What would you think about taking this week off school and going somewhere fun with your mom?"

Nola couldn't help but notice that her dad smiled as he made the offer, but slowly dropped it seconds later. She knew he was hurting, too, but she didn't know why.

She sat in silence for a few beats, unsure of how to respond. *Go somewhere fun? At a time like this?* she thought. She didn't know if she'd ever be able to have fun again.

Ignoring his question, she asked, "When are we going home?"

She didn't want to go back. The fear overwhelmed her, but it was her home. The possibility of never returning was just as terrifying as going back there.

Her mom turned around from the passenger seat and sent her an apologetic smile. "Well, your dad and I think you deserve a much better house with a bigger room. I wasn't going to tell you just yet, but we're already thinking about getting a house on the lake where Aunt Blair lives."

Nola's aunt Blair isn't her aunt at all. She's her mom's close friend whom they visit frequently, but Nola has considered her an aunt most of her life.

Aunt Blair's house has always been one of Nola's favorite places to visit: the picturesque, affluent lakeside community located a short trip down the highway from the house in which Nola grew up. The concept of making it their permanent residence would normally excite her, but nothing could cheer her up.

Nola stared back at her mom, still unsure of what to say.

Her dad chimed in again. "We can get a boat. Swim all the time. Would that make you happy? We think it would be a great change for all of us."

But Nola didn't want change. What she really wanted was for everything to go back to normal. To teleport into the 7:00 p.m. Yesterday version of herself where she could beg her parents not to leave for the party so Mia could be saved.

Chick, Donna, and Nola sat in silence for the rest of the short trip until they pulled into the police station. Her parents had both been there individually last night as well, but Nola didn't know why.

Yet here they are again, together, waiting for her to imitate something terrible she saw on paper.

"Use any of these colors you want and let me know if it's too hard, okay?" Jack says from across the table, his fingers clasped together. "I know you don't want to think about him, but showing us what he looked like is going to help us catch the bad guy who did this. Does that sound good?"

Nola takes a moment before nodding her head and reaching for the black colored pencil. Much of what she could remember about the man was literally black and white, since he was void of color. As much as eight-year-old Nola wants to grab the Razzle Dazzle Rose or the Mango or the Shamrock pencils, she instead debates between the colors labeled Outer Space and Black. Which would better mimic his midnight holes for eyes, or the dark thread etched into his mask? Or his clothes that all seemingly blended together?

A piece of printer paper lies in front of her, blank and glossy, begging to be filled up with beautiful art. She doesn't draw much anymore, but when she does, her typical works include flowers or made-up characters for a show she wishes existed on Cartoon Network or Nickelodeon. They're usually talking animals or cool, teenage girls with superpowers. She even sometimes likes to draw creatures that she heard about on her dad's show, like ghosts—but with smiles on their faces—or gentler versions of sea monsters or forest cryptids. Never has she scribbled something that scared her. And she hates that she has to start now.

Donna and Chick rub Nola's back in solidarity, giving her the go-ahead to begin. Drawing his face would mean thinking about it, concentrating on it. She starts with his clothes first instead. Nola decides not to include the scene itself because she's not very skilled at drawing stairs or furniture, and she doesn't want to mess this up. But there's a stack of paper next to Jack in case she does.

When Nola gets to the point where it looks as though she's composed the Headless Horseman sans jack-o'-lantern, she starts on the villain's face, making it large enough so she can detail the stitching. She can't decide if it's more daunting to begin with his eyes or mouth, but ultimately determines that she doesn't want his eyes staring at her as she finishes up the rest.

When she finally gets to the eyes, her heart is pounding inside her chest. She can feel it in every part of her body, the fear seeping into each pore across her skin. Nola grips the colored pencil with tenacity as her hand becomes clammy with sweat. After a deep breath, she completes the dark eyes of the man from the bottom of the stairs at rapid speed. As soon as she finishes, she pushes it toward Jack and stares down at her lap, not wanting to look at what she's penciled.

"For the record, can you describe why you drew the person this way and how accurately it matches what you saw last night, Nola?" Jack asks in a soft tone, directing his voice toward the recorder on the table.

"This is what I saw. This is what it looked like," Nola replies.

"When you say 'it,' what are you referring to?" Jack asks.

Chick leans his head back in frustration, already thinking too much is being asked of his young daughter.

"The bad person who killed Mia." Nola has a hard time saying her babysitter's name without bursting into tears again. But she doesn't think she could cry even if she tried, feeling like a dried-up well; every droplet she could muster already has been sucked out of her.

"Is there anything else you can share regarding his appearance? His voice, his mannerisms, anything like that?"

"I didn't hear it speak. And I barely saw it move."

"Right. Thank you, Nola. I keep saying 'him' when we don't know their gender. Unless something made you assume one over the other?"

Nola pauses to think. "It didn't have hair that I could see. But maybe it did have some, and it was under the mask."

"What makes you feel certain they were wearing a mask?" Jack inquires.

Nola lets out a shaky sigh and finally stares down at her creation. "Its face didn't look human."

18

NOLA

I get my dad's voicemail again as I pace around my dining area.

How would something from an evidence box that he supposedly has make its way anonymously and cryptically into my mailbox? I consider sending a photo of this to Jack, but I don't see the point. He clearly doesn't want me to get involved. If I show him what I just received, who knows what he would say or do.

Would he blame my dad? Think I made this up? Take my theory that He is back more seriously? Because of the uncertainty, I think it's best I keep this to myself for now. The last thing I want is for Jack to grow suspicious of my dad. Talking about the mailer does the opposite. Besides, I'm sure Jack has been trying to contact my dad as much as I have. Surely, I'll receive answers for this ominous package soon—whether they come from my dad's mouth or not. Until then, now that I'm home, it's time to learn everything I can online about the murders.

Curling up in the corner of my sofa, I get down to business. But when I open my laptop, my fingers freeze. I haven't a single clue what I'll find when I search Him.

Growing up, I had imagined He would have become a hometown legend, something our city would be known for. But no one talked about Him in school or around town that I can remember—and I would remember. It's probably because people don't typically glorify serial killers like they would, say, folklore. Or, at least, they shouldn't. For example, in the tiny town of Fouke, Arkansas, there are reports of a beast called the Boggy Creek Monster. He's been witnessed countless times since at least 1964, stalking people in the woods and leaving three-toed footprints behind. This creature and its story have become such a pillar in their community that they opened a convenience store called the Monster Mart. It has a life-size figure of him outside the shop that visitors can take a photo with, and a giant bust of his head atop the shop's sign, which states in small print beneath: FOUKE, HOME OF THE LEGENDARY BOGGY CREEK MONSTER. They've elevated the myth into the ultimate tourist attraction. And I'd bet that's because he didn't knowingly take the lives of at least seven innocent people and permanently destroy many others'. After hearing about the Boggy Creek Monster on *Night Watch* as a kid, I always imagined He would have the same impact on my city. Thankfully, He didn't.

My fingers press the letters T-H-E H-I-D-I-N-G M-A-N one by one as though I'm new to typing, before my right middle finger smacks the Return key. The first link I see at the top of the search page reads, "The Hiding Man: Portland's Most Prolific Serial Killer."

I command-click the link to add it to my tabs as I continue scanning the selections. At the top of the main search is a display of five photos related to the Hiding Man. A couple of them are from outside of victims' homes at the time of the murders—ambulances and law enforcement all over the scene. Another is an illustrated map of where the murders took place, which was seemingly created by internet sleuths. I click View All under the images to find endless rows of others. Here, I find a large display of smiling screenshots of the victims, linking to their obituaries.

Suddenly, I meet eyes with a familiar face, and my heart nearly explodes. It's Mia. Bright blond hair, an exaggerated but authentic smile. It's her high school senior yearbook photo, taken around three years before she died and two years before I met her. Just like the others, the photo originates from her obituary. I click on it and read the page.

Mia Ann Parsons was taken from us on December 18, 2004, after 21 years earthside. Every day of those 21 years, she lived with joy in her heart, with the love she had for her friends and family being evident in all that she did. She was outgoing, funny, intelligent, and always there for her younger siblings and peers. In high school, she earned exemplary grades while still making time for extracurriculars like theater and gardening club. She loved kids and relished the idea of becoming a mother someday. In the meantime, she babysat for multiple families and enjoyed every bit of it. It was doing what she loved that ended her short yet full life.

The last sentence stings the most. I feel more responsible than ever.

The page goes on to list her surviving family members, which include everyone from her sister, brother, parents, and more, except one of her grandfathers, whom she "joined upon death." It's only now that I learn that Mia had siblings. I wonder if she ever brought them up in the past. We mostly danced, watched raunchy movies my parents wouldn't have liked, and talked about what was going on in *my* tiny life—we rarely focused on her. The only thing I remember from Mia's personal life was talks of her doting older boyfriend.

Never learning his name, I type *Mia Parsons Boyfriend Murder Portland* into the Google search bar, but I don't get any hits. If I knew his name, I'd try to find him.

I don't know any of the others victims' names or anything about what happened to them or when; just that there were six connected deaths that came before and after Mia. I go back to the original tab I saved—"The Hiding Man: Portland's Most Prolific Serial Killer"—and study its contents.

The Hiding Man is the moniker of an unidentified serial killer who operated in Northern Oregon in the early 2000s. The Hiding Man murdered seven known victims in the Portland area between September 2004 and February 2005, most of which took place in the victims' own homes. At least one person has survived him unharmed.

Are they talking about me?

The Hiding Man's name was created shortly after they took their first victim's life: Jamie York. The Portland Police Department received an anonymous typewritten letter two days later featuring a poem, believed to have been written by the killer. After reports of the victims being stalked or tormented before their deaths made way into the media, local Portland news station KPLN officially coined the killer's title based on the infamous poem. All known victims experienced the sense of being watched or followed, but none of them were sure by whom. All but one of the attacks took place while the victims were home alone, and each of them had their throats cleanly slit by a knife. Police believe the victims were attacked from behind after the killer stealthily approached, which would explain the lack of defensive wounds on each victim. As of 2024, no suspect names have been made public.

Confirmed murders:

- Jamie York, 24, had her throat slit in her home on Albany Drive, in the Northeast Portland neighborhood of Alberta Arts District, on September 19, 2004.
- Jasey Levy, 27, had her throat slit in her home on Berry Boulevard, in the Southeast Portland neighborhood of Sellwood—Moreland, on October 9, 2004.
- Kendra Lloyd, 25, had her throat slit in her home on Pollack Street, in the Northwest Portland neighborhood of the Pearl District, on November 14, 2004.

- Carrie Fenton, 33, had her throat slit in her home on Eggland Street, in the Southeast Portland neighborhood of Mt. Tabor, on December 6, 2004.
- Mia Parsons, 21, had her throat slit while babysitting in the Southwest Portland neighborhood of Goose Hollow, on December 18, 2004. She was killed, while the child she was reportedly watching was left unharmed.

Physically? Yes. Mentally? Severely harmed.

I feel my heartbeat in my face as I read the lines over again, astonished that I'm briefly mentioned. These two sentences about Mia make it all feel that much more real. I continue reading.

- Jasmine Petri, 25, had her throat slit in her home on Stapleton Road, in the Southeast Portland neighborhood of Mt. Tabor, on January 29, 2005.
- Doniesha Wilks, 23, had her throat slit in her home on Vania Street, in the Southeast Portland neighborhood of Hawthorne, on February 20, 2005.

The article goes on to include theories of who the killer could be based on the Buck knife that was believed to be used in each slaying, without listing any names. Many believe he could be a hunter or an outdoorsman. It also details more about what the victims had experienced before they were killed; each had noted things disappearing from their home, seeing a figure in the window, or feeling like they were being watched.

Just like Felicity.

I don't know how Felicity died or what the scene of her murder looked like, but she saw someone wearing a mask, and considering all the strange things that were happening around her house, it all seems too similar to be a coincidence.

Among the information of what the victims had seen before they died was a detailed account of Jasey Levy's story, his second-known victim. There's a screengrab of a newspaper clipping from the time, which includes a small paragraph about her murder and a photo of something at the scene: a note.

The clipping reads:

> Jasey Levy, 27, was found brutally slain in her Sellwood home while both female roommates were out for the evening. Jasey, a Jewish Studies teacher at a private Jewish school in Portland, left a cryptic message at the desk in her bedroom. First, a warning, then, two Yiddish curses.

The note is hard to read even if it was in English—which it isn't—due to the fuzzy black-and-white image from the newspaper. But below the photo, it states, "Translation: The phantom is coming to take my soul. If he can come for me, he might come for you next."

The curses beneath this horrifying note, according to this article, translate to "He should crap blood and pus," and "He should be transformed into a chandelier, to hang by day and to burn by night."

Having written these forewarning messages, she had to have known she was being watched and, moreover, that someone evil was coming after her.

The bottom of the page reads, "Also see: *The Hiding Man of Washington.*" In the italicized words, there is a link with even more murders, taking place farther north in Washington State months after his final known Portland victim's death.

There were three similar murders in and around Tacoma in July 2005, September 2005, and then in July 2006.

Twenty-nine-year-old Abigail Hendricks, twenty-three-year-old Jennifer King, and thirty-one-year-old Alex Sanders, all murdered in the same fashion as the Hiding Man Seven. Throats slashed, no DNA evidence, no suspects.

Same guy, or copycat? I wonder.

I click the other tab, returning to Google Images, and scroll to see what else I can find. Among real photos from when it all happened, there is a small collection of drawings of Him. I click the link of one of them to see how someone was able to come up with a sketch at all since I'm the only person who has ever seen Him. It takes me to a Reddit thread titled r/ThePortlandHidingMan. I read the paragraph above the image.

Hey guys! I just moved to Portland, so I've been deep diving into this case lately. I wanted to draw up my version of what the surviving victim of The Hiding Man described to the police back in the day. I found a Newspapers.com article (clipped below) where she explains what she saw from her window. The guy is even creepier than I imagined.

Below it are two photographs: one of a small newspaper clipping that contains a quote describing his general appearance, which someone saw through their neighbor's window; and the other is a photo of the artwork on the poster's desk. The resemblance is quite similar to the one I drew myself at age eight, sans some of the stitching.

The post was made two years ago and has five comments below it. A commenter asked:

How would they be able to describe him? Didn't everyone who saw him die?

In response, the original poster wrote,

A lot of information hasn't been released, but based on what I read in the paper, there's been witnesses. Or, at least one. You can read the clipping in the post.

They responded:

How did she survive him? Can you link me to it?

The reply was:

I found it somewhere online. There are drawings besides mine from other armchair detectives using the same person's quote. Go harass them about it.

As I scan the comments, a memory pops into my head. Back then, my mom told me that Jack said another girl saw the killer, and somehow, I haven't conceptualized even once who she is or what she witnessed. I think that detail got buried under everything else. The newspaper clipping doesn't include the person's name, but I can guess she was the one speaking.

Skeptical, I'm scrolling through the responses when I come across a commenter claiming to be said girl.

> I'm the girl you're talking about. When I was a kid, I saw him through my window after he killed my neighbor. What do you want to know?

Her comment was posted ten months ago—a year after the post was made—and has zero replies. I consider that she could be a fake based on how openly she's putting the information out there, but I click on her profile anyway. She has replied to multiple posts under the same subreddit—r/ThePortlandHidingMan—along with other random, unrelated forums. Her most recent comment was just last week, meaning she's still an active user.

All her Hiding Man comments are alike, so I wonder if she herself is trying to get answers or finally talk to someone about an ordeal that has plagued her for years, like I'm doing now.

Her profile doesn't include her name, just an obscure username and an app-generated avatar. I go out on a limb and message her privately, figuring I have nothing to lose.

> Hi. I've seen your comments about The Hiding Man. I saw him too. If you're still in the area—or even if you're not—please message me. I think He's come back. And He's killing again.

19

NOLA

I hit the gas on my Jeep and make the five-minute drive to my dad's house. Since he still isn't returning my calls, my only option is to confront him personally about the suspicious mail I received and hope he has a good explanation.

I pull up to his house which, just like last time, boasts a vacant cement driveway. Before using my key to let myself in as I did two nights ago, I rap my knuckles on the red front door and press the doorbell over and over. Roughly thirty seconds of this goes by with a few shouts of "Dad? It's me," until I decide I've waited too long. I slip my key into the lock once again, ready to turn it and push my way inside.

As I do, my hand is yanked forward with the handle still in my grasp, causing me to stumble into the doorway. My dad, who unlocked the door and opened it that very moment, looks vaguely disheveled and half asleep.

"Jesus, honey. Are you trying to wake the neighborhood?" he says groggily while closing the door behind me. He's sporting a charcoal pullover and matching sweatpants, his salted dark hair fussed like he jumped right out of bed to answer the door.

"Dad, it's the late afternoon. The sun's going to set again in, like, an hour."

He rubs his eyes. "Oh. Really? Well, it's Sunday." He pauses. "Isn't it?"

Yes, man. Get it together.

"Have you been sleeping all day? I called you a bunch," I say, walking into his living room.

He pauses to rub his eyes again before speaking, groaning a low grumble while he does. "After the signing last night, we went to Huber's and had a few too many Spanish coffees," he says, rubbing the back of his head. "I've been sleeping on and off, watching some old black-and-whites. You know me."

Huber's is the city's oldest restaurant, established in the 1870s. They're famous for their Spanish coffee, but it's not just the cocktail that people go there for, it's the show that comes along with it. A strapping man in a dress shirt and waistcoat will pour golden rum into your glass from three feet high and light the liquor on fire in an experience that leaves you cradling a warm glass with a heavy dose of Kahlua and coffee. It's the perfect after-party spot if you have nice taste.

"Sounds fun. But I was worried about you."

"Again? Sweetie." He chuckles. "I'm fine. I'm always fine." He glances at the mailer in my hand. "This for me?"

Before opening it, I ask him flat out, "Did you leave this for me in my mailbox?"

He chuckles again. "Why, what is it?"

"Did you put something in my mailbox, Dad?" I say, holding the envelope behind my head now so he can't see it until he gives me a real answer.

"No," he answers firmly. "What is it?"

Moving to the coffee table, I slowly pull the plastic bag containing the drawing out of the envelope.

"This was in my mailbox today. It doesn't have a return address or even my own address on it. But it was sealed when I grabbed it out of my mailbox."

I flip it over, showcasing the artwork I drew as a kid, and hand it to him. I don't explain what it is because I know he'll remember it.

He studies it, puzzled. "This is your drawing," he says slowly. "How do you have this? I thought I did."

"So, you do have the evidence boxes that are missing from Jack's office?"

"Well, yeah. I took them for my book a couple years ago, but I don't think Jack knows that." His face flattens. "Does he know that now?"

"Yup. You're in trouble," I say lightly.

"I've been meaning to return them. I just don't know how," he says, leaning back in the sofa and running his fingers through his hair. "I honestly sort of forgot I had them. I haven't looked through the boxes since I finished the book earlier this year." He glances at me, gauging my reaction to the mention of his book.

I let it go. "But you remember seeing this drawing in one of the boxes when you did look in them?"

He again fixes his position on the sofa. "Of course. Because I remember when you drew it, so I knew exactly what it was when I had pulled it out. It helped me describe him for my book." He looks at me with more guilt. "I should have returned them."

I'm surprised he's taking responsibility, but that doesn't answer my burning questions. "Is this not weird to you? Like, if you didn't send me this, then who did? Where are the boxes now?"

"Yeah, I mean, I-I don't know," he stumbles. "They should be in my office closet." He points at his office door, which is closed. We both stand and walk inside.

His office is dark, with mahogany wood accents throughout, matching the kitchen cabinets and the hardwood paneling outside his house. It would almost resemble a space that a curly-mustached professor would keep if it weren't for the sleek, mod details.

My dad draws the curtains and bathes the room in light, making our search easier. He pulls open the door to the closet and flicks on the bulb inside, then sifts through various boxes. He appears to use this closet for storage and files, and many of the boxes look similar, or even identical.

"What the hell," he grunts, lifting boxes to make sure those containing vital evidence to an unsolved murder case aren't hiding somewhere. His fingers touch the shelf that's level with his eyes. "I know I had them up here on this shelf." He points to the stack on the closet floor. "And they're not down here, either. These are filled with book outlines, and research, and manuscripts."

"Did you take them anywhere?" I ask inquisitively.

"No way. They never left my office after I brought them home that day."

"Did you look at them somewhere else in the house? Maybe they're in your car or the garage or your bedroom," I suggest.

"I only looked through them in here where I could keep them organized. I didn't move them around on purpose so *this* wouldn't happen." He lightly kicks the door closed. "Shit."

"Okay, calm down, Dad," I say, putting my hands on his shoulders.

"They have to be here somewhere. They didn't just walk out of the house."

"Then where are they?" he asks with a sigh. "I'm turning into such an old man. I've misplaced so many things lately. And now this."

Lowering my arms, I ask, "What do you mean? What else has gone missing?"

"Little things, like my keys or my reading glasses. Stuff like that."

"And did you find them again?"

"Most of it, yeah. They were just simple misplacements. These evidence boxes aren't. And they're big and heavy. They're not the kind of items you can misplace," he says, looking around the room. "I know they were here. I'm sure of it."

I pace across the room and lean against his desk. "This is really freaking me out now," I admit. "Someone sent me my own drawing from when I was eight years old. A drawing that lived in an evidence box that *you* have had possession of but is now missing. So, what does that mean?"

My phone buzzes in my pocket before he can answer. I dig it out to find a Reddit notification from the girl I messaged earlier.

She responded.

Hi, I'm Mary. Yes, I'm still in the area. What do you mean he's back… Text or call me and let's talk.

20

NOLA

I haven't the slightest idea what I'm looking for as I enter Moonie's diner.

After we chatted back and forth on text for a few minutes, Mary asked me to meet her in person at a nearby late-night diner that I haven't been to since my early twenties. It was a favorite post-bar spot of my friend group's, yearning for burgers after a night of drinking. It holds fond memories.

Mary and I were going to discuss everything on a phone call, but since we live in the same general area, we figured this was the best way to do it. Plus, this gives me the opportunity to size her up in person—making sure she's legitimate. But something about this plan is forming a pit in my stomach since I'm already trusting this stranger with my time. What if she's loony? Or not who she says she is? I consider that she could be the killer in disguise, baiting me to a particular location. Though, I'm the one who reached out to her, so the chance of that being true feels slim.

Before leaving my dad's house, I warned him to lock his doors, stay by his phone, and avoid talking to Jack if he could—for now. I need to buy some time until I know more about what this girl has seen and how it can possibly help me.

The diner is a standalone building that appears to be painted some shade of green, but the bright, neon DINER sign is flooding the entire exterior in a muffled red glow. The same tone of red blares from their OPEN and COFFEE signs hanging in the windows around it and lighting the wet sidewalk, too, as dusk turns to night. I relish the autumn season, but—particularly this week—am not a fan of the early November sunsets, desperate for as much daylight as I can get. Or rather, as little darkness as possible.

A faint bell rings daintily above my head as I open the front door and peer around the room, unsure of what Mary even looks. The diner isn't busy, but most of the occupied tables are taken up by small families or couples, chowing down on anything from pancake stacks to burgers and tater tots.

I see one booth taken up by a man sitting alone, and my heart clenches a bit at the thought that this could be the person pretending to be Mary. He's wearing a black, hooded sweatshirt and is staring into his coffee.

To my right in the far corner, isolated from the other inhabited tables, is a young woman sitting alone. She's looking at me. As I make eye contact, she raises her hand to wave with a curious expression, confirming that she must be Mary.

"Hi, I'm Nola," I say, sliding into the opposite side of the matte, emerald laminate booth. I immediately regret giving my real name, having planned to use a fake one to err on the side of caution.

Too late.

I place my hands on the English chestnut table, admiring the place's cozy ambiance that falls somewhere between classic diner and Irish pub.

"Hi, I'm Mary. I'm glad we could meet amongst all the hideousness surrounding the subject matter," she says with a light smile.

"Me too." I'm not sure where to start. I have jitters, like I'm on a blind date. She looks around my age, maybe a few years older. Her hair is brilliantly red, her face naturally beautiful, but her glasses and buttoned cardigan give her an endearing look.

"I guess I'll just jump right in," she offers. "I'm very interested in why you believe he's back, but I can start by telling you what I saw back then, and you can do the same?"

"That sounds good," I reply, tucking hair behind my ear.

Just as she opens her mouth to speak again, a waitress approaches our table holding a small notepad.

"Evening! I'll be helping you out tonight," she says with a smile, sliding a menu to each of us. "Not sure if either of you have been here before, but we're known for our all-day breakfast. We also have a dinner menu featuring many American classics. And our pie today is Marionberry."

I haven't eaten dinner, but considering the number of nerves that are firing inside me, I don't have much of an appetite. Without even looking at the menu, I opt for a Diet Coke and side of French fries, while Mary requests a strawberry milkshake, which is exactly the type of thing I thought she'd order. I smile at her, and the waitress walks away to fetch our drinks.

"So," Mary begins, picking at a hangnail on her thumb. "I was almost thirteen when Carrie was killed—Carrie Fenton, the Hiding Man's fourth known victim." As she speaks, I look around to see if

149

anyone is listening in. But luckily, no one's sitting in this corner of the restaurant with us.

She continues: "It's weird to think I'm coming up on the age she was when it all happened." She stares at her hands before shaking her head and fixing her gaze back on me. "We lived on a quiet, residential street—we knew our neighbors. And I would often sit in my window reading because I had one of those window nooks in my second-floor bedroom. Sometimes, I would get distracted if a car drove down my street or I heard something outside. Well, on this one night, I was up way past my bedtime devouring a new book in this fantasy series I loved, and I kept noticing a car drive by, so I was constantly looking down at the street. We lived in a nice neighborhood that had twenty-four-hour surveillance where a patrol car would drive around all the time. And I noticed this a lot when I read in my nook in general." She swallows, clicking her tongue. "I actually liked when I saw them because it made me feel less alone, like someone was watching out for me. But anyway. On this night after looking down to watch the patrol car drive by a few times before they went through the rest of the neighborhood, I noticed Carrie through her downstairs window."

Our drinks are dropped off, and we both take a quick sip.

"I wasn't, like, some Peeping Jane. I just wondered what she was doing at that hour by herself, since it was around one in the morning, when everyone else had their lights out. And I think I had this minor fascination for her as a budding teenager, because I thought she had it all, you know? She was beautiful, successful. Had a house, a career. I mean, when you're that age, you just want to be older."

I nod because this was exactly how I felt about Mia.

Mary takes another sip of milkshake.

"No, I get what you mean," I say.

The fries are dropped off, and I motion to Mary to share them with me. We both eat one. My fry is piping hot and salty.

"I'm thankful to this day that I was watching her, because I was the only person who could tell the police anything at all."

"And what did you tell them?" I ask, patting the butt of a ketchup bottle and squirting thick sauce into the basket.

"She was alone in her living room watching TV, and I looked away for a while because nothing was going on with her, she was just sitting there by herself. So, I put my attention back in my book. And it must have been fifteen minutes later when I saw the lights go out in the corner of my eye. I thought she was going to sleep, but then I thought I heard what sounded like a scream—just one. And I was so scared that I turned off my reading light and listened for more. And then, after staring at her house in silence for what felt like ages, I finally saw a face in the window."

Mary almost knocks her milkshake glass over with all her drastic hand motions, so she pushes it to the end of the table and continues.

"I'm hiding behind my own curtain and see a white face emerge from her dark dining room and close her curtain quickly. All I saw was their face. It was so bright in the darkness, brighter than a real face would be. And its features were thin and hard to make out, so putting all that together is what made me think this was some sort of mask. But I never saw anyone exit the house after that." Mary chews on another fry, then waves it around like a wand as she continues her story. "She had a small patch of forest as her backyard, so I wondered if someone had come in that way—but I knew something bad had happened. I was the one who called the police."

"Did you call them right after seeing him?"

"I didn't want to wake up my parents in case it was nothing, and I knew how to call the police. I was practically a teenager. But they both worked early the next morning, which I think was, like, a Monday. So, I didn't tell them right away and just called the police and explained the scream, the lights, and the person in the window. Then later, they asked me to draw the person I saw, which I did, but not very well, since I couldn't make much out from across the street. I just drew a white mask with slices for a mouth, nose, and eyes." She grabs her milkshake glass and dips a fry into it.

"Did you know her well? Or know if she had been seeing anything or experiencing anything before she died?"

"She and my mom were pretty close. My mom had me when she was twenty, so she was around Carrie's age when she was killed. And since I was the one to call the police, my parents couldn't hide anything from me. I had inserted myself into the situation that way, so my mom told me some stories." Mary pushes her glasses up her nose. "Carrie had been coming around our house more in the weeks leading up to that night—which I remember happening. My mom said she didn't want to be home alone. I don't know if she had a boyfriend or anything, but she was separated from her husband and didn't have kids. I'm sure police investigated her husband, but I never met him, so I can't speak on his personality and potential serial-killing capability."

"Did you guys have to move after it happened?" I ask.

"As disturbing as it sounds, we didn't. But it was hard having her house in our faces all the time," Mary says sincerely. "I started reading in my bed instead of my window nook, and eventually her house went up for sale. And to our surprise, it didn't take long for a family to move in. But that definitely helped us get back into a normal neighborhood swing—having life across the street again." Mary stirs her milkshake in a daze for a moment before snapping out of it. "And nothing scary like that happened in our neighborhood again."

"How's everything tasting over here?" our waitress asks after suddenly appearing.

"Great," Mary and I say in unison.

"Can I get you guys anything else? Dinner?"

"Um," I start. "I'm good for now." Mary agrees, and the woman smiles, nods, and walks away.

"So. What did you see?" Mary asks me.

Considering most of the people in my life don't even know this story, I'm hesitant to tell it to a complete stranger just because she told me hers. She already knows my first name and I met her on the internet today.

What am I even thinking by being here? I can't deny that there's something trustworthy about her. Maybe it's her kindhearted nature and gentle voice that eases me, or the fact that we have something dreadful in common: We've both seen a monster in the flesh.

Keeping my voice low, I decide to tell her what I saw, but without revealing specific details. I don't tell her Mia's name or the fact that she was my babysitter, and she doesn't ask. All I mention is that it happened to my friend while I was young, and that I came downstairs to check on her and found Him at the bottom of the stairs. To embellish my version, I focus on the mask and the power going out but don't note the message in blood.

"I can't believe you were in the same room as him," she says with horror and pity on her face.

"Yeah. It was hard for a few years after that. And now things seem to be circling back, so it's good to know I'm not crazy and that you saw Him, too," I say earnestly.

"What makes you say that? Have you seen him again? Or heard anything?" Mary asks.

I form my words in my head before I speak. "Did you hear about the murder in Nob Hill the other night?"

"Only very briefly through a friend," Mary says slowly. "I think it happened pretty close to my house."

It's no surprise she isn't well informed since the major news headlines haven't picked it up without the release of Felicity's name. Jack and his department are clearly trying to keep her identity under the radar. Mentions of the murder surfaced in a couple local articles this weekend, but that's about it.

Responding to Mary, I leave out the fact that I'm a paranormal radio host and that I received a call from the victim. Instead, I tell her the same basic details that can be found online right now.

"I can't say for sure they're connected, but I think it was Him. I have inside information that she was spooked by a masked man in her window before she died. And she described Him exactly as you and I have."

Now I really sound crazy.

"Interesting," she says skeptically. "Are the police looking into it?"

Her skeptical tone is making me wonder why I even met up with her—as if gaining the account of her sighting would help me in any way. Suddenly, this all seems pointless. I think I just wanted someone to verify that He exists, that I'm not making Him up. It's silly to me now.

I wave for the bill and squash the conversation. "Yup, they're all over it," I lie. I check the time on my phone. "I'm sorry. I really have to go."

She starts to speak but I interrupt quickly. "It was nice meeting you, Mary. Thanks for sharing your story with me. Take care of yourself." I slam down a $20 bill and jog out the diner's door.

My car is parked out on the street, roughly a block away. As I speed-walk to it, I grab my phone to dial Harvey. The moon above is glowing and half-visible among the clouds. The asphalt is slick and drenched when I cross the street to a more populated area and recognize my car parked about two storefronts ahead.

After I spot it, I notice someone standing near my rear passenger door, looking directly at me. At first, they're just a dark shape. I relax my pace, giving myself more time to think of what to do. They're dressed in black, and I can make out only basic features of their pasty face under a hoodie.

As I step closer, wavering between watching them and finding Harvey's contact, their face becomes clearer. It's the guy from the diner, the guy in the hoodie who was sitting at a booth by himself. My face scrunches into visible confusion as I try to decipher why he's standing next to my car, perceiving me.

I look down at my phone again and anxiously search Harvey's name, but I approach my car before I can click on it.

Keeping my eyes on the ground to avoid contact—knowing there are witnesses around to watch my back—I dart off the sidewalk toward my driver's-side door when a hand grabs my right shoulder.

"Hey!" I shout in panic, whipping around to face my supposed kidnapper.

"Nola Strate?" asks the man. "My bad for touching you. I just didn't want to miss my opportunity to talk to you. I saw you in Moonie's." He points his index finger up the street and drops the hood off his head, exposing short, sandy hair.

"How do you know my name? Who are you?" I ask, my heart still beating from the way he gripped my upper arm. He looks to be in his forties, so he should know better than to grab a woman like that.

He laughs. "Are you kidding?" He scans my face to see that I'm not. "I love your show. Huge fan."

I've only been recognized in public once before. But I guess Nicole and Harvey were right; the show is growing. Maybe this is something I have to get used to. I can only hope my next fan isn't as grabby.

"How did you know this was my car?" I ask, trying not to sound rude despite his own behavior.

"Um, lucky guess?" He smiles. "Anyway. I finally got all my friends to listen after that crazy call you got on Friday. Wicked stuff."

"Yeah, it was pretty messed up," I say, not wanting to elaborate. "Anyway. I really appreciate you listening." I give him a normal smile. He sends a bigger one back to me as I turn toward my car.

"Stay safe," he quips with a singsong tone.

"Excuse me?" I ask, returning my gaze to his.

"Your tagline for *Night Watch*. 'Stay safe out there,'" he says with air quotes and a weird arm dance.

"Oh. Right," I mutter. "Have a good night."

As I jump into my car, I finally dial Harvey, who answers with a friendly greeting.

Meanwhile, my tone is agitated. "Can you come over? I don't want to be alone. And I need to tell you something."

21

NOLA

Harvey arrives at my house at the same time I do. The car in my neighbor's driveway is gone, I notice, and there are no new—mysterious or normal—letters in my mailbox. Everything looks just as it should.

With the sun already long-set behind the mountains, I push my key in the lock as fast as possible and pull Harvey inside.

"Your cryptic calls are starting to worry me," he says as we move into my kitchen. "Why'd you want me to bring my laptop?"

I pull on the stainless steel refrigerator handle and grab a Hazy IPA from one of the shelves.

"Beer?" I ask, already pouring it into a pint glass with a slight shake in my hands. Harvey looks at me skeptically and accepts the drink.

I walk over to my bar and uncork a bottle of the first wine I see:

a local Merlot. I pour myself a glass, then unlock my back door and move out to the balcony without saying a word.

Harvey follows me out and leans against the balcony's railing, taking sips of his beer and looking out at the city with me. He turns toward me and looks into my eyes, waiting for me to speak.

"Are you hungry?" I ask, pulling out my phone and opening a food delivery app.

"I'm more interested in what's going on with you. Talk to me. Please," he says, blue eyes as earnest as can be.

I sigh. "I feel like I keep getting shut down whenever I've brought this up to someone. But I'm scared to ignore it—because something really strange is going on."

"I promise to keep an open mind," he says, opening his hands.

Dropping my phone back into my pocket, I walk to the outdoor sofa and take a seat.

"I have to start at the beginning," I say, taking a large sip of Merlot. "I know it's weird I never told you this. But when I was eight years old, my babysitter was murdered practically right in front me. I saw the guy who killed her, and police never found him."

"Whoa," Harvey says with widened eyes. "How come you've never told me this before?" His shock turns to sympathy, and he places his hand in mine. "Are you okay?"

His oversized knit sweater is soft on my skin. I move my hand to the knee of his jeans and play with a loose string, holding on to his stare. My words catch in my throat as I silently will him to kiss me, already wanting to bury the conversation.

When the moment passes, I answer. "I don't know. My family didn't want anyone to know, so we kept it mostly to ourselves."

"Damn," he says under his breath. "Why did someone kill her?"

"Do you know who the Hiding Man is?" I ask quietly.

Harvey grew up in a small town in Washington, about two hours north of here. Although it isn't far, I'm fully expecting him to have never heard that name before.

"Yeah, that serial killer?" he asks after a few seconds of pause.

"You've heard of him?"

"Just from school and stuff, I guess," he says. "Is that who you're saying killed your babysitter?"

"Yeah, so. Mia was the fifth known woman he murdered. And on the night that he killed her, I saw him in my house. I saw his mask. He followed me up to my parents' bedroom where I locked the door and called the police."

"That's heavy," Harvey says softly, still shaking his head.

"Well, remember what Felicity said on the phone? That a man in a white mask was in her window? I'm pretty sure I saw him last night," I say matter-of-factly. "That's why I called you. I feel like he's come back somehow. Or he never left."

"Does Jack know all this?"

"Jack wants me to stay out of it." I rise from the outdoor sofa, go inside, and grab the suspicious mailer from my purse. I return to Harvey and hand it to him. "This was left in my mailbox this morning with no postage or return address. This is the drawing I did of Mia's killer the day after she was murdered."

He holds it in his hands, studying the artwork. "Holy shit. He's terrifying."

"I don't know who left this for me, and I don't know why this guy would want to come back for me, but something's going on," I breathe. "It's just like how I told you I thought someone was following me."

Harvey's expression remains perplexed.

"I'm trying not to overreact or scare you or myself until Jack tells me more, but I don't want to just sit around and wait. So, I guess I'm wondering if you'll keep me company while I learn everything I can about this guy. Maybe we can try to figure out who he is ourselves," I say, gesturing to his laptop, then gulp my wine.

"You want us—two people who just make a radio show—to somehow identify a serial killer that police haven't been able to, with only our laptops?" he asks.

"I mean, not actually," I laugh, stuffing down my true panic on the matter. "Jack thinks Felicity was killed by her boyfriend. So, hopefully I'm wrong about all this. I don't think he would belittle me if he thought I was in real danger. But it would give me some peace of mind to know more. There's still a lot I haven't told you if you're willing to listen."

Although I spent time earlier doing research, I barely scratched the surface on what's out there. And any additional information I learn could help me feel more prepared if my worst nightmares come true. Or drive me further into insanity.

Harvey runs his fingers through his ear-length, wavy hair. Biting his lip, he says, "I can't say no to you. Tell me everything you know."

I fill Harvey in on my meeting with Mary, and everything else that has come up over the past few days, like my dad's new book and more about the mailer I received.

Still snuggled into my balcony's outdoor sofa, we open our laptops. I show Harvey the drawings that I can find online, and we continue searching for more information.

Harvey glances at the drawing in front of us every few seconds, and I can tell it's creeping him out as much as it is me. To get it out of our sight and keep it safe from the unpredictable weather beyond my balcony, I walk inside to drop it on the dining table and fill up my wine glass, gripping the bottle by its neck as I go back outside.

Ever since I saw someone standing under the streetlamp the other night, I've avoided my balcony. It feels like being under a magnifying glass out here, like someone is always watching. I glance over at the streetlamp in question to make sure no one's standing under it now. But as I peer down at the street, I note its emptiness, with few cars parked along the sidewalks.

With Harvey here, and the rain blanketing us, remaining outside with a watchful view doesn't seem like a bad idea.

"Did you just see something?" Harvey asks, watching me investigate.

I hesitate to speak. "No. But I saw someone standing down there the other night," I say, pointing. "Under the streetlamp. That's why I came into work all jumbled on Friday."

Harvey blows air out of his lips and places his interlocked fingers on top of his head. "Should we do this at my house instead?"

I chuckle. "Do you want him to know where you live?"

"I absolutely do not. But I don't like that this person seems to know where you live."

"Tell me about it," I say. "I'm sure everything will be okay. I wouldn't willingly put you in harm's way by being here if I really thought someone was coming."

And for the most part, I mean it. As unsettling as the events of the weekend have been, I'd probably be sleeping at the police station if I truly believed a vicious killer was after me.

"That's so thoughtful of you," he jokes.

Harvey returns to his research as I take another moment to peer down at the street, then walk to the other end of my balcony to check the side of the house where the camera and garage are located.

"'The creak, the squeak, from in the night / Is quite enough to cause a fright,'" Harvey slowly reads.

"What's that?"

"'But when you see his wielding knife / It's far too late, he'll take your life.'" Harvey squints his eyes at the bright screen. "Have you read this?"

"I don't even know what that is," I say, wanting an explanation.

"'He lurks from deep beyond the gray / He thrives as loose among the prey / Like a fox, to his hen.'" Harvey looks up at me. "'This "He" is called the Hiding Man.'"

"Who wrote that?" I ask.

"I don't know. It's in an old newspaper I just found."

"Why would someone write that?" I ask, nearly polishing off my second glass.

"Cause they're sick and probably think this whole thing is a joke," Harvey says, peering closer at the article. "Oh, wait. This was in a letter the police received. They think the killer wrote it himself."

I nod, remembering now. "I read something about that earlier. But I didn't see the poem." I grimace. "What a self-centered creep."

"Yeah, he probably felt really cool when this hit the papers."

I sit down and nestle close to Harvey, staring at the screen and reading the poem. As I do, he turns his head toward mine, only inches away.

"What?" I ask, smiling with my gaze. "I just want to read it again."

"No, yeah. Please." His arm grazes mine as I look back to the poem, reading the first sentence over and over unintentionally. Suddenly all I'm thinking about is Harvey.

Harvey clears his throat. "I'm gonna get another beer."

He places his laptop on my lap and heads inside the kitchen.

22

NOLA

As I scan the newspaper article for a source, I note that this was sent anonymously to the police department and was received two days after the first murder was committed—after Jamie York was slain in her home. It almost makes Him sound like a macabre nursery rhyme, which was likely what the killer was going for—creating some sort of villainous character for Himself.

I read it once more, the words swimming in the glare of my laptop. For just a moment, I let myself visualize that dreadful evening at my childhood home when Mia died.

These are images that, no matter how hard I try, I can't fully suppress. They always find their way back into my head, no matter how many times I cast them out.

I'm suddenly shaken from my film of memories when the sharp squeak of a rusty hinge hits my eardrum. That god-awful high-pitched sound that makes you clench your teeth and wince.

Like the whine of a dentist's instrument. It was distant enough that I know it didn't come from my balcony where I now sit, but maybe from inside the cracked door leading to the kitchen. I glance through one of the bay windows into my house to see Harvey closing the refrigerator door and pouring a fresh beer into his froth-stained pint glass.

Must have been the fridge door closing, I think.

Refrigerator doors don't squeak, a voice in my head sneers.

Yes, they do, I lie in response. *Sometimes they do.*

I let out a short sigh of relief that the sound was nothing of concern and swallow the dregs from my glass, then turn to the bottle of Merlot sitting on the wooden table in front of me to pour another.

Sometimes they do. Right?

Quiet! I shake my wine-soaked brain in my skull until the tipsy voices stop. Forcing a smile, I think of the positives. The good of the present.

Lots more wine in my kitchen.

Sexy Harvey, also in my kitchen.

Another sigh of relief. Another forced smile. And then, the gratifying lack of agitation, for a brief moment. I gulp the wine back a little too hard, making a face of disgust at the colossal dosage. The sommeliers of the world would be horrified.

My head suddenly feels heavier. The weight of three heads, at least. If I hadn't silenced the devil on my shoulder into oblivion with that last swig, she would surely be cross with me.

You weren't supposed to drink tonight, idiot, she'd say.

Stay sharp. There is a killer on the loose, she'd add.

Just like that, I get that feeling again. The feeling that I'm being watched. I sit in that fear for a moment too long while taking long glugs of wine.

"Screw it," I mutter inside the glass, my own words echoing back into my face.

Placing the stemless glass on the table, I chalk my fear up to everything I've seen and heard over the last few days.

The shadowed man on the street. That dreadful phone call. The fact that He might be back. I shake my head again as if to lose that last thought for good, casting it to the ether where it belongs. But just like before, I can't get the images out of my head. They might as well be tattooed inside my eyelids.

Setting my glass on the table stirred a rational musing. Maybe it was my coffee table that made that wretched sound. The trashed old thing has been destroyed by slanted rain and is unfashionably distressed to the touch. I give it a wiggle with my foot, and to my surprise, it remains silent. I push harder, and out comes a low groan. The opposite of a squeak, with the hum of bass.

Innocent.

Taking a deep breath, I adjust myself on the balcony's sofa. My stomach grumbles, begging for food instead of more wine. As I ponder what I have in my kitchen, I hear the sound again.

Squeak.

I shoot my head up to see where it came from this time, having heard it a bit more clearly.

The creak, the squeak, from in the night.

It's just past 8:00, and the blinds in most of the neighboring windows are drawn. It seems most people are either tucked in for the night or they've gone out on a Sunday. I assume the former, since many in this neighborhood are on the older side. Either way, I don't see clear movement.

I glance to my right at my one real neighbor's house, cloaked in shadow. A lit candle flickers above the sink in their kitchen, and the casement window is cranked half-open to the breeze. Besides the glowing light of the flame, the rest of the house is completely dark. The owners must have come home since Harvey and I did, since their driveway was empty when I arrived.

As I continue to scan the house, the sight of gentle swinging on their balcony catches my eye; the knit hammock in the corner is rocking back and forth. I shimmy further down into my outdoor sofa so as not to be seen and investigate their deck. Though something tells me I've already been spotted, unsure of how long someone has been outside—and if they've been listening to what we've been saying about Him.

Closing the laptop so my face is no longer spotlighted, my eyes adjust to the darkness in front of me and I make out a shape in the swaying hammock. I quickly glance through the window behind me, hoping Harvey is on his way outside. But he's nowhere to be seen. His freshly poured beer sits untouched on the dining table adjacent to the kitchen, which is also vacant.

Where did he go?

My body begins to quiver as I turn my attention back to my neighbor's balcony and still see the indistinct silhouette of a person, facing me. The hammock's movement is calm and controlled, making me even more afraid.

I wonder, for a moment, if I'm imagining this. If the hammock is simply oscillating from the windy weather and whatever-my-neighbor's-name-is is relaxing inside like the rest of my street—innocent of voyeurism.

Squeak.

My heart pounds in my chest as I realize the sound came from exactly where I'm looking: my neighbor's balcony. The squeaking is coming from that hammock chair.

NIGHT WATCHER

He lurks from deep beyond the gray.

I continue adjusting to the lack of light, staring hard at the hammock and sitting in utter silence and stillness like I'm lost in a jungle, striving to camouflage my body from the sight of a ravenous jaguar. Yet the more I stare, the more I know that what I'm seeing is real.

Someone is sitting in that hammock, watching me. But I can't see their face.

23

NOLA

Petrified, sunken into my outdoor sofa, unable to move, I keep my gaze locked on my neighbor's balcony.

I can spot the outline of a round head, and broad shoulders in the shadow of night. They have an outdoor sofa like I do, but a larger deck that's completely uncovered. I've tried to figure out what type of person lives in that house based on the furniture, or what I can see in the window. But it's all very basic and bland, not giving any solid identifiers to the generation or gender of its owner.

Squeak.

I shoot my head forward, putting the hammock in my right peripheral until I close my eyes and silently plead to be rescued. It seems silly to be afraid of a person who might simply be enjoying a Sunday night on their own property. But between our discussion this evening and the fact that they appear to be looking my way, red flags are flapping dramatically in my head.

Harvey still hasn't come out of the house, and I don't hear any noises coming from inside. All I can hear is the howling wind picking up speed, and the squeak from the hammock every few seconds, the mysterious neighbor making their presence known.

I slowly stand up and walk casually into my house, looking unbothered in my movement. I waltz straight into the kitchen and find it, again, empty. Harvey's beer is still sitting on the dining table, filled to the brim with liquid and foam right next to the envelope with my drawing in it. As I turn to check for him in the rest of the house, someone emerges from the hallway. Completely on edge, I yelp a quick, animalistic sound and physically jump backward. Harvey shouts even louder, scared at me being scared of him.

"Where were you?" I ask, breathless.

"Fuck." He drops his head back. "I was pissing."

"Sorry." I try to catch my breath, lowering my voice. "I just saw something out there."

"Where?"

"Someone's on the balcony of that house," I say, pointing across the room at the window, even though my blinds are closed. From where we're standing, we can't see their balcony, either.

"Okay," Harvey says curiously. "What are they doing?"

I nearly say, "They're just sitting there. But I think they're watching me." Just saying it in my head makes me sigh. It's absurd to be this startled by absolutely nothing. As if someone lounging outside their home is newsworthy.

"Never mind. They're just sitting in their hammock. I've never seen anyone out there, so it's unusual." I shake my head, chuckling. "I'm losing my mind, Harv. I mean, I'm really losing it."

"I think you just need to stop reading about this stuff. Let's put on a movie or something."

I walk out to the balcony to grab our laptops, still a bit apprehensive, only to find my neighbor's balcony unoccupied. The hammock is swinging much more turbulently from the wind than it had been a minute ago when there was weight in it, and I no longer see the silhouette of a person.

I release a short sigh, unable to do anything but feel foolish.

Moving inside, I turn on the fireplace, filling the room with warmth.

A sense of defeat washes over me, bathing me in self-doubt. The whole situation—Felicity's murder and the subsequent investigation into it—is out of my hands. And I need to stop letting it consume me before it destroys me.

"We'll figure this out, okay?" Harvey says reassuringly.

I nod and head into the kitchen with him in search of snacks, ready to put talks of Him behind me and salvage the evening. With Harvey here, I feel like I'm being guarded, like nothing bad will happen anymore.

We settle on grilled cheese, which Harvey cooks for us, and enjoy the sandwiches in my living room while we search for a lighthearted movie on TV. Getting food in my belly takes away most of my drunken haze, bringing a content grin to my face as I lean on Harvey's legs. He's positioned on the couch, still scrolling through streaming apps, and I'm sitting crisscrossed on the floor. I like being close to him, feeling his body against mine. But I don't know if he shares those thoughts. For a moment, I lay my head against his knee, and his hand gently pets my hair.

When he stops, I crawl closer to the fire, hoping he'll join me as I stare into its flames, flickering yellow and blue. Hugging my knees and taking small sips of water, I enjoy the comfort of it along with a newfound sense of peace that distracting my mind has brought me.

But since Harvey stroked my head seconds ago, I can't get it out of my mind that I want him to keep touching me.

"I can't choose," Harvey says, setting down the remote.

I swallow, pulled briefly from my thoughts of him. Smiling, I wave my hand down. "We can just hang out. As long as you can."

"I'll stay here with you all night," he offers. "If you'll have me."

My chest feels heavy at the thought. I look up at him as he joins me on the floor in front of the fireplace, and gently nod at the idea. "I'd like that."

As I stare back into the fire, biting my thumbnail, I fantasize about pulling him upstairs and into my bed. How his lips would taste, where he would put his hands. I take another sip of water.

He's facing me now, seemingly numb from the fire's comfort, too. I meet his pale, blue eyes as he stares into mine, and then down at my lips. My pulse quickens as he doesn't pull away, as though he's been reading my mind. My heartbeat rises, and I wonder for a moment if he can hear it.

"How come we've never..." I softly start to ask.

Harvey shifts slightly in his spot, but keeps close, inches from my face. "Never?"

His eyes are lightly squinted, and the word slithered out cunningly, almost provocatively. His body language is inviting as his face gets even closer, until we're almost touching.

"Don't make me say it out loud," I whisper, brushing the hem of his pullover with my fingers.

Harvey leans into my lips, tender at first, and then hard. Before I know it, we're lying against my living room rug, fiercely kissing, tongue on tongue, his mouth sweet from beer. His hand grips the base of my head and he gently pulls at my hair.

Harvey pulls away from my lips, just barely, to say, "I've wanted you for so long," then kisses my ear as his body presses me against the floor.

Tiny goosebumps rise across my skin as he drags his fingertips down past my stomach and moves his mouth to my neck. I fall deeper into his swollen lips, and he meets mine again, peeling my sweater off, then his.

Harvey pulls me off the hardwood floor and into his lap in one swift motion, and I lock my legs around the waist of his pants and roll against him. The heat from the fireplace and our bodies creates sticky, slick skin, and we don't care. I kiss him harder as we passionately tumble around the living room, sighing into each other's mouths until we feel better than we have all week.

24

NOLA

The recognizable crinkle of my down feather duvet hits my ears, and the plush caress of my pillow supports my neck instead of Harvey's fingers. Realizing I'm in my bed, I slowly open my eyes and peer around my near-pitch-black bedroom. My door is cracked open, allowing light from the hallway to pour in in the shape of a sharp triangle. I turn over, half expecting Harvey to be there, even though I have no memory of us coming in here last night. But my bed is hosting its usual party of one: me. There's no sign that Harvey was ever here, as the pillow next to me is perfectly fluffed and the duvet is flat and neat.

I venture to call his name, but as the silence rings, I can't be sure I even said it out loud—maybe just in my head. Exhaustion is getting the better of me.

Something catches my eye in the corner of the room immediately after I say—or try to say—Harvey's name. In the sofa chair underneath the mounted flat-screen TV is the shadow of a person. Their body is in the safety of darkness, just inches away from the triangular spotlight coming from the hallway. It misses their body by mere inches.

I blink rapidly. It's Harvey sitting in the chair; his eyes are open, staring blankly into nothingness.

"Harvey?" I say again, hoping to wake him from whatever trance he's in. He doesn't move, doesn't blink. His arms lie on the cushioned rests, hands gripping the edges.

I imagine he watched me until I fell asleep, knowing I didn't want to be alone. He probably brought me to bed afterward. Maybe he didn't want to be too forward by sleeping next to me and decided to keep watch from the corner of the room and slumber there instead. But based on what we did with each other last night, I don't believe that. There must be another reason he's in the chair. Maybe he couldn't sleep.

"Are you sleeping?" I whisper, even though I can see that his eyes are open. It's possible he's one of those fascinating specimens who can doze off with both eyes fixed. But it doesn't even look like he's breathing.

In the darkness, I can tell that his chest isn't rising and falling. His mouth is shut, and there's no breathing sounds coming from his nose. If he were auditioning for the roll of a mannequin or scarecrow, he'd be cast.

"Harvey, answer me," I whisper with a note of aggression, worried now. Breaking the silence is deafening.

He remains the same. I sit up slowly, preparing to crawl across my bed and either wave my hand in his face or check his pulse, when his body suddenly jerks forward. I launch backward, startled from his unexpected movement. He's leaning forward enough to now be visible in the strip of light coming from the hallway, but it's not Harvey's face anymore. Bent over and staring directly at me is Him. In this light, his black eyes are visible under the mask, unblinking and bottomless. I let out the loudest scream I can, unsure of where to go or what to do.

He's finally going to get me.

But instead, I awake, still letting out a yelp, but much quieter than the one I released moments ago in the fictitious world of my dozing subconscious. Only now, I'm on my living room floor where I fell asleep in Harvey's arms. I was only having a nightmare.

The fireplace is turned off, but the glowing kitchen light is softly illuminating the living room opposite it. The analog clock on my wall ticks away, showing 6:38 and 23 seconds, 24 seconds, 25 seconds. Twenty minutes ahead of sunrise, the glimmer of Monday peeks from behind the mountains out the big windows, and everything feels right. There's no bad man in the room. There's no sense of danger. I'm safe, with Harvey's hand cradling my hip bone. I think about being intimate last night. Being told he wanted to be with me, too—the reality of it surpassing expectations. Feeling all the fear and worry and isolation dissolve on his lips.

I smile and pull my sleeves over my hands, hugging my chest and turning over to look at Harvey. He's sound asleep, facing the ceiling. I stare at his tousled hair, diamond jawline, all of him, smitten at the sight of him in nothing but black boxer briefs, exposing small tattoos across his chest and arms.

As of the second our mouths met last night, I felt everything settle into place. No more personal investigations, no more stoking panic. No more exaggerating and looking into every little thing that seems off—like my neighbor sitting on their own balcony or a local walking under a streetlamp. The stress of the past few days caused me to hallucinate Him in the Powell's stairwell during a wine-fueled delirium. I know that now.

I also know what I heard in that call with Felicity, but jumping to conclusions and presuming the worst is pointless. I'm not a detective, I'm a radio host—just like Harvey pointed out last night before googling nonsense with me for an hour. It's true: A horrific thing happened in this city twenty years ago. Am I just going to believe that no one has been murdered in this place of 650,000 people since? And believe that He is the only bad person who has tormented this area? Jack said it himself: Felicity had a boyfriend who's nowhere to be found. There were strange texts between them and, although he might not have proved murderous before, who knows what he's capable of? Jack will locate him and question him, and if it doesn't turn out that he's the culprit, they'll figure out who is. It has nothing to do with me.

I breathe out a sigh and gently run my fingers through Harvey's wavy, chocolate locks until I suddenly feel something wet and sticky. Oblivious to what it could be, I pull my hand back to see that my fingertips are now covered in a gooey, red substance.

Blood?

I shoot up and shake Harvey, but he's not responding. I lean over his body, pull his head onto my knee, and inspect his scalp. He has a large gash near the back of his head. It's only then that I notice a small pool of blood on the floor where his head had been.

Resting his head back down, I look around everywhere for my phone or Harvey's, nearly slipping on a fallen taper candle on my way around the room. Curious how it got on the floor, I kick it under the couch and run all over, unable to find either phone. They're not in the bathroom or the dining room or in our pockets or under our bodies.

It's during my search that I notice the envelope containing my childhood drawing of Him is no longer on the dining table, or anywhere in the room. I run to the balcony door to check if we left our phones outside somehow, only to realize that the door is unlocked.

No, no, no.

Did we forget to lock it last night?

Before leaving the balcony, I scan down below on the street to see if any neighbors are taking a sunrise walk with their cell phone on their hip. But the road is as quiet as the homes surrounding it.

"Shit!" I say out loud, debating on screaming bloody murder to wake everyone up. As I start to run back inside, I promptly turn around, jog back to the balcony railing, and scream, "Help! Help!" at the top of my lungs. "Someone! Call the police!" Losing precious time and knowing I can't solely trust that someone will hear me, I go back inside to keep searching for a phone.

It's times like this a house phone would come in handy—though with the overnight storm and my luck, the line would be dead, just like Harvey might be.

I feel vulnerable, violated. Did someone come into my house last night and hurt him? Or did something happen before we went to sleep that I don't remember? I'm frantically trying to recollect everything that happened before we fell asleep. All I remember from the end of last night is that we slept together and stayed up talking afterward before lying by the fireplace and nodding off. I don't even think we intended on falling asleep on the floor, but that was what happened.

I sprint into the kitchen, screaming for Harvey to wake up and needing help faster than I can get it. As I scan the kitchen countertops for any sign of our devices, I notice my cell phone sitting next to the sink.

How did it get over here?

I grab it and rapidly dial 911, my hands vigorously shaking. I run back to Harvey's body to check for a pulse as the operator asks for my location and emergency.

25

JACK

awn is breaking through the cheap, aluminum blinds in Jack's office. He's barely left his desk chair since he returned from the scene of Felicity's murder and is beginning to think he never will. He stayed there into the night after Nola left yesterday and finally returned home far too late to his wife, Tammy, who was disappointed that he'd missed Sunday dinner with her parents.

"You're hardly resting. And don't you think you're getting to be too old to take on these kinds of cases?" Tammy lightly jabbed when Jack arrived home around midnight looking for leftovers.

Jack chuckled. "If I wasn't so tired, I think I'd be offended."

Tammy set a plate of roast chicken and mashed potatoes on the kitchen counter next to him. "I just don't want to see you losing yourself like you did with..." Her voice trailed off.

But he knew exactly what she was going to say. *...like you did with the Hiding Man case.*

"I know I was absent back then. The situation wasn't ideal for me, I can assure you."

"Absent?" Tammy quickly asked. She started pacing. "That case nearly broke up this family. You were rarely home. You weren't eating, sleeping." She paused and stared at Jack.

Jack wanted to erupt. The impact of letting down the victims' families, the community, the Strates, and his own family never quite left him. He's already weighed the pros and cons of leaving this job behind and starting new with Tammy and Ethan elsewhere. But he knows he can't give up.

"I won't let that happen again," Jack promised. Instead of arguing or letting his emotions on the matter taint an already tainted day, he kissed his wife in the dim kitchen light and held her for a long while.

Jack picks up his Best Detective Ever mug that his son bought for his birthday two years ago and takes a mouthful of sludgy coffee that had been sitting at the bottom of yesterday's pot. As pathetic as it makes him feel, he will appreciate when Minnie arrives at the office and makes a fresh pot for everyone.

He can feel his eyes sinking deeper into his skull as the lack of sleep settles and takes over. He nods off for what feels like a split second but ends up being a few minutes before he slaps his cheeks and manually pulls his eyes open. He must stay awake. There is too much to do.

Before he left his office for the night around six hours ago, he had confirmed that the shops within the same block of Felicity Morton's house didn't have surveillance cameras pointed toward the street, and the ones he was able to access on the surrounding streets didn't show anything suspicious. Instead, they showed countless cars driving around at all hours of the day with no sign as to where they were going or coming from. The shops were long closed by the time her murder occurred late Friday evening, and all the neighbors reported being asleep or out of the house when it did. Having questioned every person on her block, he knew none of them reported hearing or seeing anything nefarious in the hours leading up to the killing. Just normal neighborhood quietude. Figures.

The one piece of progress he did make this weekend seemed significant, but only led to more questions: Felicity's boyfriend, Connie Sturgis, had an airtight alibi for the entire night she died.

After Jack finally tracked him down, Connie explained that the reason he hadn't answered Jack's other calls was because he was on a fishing boat off the Puget Sound, nearly three hours north by car. Connie had taken a job as a longline deckhand a few weeks ago, since he had experience from his days living on the New England seashore. The job, based in Seattle, required him to work on board a fishing vessel off the coasts of Washington and Alaska. He had been out on the bitter sea training around the same time someone sliced his ex-girlfriend's throat.

Jack knows it's a strenuous job that can require around twelve hours of work a day, with the shifts customarily being overnights and seasonal. Six p.m. to six a.m. hauling gear and operating the ship's deck, with the dank smell of Greenland turbot and Pacific cod in your nostrils while you do it. Suddenly, Jack's job doesn't seem so bad.

Connie's shock and grief were discernible on the phone, since, according to the texts between them, he'd wanted to salvage his relationship with Felicity. She didn't, Connie explained, which was why he'd moved to Seattle, gotten a new job, and was trying to move on with his life. Of course, this all seemed rather convenient.

Jack almost made the drive up to Seattle himself, but after speaking with Connie's supervisor and reviewing some evidence from his new job, it was clear that Connie was telling the truth. He was nowhere near Felicity's house that night or on the surrounding days.

So here Jack sits at his desk with no potential suspects and no motive for this woman's murder. He's looking at a list of all the clients Felicity was actively and previously seeing, having files for a handful of them already.

Kara Swenson. Julia Carlson. Benjamin "Benji" Moor. The list goes on.

Kara Swenson was seeing Ms. Morton to help deal with losing her mother, which happened four months ago. Julia Carlson—a longtime patient—was seeing her for OCD, Benji Moor for emotional and physical abuse committed by his own father.

Jack puts a pin in Benji's file, interested in chatting with his father, Eddie, as well as his mother. He wonders if Felicity had any other clients with deep parental conflicts, and he plans to check when he receives the rest of the files. Surely there will be others that stand out.

All he's looking for is proof that someone who frequented her office could be capable of harming her or have reason to. But just like Felicity's friend Gale Thompson said, she didn't see patients over the age of twelve, so the likelihood of one of them being behind this is pretty much zero.

If her murder is work related, Jack bets one of the children's parents would be responsible. Or even possibly a colleague of hers.

On the other hand, Jack realizes that sometimes there isn't a motive. Or a motive strong enough to fit the crime against the deceased victim. Sometimes, people just want to commit violence against someone else—anyone else. And it doesn't matter who it is. They make up a reason this person should be killed, based on a time when they were wronged themselves. Causing violence to fill an unfillable hole.

This theory has come to mind many times over the years that Jack pored over the Hiding Man case. No matter how hard he tried, he couldn't find a connection between the victims. They all lived in different neighborhoods, were around the same age but not exactly the same, and had completely different jobs and lifestyles.

Jamie was a bartender. Jasey, a hairdresser. Kendra, a social worker. Carrie, a winery owner. Mia, a babysitter. Jasmine, a barista. Doniesha, a bookkeeper. Back then, Jack tracked all their recent bank statements, phone records, figured out where they ate, drank, shopped, who they dated, who they were friends with. No matter how hard he looked, they didn't seem to cross paths. The city isn't tremendous in size, so they naturally ended up on the same jaunts here and there, but not enough for one single person or a group of people to be connected to each of them. So why did someone do this, and how?

Jack takes another sip of coffee—which is now cold—and immediately spits it back into his mug. He stands up and does some jumping jacks, instantly feeling ridiculous and stopping himself right as his tie smacks his nose on the way down.

He walks over to his office door and peers out over the rest of the floor, taking in a deserted scene. Locking eyes on the property room, Jack remembers that he never heard back from Chick regarding whether or not he still has those evidence boxes. It's high time he reviews the contents of those files and compares them to Felicity's case. But Jack has been so busy with her investigation that he hasn't had the bandwidth to chase after Chick about the boxes, or finish checking the others from the property room. He needs to get Mia's and Jasmine's back before someone else comes looking and all the evidence from said boxes becomes inadmissible. Today will be the day he tracks Chick down.

As Jack returns to his desk, his cell phone buzzes loudly, startling him out of his tired fog. Looking at the time on the wall, 7:09 a.m., he wonders who would be calling him at such an early hour. Jack lets out an audible groan as he walks over to pick it up.

It's Officer Austin Torrance. He answers the call before it can go to voicemail, unsure why he could be calling but mentally begging that it's not what he thinks it is.

"Detective De Lacey," Jack says into his smartphone.

"Hey, it's Officer Torrance. We have another body."

26

NOLA

The emergency dispatcher asks me to stay on the phone with her as police are dispatched to my house, instructing me to check Harvey's pulse. She tells me to inspect the radial artery in his wrist using my thumb, as well as the carotid artery on either side of his neck. My hands are shaking violently; my own pulse is going faster than it has since I was last on the phone with a 911 dispatcher. How I'll be able to hush my nerves is beyond me.

I put her on speaker so I can study both spots for a pulse, sobbing and leaning over Harvey's body, begging that he's still alive. I check his neck first and detect a low pulse.

"I feel a beat," I blubber into the phone.

Or at least I think I do. It's hard to know if it's his or mine, or if I'm making the thump up entirely with wishful thinking.

"Can you tell how many seconds are between each beat?" the dispatcher asks.

I suck in deep, steadied breaths, trying to relax—my face wet all over. Slowing my own heart rate down to its normal beat will help me help Harvey.

After a final exhale, I firmly press my thumb under his jawline and try to count, which is harder than I thought it would be considering how much I'm still shaking.

Stop wasting time. You're killing him.

Tears brim in my eyes again, knowing my lack of ability to do what I need to do right now could change everything. It could be the difference between Harvey living or dying.

"I'm not sure. At least a few seconds," I manage to say through sniffs and gasps.

His face is angelic and beautiful—his expression tranquil. I stroke his cheek, feebly whispering, "Stay with me. Stay with me."

"Is his head actively bleeding?"

Without jerking his body, I pull his head further into my lap and separate his hair like I did minutes ago, looking for the gash.

"I can't tell. It doesn't seem like it still is but there's a lot of blood around it."

"Grab a clean towel and lightly press it to his head. Then let me know if it soaks through," the dispatcher instructs.

I run into the kitchen and find an unused, white cotton dish towel, then do as she tells me. After holding it lightly to his injury for about ten seconds, it doesn't soak through, and I explain this.

"Police and EMTs should be there in just a couple of minutes. Just stay with me on the phone and keep that same pressure."

"Okay," I squeal. "Do you think his heartbeat is too spaced out? Is he going to be okay?"

"The EMTs will assess him as soon as they arrive. Just hang in there. Any minute now and they'll be at your door, ma'am." Her tone is professional, barely sympathetic. I wonder how many calls like this she has gotten throughout her career.

"Should I be applying only light pressure or be pushing down on his head?" I ask. The last thing I need is to get this wrong.

She breathes out heavily. "This is a difficult situation because we can't be sure if his skull is fractured. Pressing on his injuries could do him great harm. Can you grab an ice pack and gently apply it to the wound? Make sure there is a towel over it."

I return to the kitchen, feeling like I'm in a relay race with all the back-and-forth sprinting I've been doing since I woke up. Sifting through my mostly barren freezer, the only frozen bag of anything is a pouch of chimichurri rice that's been in there for months. I can smell the spices through the bag, but it'll have to do.

As I return to Harvey, the dispatcher asks, "You're sure no one is in the house with you?"

Through my panic since noticing the blood, that thought didn't even cross my mind. But now that it's in my head, nausea and fear beat across me. I haven't heard or seen anything since I woke up—not like I was paying much attention anyway. But as scary as that question is, I almost wish He was here so I could take all my emotions out on Him for what I know He did to Harvey. I certainly didn't do this myself, and there's no weapon lying around that could indicate how this even occurred. One moment we were falling asleep in bliss, and the next, I see him battered, bloodied, and unconscious. There was no in-between.

I can't help but wonder why He would bash Harvey's head instead of his usual slice of the throat. Did Felicity die by blunt force trauma? Or did He use a knife on her? I rack my brain for an answer that doesn't exist in me.

"I don't think anyone else is here anymore," I say, putting the bag on Harvey's head. "Okay, I have a frozen bag. What do I do?"

"Just place it gently on the wound and hold it there. We want to control the bleeding."

I do as I'm told, and Harvey remains lying beside me, breathing ever so slowly through his nose, but fast enough that I can feel the air come out when I hold my finger on his stubbled upper lip.

I scan the rest of his body, and only then do I notice small beads of blood under the light brown hairs on Harvey's right calf. Leaning over to get a better look, I keep the bag fastened with my right hand, my long, blond hair tickling his stomach as I hover.

When I realize that it's not a cut after all, but a word, I almost vomit in his lap.

N-O-L-A is carved thinly into his calf, taking up about four inches of space.

I audibly gasp and fall backward in shock, nearly cracking my skull against the wall of the fireplace. My phone fumbles out of my hand.

"Is everything all right?" I hear the woman ask through my cell phone's speaker, which is now sitting next to me on the floor. I pick it up.

"My name," I breathe. "It's written on his leg."

Not written. *Carved.* My name is branded on his skin.

"What do you mean?" she asks.

"It's bleeding. Someone carved my name into him."

"What?" she says, before quickly following up with, "Is it actively bleeding or is the blood dry? Don't touch it, just look at it."

I lean over again as my heartbeat speeds up. Any harder and it'll detonate.

"It doesn't look fresh but it's not crusting. It's almost congealed."

There's a moment of silence on her end as she thinks about what I'm saying. I can practically read her mind.

188

"I didn't do this," I add.

Another short moment of silence. I continue to hold the frozen bag against Harvey's head.

"Did you two get into a fight before you went to sleep last night that you may not be remembering?"

"No," I say sternly. "I'm not forgetting anything. I told you. We went to sleep, and I woke up to find him like this. I have no idea how he got injured. Or why or how my name is on his leg!"

Unbeknownst to the dispatcher, I, of course, have a clear idea, but logically putting together how it happened without me waking up is impossible to know.

"Okay, stay with me," she repeats.

Another minute goes by consisting of me feeling utterly helpless and Harvey barely clinging to life. Then suddenly, Harvey's eyes flutter. Before I can even say his name aloud, he lets out a faint groan from his lips.

"Harvey? Can you hear me?" I ask, still holding the chimichurri rice bag to his head.

"Hey," he grunts with closed eyes. He sounds like he's fading.

"Hi," I shout a little too loudly.

He squints up at me and takes a big breath in. "What happened? Where am I?"

"You're in my house. There was an accident. Do you remember anything?" The words are flying out of me so quickly that I don't even know if he'll understand them.

He continues to squint his eyes and gently peer around the room. When he looks back at me, he forms a small smile. "Hey," he says again. This time, softer. Like the positive events of last night are flooding back to him.

"Hi," I breathe, a tear dropping onto his hair.

His face returns to confusion as he tilts his head up toward the bag on his head. "It feels a little early for lunch. What is that?"

There's that sense of humor I love so dearly.

"Is he talking?" the dispatcher asks.

"Yes," I shout to my phone sitting on the hardwood floor next to Harvey and me.

"Okay, do not move him. Do not move his head. Keep him lying still until help arrives. And keep him talking."

Harvey winces. "My head hurts like hell."

I don't want to tell him how much he bled or what it looks like, so I steer clear of the subject.

"I know. The ambulance is almost here. Just hang in there. Everything's going to be okay."

I glance at the carving in his leg, wondering when he'll notice it. Feelings of guilt boil over knowing it's my name. Knowing he's hurt because of me. And now, police are going to think I did this to him and left a likely permanent mark on his body. Like some sort of sick tattoo crafted by an equally sick human being.

Why would He do that? I wonder.

Was it some sort of message that He's coming for me? Or is He trying to frame me?

Harvey swallows and looks around the room only using his eyes. Then he looks right at me. Suddenly, there's fear in his expression, like he's remembering something. "I saw him, Nola," Harvey whispers. "He was here. In the house."

Three loud knocks pound on the door, startling both of us. I don't hear any sirens, so I hesitate for a moment until one word comes from the other side of my front door: "Police!"

At the same time, the dispatcher says, "Okay, Nola, the police are at your door." I hang up the phone with a quick thank-you, wanting to get to the door as fast as I can.

Gently placing Harvey's head against a pillow from the sofa, I say, "Help is here. You're going to be okay."

I unlock the door, and the EMTs rush past me with medical bags and a stretcher in hand. Following them is a police officer.

"Are you the one who called?" he asks.

"Yes. I'm Nola Strate. My friend is in there. Harvey Stephens. He's badly injured but he just woke up."

"I'm Officer Nelson. I need you to tell me everything that happened from the beginning."

I wipe my tear-stained cheeks and sit down at the bottom of the staircase with him. The officer gets out his notepad, and I tell him everything I told the dispatcher on the phone. About how our night went, about what I woke up to, and additionally, about my potential stalker. But I don't want to mention my belief that it's Him. For now, He is the Stalker.

Glancing at the dining room table across the room, I note once more that the envelope containing the terrifying drawing is gone. Did He take it when He left this morning, hoping I wouldn't bring it to the police as proof? My fingers meet my forehead when it dawns on me that I didn't even snap a photo of it.

"You think someone came into the house, hit him, and left? Without waking you up?"

I look down and roll my eyes without letting him see, clenching my teeth harder than ever.

"Yes. I can't explain it, either. But that's the only plausible explanation. And Harvey just told me he saw someone in the house. Ask him."

To Officer Nelson, this scenario is far from plausible. And he doesn't try to hide his opinion when he takes a deep breath.

"Can you tell me the man's name then? This supposed stalker of yours?"

I can't tell him that I don't know. And I don't want to say the only name I do have: the Hiding Man. That will surely get a laugh out of this asshole.

"Can I speak with Detective Jack De Lacey about this? He knows a lot about it already and I think it would just be easier that way."

"I don't know who that is, and even if I did, I'm the one you need to speak with about this because I'm the one who's here," he says with a semi-snarky tone. As he finishes his sentence, the EMTs come barreling around the corner with Harvey strapped to a stretcher.

"Is he going to be all right?" I ask them. I know they probably can't tell me, but I try anyway.

Harvey holds up a thumb as they take him past, making one of the EMTs say, "That's a good sign."

I turn to the officer again. "Look. I don't have any answers, and I did not do this myself. When Harvey gets to the hospital, I think you should speak with him about what he saw. Because I didn't see a damn thing."

He scribbles something down on his notepad and says, "Oh, I will definitely be speaking with Mr. Stephens."

"Can I please go with him to the hospital?" I ask, not wanting to be away from Harvey.

The officer mulls it over for a few seconds before deciding he's heard enough from me, and that I'm free to leave. As Harvey is carefully loaded up into the back of the ambulance, I walk out to my driveway behind them and peer up at the sky—which is gray with notes of gold under several clouds that are low enough to catch the day's new rays.

The men secure Harvey into place and usher me to the end of the padded bench next to them—but I decide to follow in my car instead. As the ambulance doors close, I walk the few feet to my own vehicle.

Approaching my driver's-side door, I see something in my neighbor's window. The driveway remains uninhabited by cars, just like it was last night when Harvey and I got to my house, not long before I saw someone swinging in their hammock.

Part of someone's face peers from behind a curtain in the front room of their house. This is the first time—other than last night— that I've spotted someone there. And they're looking right at us. As I stare hard back at them, trying to study their appearance through the window, they rapidly pull the curtain closed.

27

JACK

A young woman was murdered just six blocks over from Felicity's house last night, on the ever-quiet, vintage block of Truman Street. Jack and the rest of his department were astonished to learn yet another young woman had been killed in this neighborhood. It's an urban neighborhood that isn't known for its crime, but rather its young professionals, dog-friendliness, and charming local businesses. Any part of the city can suffer the occasional broken car window, but not two brutal murders seemingly committed by the same person in such quick succession.

Jack arrived at the crime scene within minutes of receiving the call from Officer Austin Torrance, who gave Jack a nod as he stepped out of his sedan on the orange leaf-covered road that is Truman Street. There are multiple officers standing outside Mary's house, one of whom is busy speaking to an elderly woman. She's dressed in a matching floral pajama set covered mostly by an eggplant windbreaker with the hood up, shielding her from the drizzling wetness misting the air. She's holding a small Yorkshire terrier under her right arm, rocking it softly like a baby. When Officer Bob Cantor sees Jack, he waves him over. All Jack knows at this point is that a young woman was found murdered in her home early this morning by her next-door neighbor. And that the MO matched that of Felicity Morton's murder from three nights ago.

Jack's mind immediately goes back to the Hiding Man, since at this point, he's trying to draw similarities and differences so he can rule any connection in or out. Two murders in one weekend is a lot, even for the masked killer. Jack knows very well that the Hiding Man's victims were murdered within a month or more of each other. So why would he start killing faster now? Yet another reason to believe it's a different person.

"Mrs. Brighton, this is Detective De Lacey. Detective, this is the victim's next-door neighbor. She called us this morning after finding her." Officer Cantor turns to Mrs. Brighton and adds, "He's going to get the rest of your statement now." He nods at Jack and quietly hands him a slip of paper hosting basic details of the victim—Mary Clairemont—as he walks away.

Jack almost protests, wanting to hear more about the case before collecting the woman's statement. But instead he gives the dog a smile and looks up at the woman. "Hello, Mrs. Brighton. Would you mind starting from the beginning again so I can get the full picture?" He squints from the light rain. He would move them to a different spot, but partially leafless tree branches hanging above their heads are catching most of the droplets.

The elderly woman's face is doughy and supple, but emotionally hard. There are remnants of tears atop her eyebags, and Jack can already tell she's had a strenuous morning.

"Hello, Detective," she says hoarsely, clearing her throat. "I suppose I'll start from last night." She swallows. "My husband and I are typically in bed quite early—maybe by seven. But recently I've been waking up at midnight to take a new medication, and then I'll go right back to sleep. Thankfully I'm almost done with that stuff," she says, consistently sniffing. "Anyhow. Last night I forgot to set out a glass of water on my bedstand, so I went to the kitchen. And that's when I heard a ruckus next door."

"What kind of ruckus?" Jack asks. He looks at the house and notices that it's a duplex. "And might I ask as well, does your kitchen share a wall with Ms. Clairemont's home?"

"Yes, it does. And that's where I heard the sound, coming from the other side of my kitchen wall. Now, I haven't been in her house in quite some time—not since the previous tenants lived in there. So, I'm not positive what room is on the other side of my kitchen. But I heard some sort of thumping sound. Nothing more, nothing too loud."

"And how did you find Ms. Clairemont?"

"I kept hearing something pawing at my door this morning, and when I opened it, this little guy was sitting there," she says, looking at the dog. "This is Franklin. He's Mary's. She's always taking him on walks, so I see them pass my window most days. I know her roommate is out of town, so I wondered if she had gone with her, and somehow the little guy got out. I walked over to her porch to see what was going on and her front door was open a crack, which I found odd as it was so early. But then, of course, it made sense as to how the dog had gotten out."

"About what time was this?"

"Let's see. I woke up at six and puttered around the house for a while. Then I made some breakfast for my husband. It must have been 6:45 or so by then. I called you guys right away."

Jack checks his watch. It's 7:25 now.

"And what did you do after finding the door unlocked? Did you touch the door? Did you open it?" Jack asks lightly.

"I sure as hell didn't expect anything had happened to the girl. I planned to drop the dog inside her doorway and then close the door to keep him in. I thought maybe the wind had swept it open last night," she says, still visibly upset. "I didn't want to be snooping in her home, but when I leaned in to drop the dog in, I couldn't help but notice someone in the corner of my eye. It was Mary, lying there. A few feet inside. That poor girl was so kind to my husband and me. Unlike her roommate."

"What do you know about the roommate?"

"I don't know a last name, but her first is Mabel. Mabel and Mary—it was easy to remember. I saw her loading a car with a suitcase on Saturday and haven't seen her since, so I assumed she was out of town."

"And what makes you say she wasn't nice?" Jack presses.

"I haven't spoken to her many times, but she was always standoffish. Not like Mary. Mary would wave and say hello. She's come around a couple times to look at old pictures with me. But Mabel never came with her."

Jack nods. "Thank you, ma'am. This is all very helpful. Did your husband see or hear anything last night or this morning?" Jack scans the scene for an elderly man and finds him on what is likely his own front porch speaking with Officer Cantor. If he's correct, the victims' portion of the building is situated on the left, with the Brightons' to the right.

"Only what I told him. That man sleeps like a bear. Snores like one, too," she admits, shaking her head. "Say, could I keep this little guy? The poor thing needs a home now, doesn't he?"

Jack thinks on it a moment. "We'll want to notify her family and see if they'd prefer to take him. If not, I'm sure you could."

She gives the dog a squeeze and nods her head.

Jack thanks Mrs. Brighton for her time and assesses the scene.

Between his exhaustion and the unthinkably devastating news of a second homicide, Jack is surprised he's on two feet. Ms. Claire-mont's death will surely hit the news soon, and the city will begin to group her murder with Felicity's. It's only a matter of time before the media gets ahold of Felicity's information as well, and compari-sons are made. As of now, most people only know that someone was murdered. But they don't know how or who—not yet. He can see the headlines now: Two Bodies in Two Days: Has a Serial Killer Come Back to Portland?

Part of him hopes the city becomes alert to this immediately, with people watching their backs more than they usually would and taking notice of strange occurrences. Perhaps that would make it easier to catch whoever is behind these two crimes. That, or it would lead to false confessions, countless tips that go nowhere, and more pressure on his shoulders. Jack hasn't been informed of Ms. Claire-mont's wounds or cause of death yet, but he can guess.

"I can't believe there's another one. I'm betting it's the same guy," Officer Austin Torrance says as he approaches Jack.

"Hit me," Jack says with a sigh.

"Mary Clairemont. Thirty-two years old. Still waiting to learn how long she's lived in the house, but she's been here at least a year, according to Mrs. Brighton," Officer Torrance reads from his notepad.

Since Austin Torrance first said her name, it's been ringing in his head. There's something familiar about it.

Officer Torrance continues, "No sign of forced entry in the house, though her front door was cracked open upon discovery. Mary's body was found just inside at the entrance of the living room, and her throat was slit. Since there doesn't appear to be signs of a struggle inside, we can surmise she was likely caught off guard."

Jack massages his temples. He sensed that her cause of death would be the same as the first murder, but hoped he was wrong. Not that two killers on the loose is what he wishes for, either.

"Is there any indication that she was ambushed as she walked into her house?" Jack asks.

"I mean, according to the scene, it's definitely possible. But she isn't wearing shoes and her purse is in the kitchen. So, unless she was checking the mailbox or something, I doubt it. We're still trying to figure out when she was last seen," Officer Torrance admits.

"Back door?"

"It's locked. It goes into a courtyard that's shared with the Brightons. We only glanced back there if you want to take a better look."

"Will do." Jack nods. "Anything else?"

"Not really. Her phone's next to her purse in the kitchen if you want to take that back to the station and contact her family and friends. Tell them what happened."

"Lucky me," Jack breathes.

Jack heads inside the brick duplex to check on the body, and bag Mary's phone, purse, and anything else that looks important. When he walks through the white, wooden front door of the historic, red-brick building, he spots Mary immediately.

She's lying face down on the beige carpet that spans her living room while a forensics team works around her. The scent of death is billowing around them. Jack carefully walks around the scene, eyeing the floor, the walls—everything. He moves to the living room window and spies closed blinds, trying to picture the evening Mary had. Had someone been watching her? Was she caught off guard after leaving the front door unlocked? Or did she let her killer—someone she knew—inside her home, only for something to go wrong?

Using a newly gloved hand, he peeks through the blinds with his index and middle fingers, separating them enough to see out. There's a large tree out front—the one he questioned Mrs. Brighton underneath—but otherwise, the street is quite open. The house across the way has even more trees covering their property, making it unlikely they would have seen anything. He makes a mental note to speak with them anyway once he wraps up in the house.

Heading into the kitchen, Jack finds Mary's purse, keys, and wallet—seemingly untouched. Already it appears the perpetrator wasn't looking for money or valuables. Though, strangely, Mary's license is missing from her wallet.

The kitchen is small and unassuming, with white cabinets and granite countertops that look like they were updated somewhat recently. On the counter sits a loaf of bread that was purchased from a bakery just up the street. A serrated knife with minuscule crumbs on its blade lies on the brown paper bag the bread came in, and a bell of butter is flipped open. Jack jots this down, considering that Mary might have been awake and having a snack before she was killed. The second of two doors in the house is located in the kitchen with a chain lock secured in place. A short, beige curtain covers the window that takes up the top half of the door, proving to Jack that she didn't attempt to go out this way, and neither did whoever took her life.

He walks across the rest of the first floor before ascending the staircase looking for the girls' bedrooms on the second floor. At the top of the stairs, he finds both. First, he checks the roommate's room and finds an old California driver's license in a drawer. The address is a place in San Francisco and the name listed is Mabel Fine. She's the same age as Mary, and from her picture alone, looks like a normal girl—whatever that means. Many of her clothes and belongings remain in the room, verifying to Jack that she is simply on a trip. But where? What does she know—if anything?

Across the hall is Mary's room. Jack enters to find a clean, organized living space with no traces of disturbance. Her bed is made, indicating to Jack that she hadn't been sleeping—or even trying to—when she was killed. This leads him to believe that she was already downstairs when the killer entered the house. It's likely the perp didn't even enter the second level, but he could have seen her in here at some point if he had been watching her. Was this how he knew her roommate wasn't home, and that Mary was alone?

The curtains are open, and the window faces down to Truman Street below. On her desk, there's a stack of novels, a crocheting kit, and a desktop computer that is password protected. Jack looks around, defenseless to the painful knowledge that her family will have to come into this bedroom and see the serenity of the space she occupied while she was alive. They'll have to sift through her personal things and find a new home for them. And Jack's the one responsible for notifying them of this. He's the one who has to tell them that their beloved daughter, possible sister, and friend, is dead.

Jack finishes up inside the home, trashes his gloves, and walks out to the street to view the building—seeing what the killer would have seen. There are eight colonial windows at the front of the home—displayed on the first and second floors—multiple iron-gated faux balconies, and a front garden that takes up a few feet of space between the house and the sidewalk. There's no proper driveway for any of the four residents, though street parking appears ample. From the street, Jack looks up at Mary's bedroom window to see nothing but the reflection of the tree in it. Though he can imagine that at night, when a light is on inside, much more can be witnessed. Glancing at the left side of the house where a short staircase leads to the back of the building, Jack wonders if he'll find anything of importance.

Officer Torrance described a courtyard, so Jack walks up and finds himself there. Both Mary's and the Brightons' homes have back doors leading to this area, where there is a private garden space. An alleyway at the far end connects to the street behind which, Jack notes, would have allowed the killer to enter or exit this way without being seen. Jack carefully inspects this outdoor space and the path through the alley, looking for any clues. The rain would have washed away any detectible footprints, so the chances of him finding anything useful is slim. But near the end of the alley where it meets the next street, Jack spots something on the ground. Considering the section isn't secured, it doesn't appear any of the officers have come back here yet.

He grabs a plastic bag from his pocket—something he always keeps stored on him for situations like this—and inverts it, shoving his hand into the makeshift glove. On the ground is a leather wallet. Without quite picking it up, Jack crouches down and flips open one side of the bill, looking for any indication of who the wallet belongs to. And right there in the left front screened slot is an Oregon license with a name and photo he knows better than most.

28

NOLA

A purple-smocked nurse places a tray of food on the overbed table that she'd situated in Harvey's lap just minutes ago.

"Breakfast is served," she says with a grin. "You doin' okay, hon?"

"As good as I can be. Thanks," he replies kindly.

The nurse sends him a soft smile and a double thumbs-up before leaving the room.

The tray includes a plastic cup of orange juice with a foil lid, a plain bagel also sealed in plastic, a single-serve pouch of cream cheese, a tiny box of Honey Nut Cheerios, and a carton of 2 percent milk.

"You lucky man," I joke. "They're really giving you the gourmet stuff."

Harvey playfully sneers and opens the cereal box, then pops individual Os in his mouth. "Hey, at least I'm alive. Thanks to you."

"Please. I freaked out more than I helped," I say. "Seriously, though, I can go grab you a real bagel with all the fixings. Or a smoothie or something?"

Harvey sends me an appreciative smile. "Thanks, but this is fine for now. Lunch, however. That might require outside forces. I don't even want to know what's on the menu here."

"Whatever you need."

"You must be hungry. You want some of this?" he asks, meaning it.

"That is just so tempting," I laugh.

Harvey is propped up in his hospital bed while I sit in the burgundy upholstered chair next to him, sipping a terrible cup of coffee that I snagged from the cafeteria downstairs. *Edward Scissorhands* is playing on the little TV hanging on the wall in front of his bed. It's the brightest thing in the room, with the overhead lights turned down to avoid visual overstimulation. A small lamp sits on the table next to him so he can see his food. Technically, he shouldn't even have the TV on, but it's bringing him a sense of comfort and he's trying not to focus on it too much. It's mostly about the sound anyway.

It's bleak in here. Some decorator made a failed attempt to soften the space with a horrible periwinkle paint job that makes it feel more like a decrepit nursery than a regular hospital room. But I guess it's better than white. Everything else in here is. White, that is. White sheets, white gated Gatch bed, white glossy floors, white fluorescent lights, white curtains. Like I said, bleak. But they assigned Harvey his own room with a single window to the outside world, which is better than what some of the others in this place get, having to share rooms or choke in the claustrophobia that is four solid walls. Every minute or so, a patient wheels past our room, or nurses and doctors will jog at an alarming pace, signaling that something urgent is happening down the hall. The sounds of people moaning in pain pass infrequently, but enough to strengthen the anticipation of discharge.

I glance at Harvey's right calf, my messily etched name covered with a large bandage. He catches me staring.

"It's kind of cool, you know," he says, pulling the foil off his juice cup. "Most guys get their girlfriend's names tattooed. Not me. I'm way tougher than that."

I wheeze a quiet laugh. "You're taking this far too well," I say. "You sure your head's all right?"

"Oh, definitely not."

Harvey tears pieces of bagel and squeezes small amounts of cream cheese on top before popping them into his mouth. His head is wrapped in gauze that meets under his chin to cover the injury at the crown area, but again, he seems to be taking it all in stride.

"I look ridiculous, huh?" he asks.

I didn't realize I was still staring at him. I'm so happy he didn't die this morning that I can't stop looking at the guy. He was who knew how close to lying on an embalming table today instead of in a hospital bed.

"You've never looked hotter," I tease.

"It's the gown, isn't it? You can see my ass through the back, you know," Harvey says.

"Oh, I'd love to see that."

The doctor thinks that Harvey was hit with a blunt object of some kind that caused a concussion severe enough to make him lose consciousness. What that object is, the police are still trying to figure out.

As far as when it happened, we just can't tell. From the blow, he could have been passed out for minutes or hours, leaving the window for the attacker to enter and exit my house wide open. Police considered the fact that my balcony door was unlocked, and the fact that Harvey confirmed it was not me who hit him—although he can't remember what exactly happened. But he knows I would never and could never do anything like that, and he recalls seeing his face. Though, admittedly, he said the memory is foggy.

With everything we were researching last night, could it have been anyone other than Him? I can't put my finger on why He would hurt Harvey and leave me untouched, but I'm determined to find out.

When we got to the hospital this morning, Harvey told me and the police officer that he only remembers one thing before his vision went black: a man with a white face standing over him. He doesn't know why he woke up—whether he heard a noise or was touched in some way—but he has this singular, muggy image in his head. The officer wasn't too convinced that this was true, especially when Harvey compared the face that he saw to the images he was looking at hours earlier. The officer said the person with a white face standing over him was probably a nightmare. But then how does he explain the injury?

The ever-skeptical officer, a second time, had said, "Are you sure you saw that in person? It wasn't a dream or hallucination based off the pictures you looked at?"

Part of me understood why he asked that. It's a logical question when the person you're talking to just suffered a traumatic head injury where their brain literally bounced around in their skull. He seemed to take Harvey's confident "Yes, I'm sure" with a grain of salt.

I think back to the person in the window before we left my house. Was it just my neighbor being nosy and taking notice that an ambulance and police cars were out on the street so early in the morning? The strangest part to me is that they didn't come out to make sure everyone was okay, and, on a completely different note, that was only the second time I have seen any kind of movement in that house. I've lived next door for over a year, and until last night, hadn't seen any trace of a real human. I elected not to tell the officer about this sighting, since it doesn't scream "malice," but I'll most definitely be watching out for them from now on.

"Oh, my baby," says Harvey's mom, Cynthia, as she suddenly walks through the open door. Harvey expresses a mixture of embarrassment by her wording and joy that she's present.

"Hi, Mom," he says, squeezing her hand. He's trying to keep himself as still as possible, making a hug out of his words.

"Hi, Nola," she says with a warm grin, her bright whites shining in my face. "Thank you for being here with him." Her wavy, dirty blond hair is down on her shoulders, with her tight, black workout clothes covered by a cream, fur-lined windbreaker.

Cynthia moved to the outskirts of Portland from Washington a couple years ago to be close to Harvey, her only child. His dad died when he was young, so Harvey is all Cynthia really has—surely making today's events the scariest thing she can imagine.

I greet her back and apologize for what happened.

"It's not your fault," Harvey says.

"Don't blame yourself," Cynthia adds. "Are you in pain?" she asks Harvey.

"My head is killing me. The doctor said my brain could bleed if I take any pain meds in the next few hours."

"They're supposed to bring him some Tylenol soon, though," I chime. "They said that's safe to start with, but probably won't help too much."

"Thank you, Nola. I'll go find the nurse and get you some,"

Cynthia says, walking over to me and dropping her purse on the adjacent table.

"I'm so sorry. I feel responsible," I say again.

Cynthia briefly sits in the chair next to me. She puts her hands in mine and says, "Sweetie, this isn't your fault. Do they know who did it? Do they know anything?"

I exchange glances with Harvey, unsure of how much to say.

He does it for me. "I think Nola's in danger. Someone's been following her, and I'm sure I saw him last night," he starts confidently. "We think the person who did this to me is responsible for a murder that just happened across town."

"What?" she asks, shaking her head. "A killer is after you?"

We both sigh, knowing how far-fetched it sounds without the full story.

"And are you talking about the murder from Friday night? Felicity Morton?"

We're both shocked that she knows about Felicity's death since it hasn't hit mainstream news yet and I haven't seen her full name in any articles.

I ignore her original question and ask, "How did you know that?"

"My coworker Gale is the one who found her. I learned about it this morning right before I came here." She waves her phone in the air. "I would have learned at work if I had a chance to go in, but we have a group chat for all the office ladies at the school."

As if this city could feel any smaller.

Harvey tells her about the phone call we received on *Night Watch*. She's aghast, and wonders why Harvey hadn't told her before now and how no one in her group chat knew about it.

"All the ladies thought it had to be a lover's dispute, but her boyfriend didn't do it," Cynthia says.

"What makes you say that?" I ask. Although I didn't believe it was that cut-and-dried, I'm still surprised at her words.

"I guess he's been up in Seattle. That's what's floating around the group chat," she says.

If this wasn't a hideous act of domestic violence committed by her boyfriend, that leaves one possible suspect in my mind. But no one knows where He is, how to find Him, nor what his plans are.

I glance at Harvey, who is gripping his head and silently wincing.

"I'm gonna shut up for a bit and let you rest," Cynthia says to Harvey. "But I'd really like to hear more about this after his pain meds kick in. I'll go grab that nurse now." She rises from her chair.

Just then, an officer walks into the room. I thought they'd be done questioning us, so I wasn't expecting him to stop by again.

Officer Nelson looks between me and Harvey before settling officially on Harvey. "We may have a witness who thinks he saw the person that attacked you." He looks at me and adds, "Your neighbor."

29

NOLA

My neighbor?

My mind goes nowhere except to my next-door neighbor, of course. This means they were watching me on the balcony last night, and from their front window at the crack of dawn this morning. They must have been awake whenever Harvey's attacker entered my house. Or were they the ones responsible, and this is part of their clichéd move to insert themselves into the investigation? Either way, all of this not-knowing is really starting to rattle me. But I finally understand why girls in horror movies don't just hop on a plane and get as far away as they can. I can't leave my dad and Harvey to deal with all of this by themselves, no matter how much I want to put it behind me.

"Can you tell us what exactly they called in with?" I ask Officer Nelson eagerly.

He steps into the room and closes the door halfway, causing me to rise from my seat and walk toward Harvey's bed. Harvey has stopped eating now, and pushes away the tray with most of the food untouched.

Before he can reply, Cynthia returns to the room saying, "All right, honey. The nurse will be right in with the Tylenol." When she sees the officer, she adds, "Hello."

"Morning," he says, nodding. "I was just telling them that a neighbor may have seen something." He reaches out his hand to shake hers, and they exchange names.

Officer Nelson's face is swarthy and hard, like he recently moved to our shadowed corner of the United States from the sunny tropics. His shoulders are tense, giving him the demeanor of a man who means business and nothing but. Concern flutters his eyes, making the rest of us get the same feeling.

"He saw someone running out of your house around five o'clock this morning holding something. The neighbor was standing a ways away, so he couldn't tell what it was."

I surmised that had to have happened, but hearing it out loud makes it that much more terrifying.

I feel sick thinking about a stranger in the night running out of my house. Knowing I was asleep while this all happened gives me the darkest sense of dread.

"What?" Cynthia asks, disturbed. "Did they see anything else?"

"All I can tell you is that the neighbor lives a few houses down the hill from Ms. Strate here, and they were out walking their dog very early this morning."

A few houses down the hill?

That would mean this wasn't my next-door neighbor, but someone else that I've likely never met, as everyone in my neighborhood remains a stranger.

I take a deep breath and wait for the officer to give more details, thankful this person came forward at all.

"The neighbor was surprised to see someone else was out at that hour, so he watched them as they came out of your house and bolted down the street. I have a guy going there now to see if he can find anything on the road and check if any other neighbors saw anything."

"Did he give a description of the person?" I ask.

"Well, it was dark out at that time—this was before sunrise. All he could see was the shadow," Officer Nelson says, shrugging. "He was skeptical of them since they were running but, as I'm sure you're aware of, you live in a safe neighborhood—so he didn't think it could have been anyone causing harm. He called us when he saw the squad cars outside of your house an hour later. All he noted was that the person was fast."

"Are you not suspicious of this neighbor?" I ask, playing devil's advocate. We can't be too careful right now. "How did he happen to also notice when you guys showed up? It just seems a little funny."

"I agree," Cynthia says, now crossing her arms.

I'm not particularly suspicious of the guy, but who knows. I'm not even sure which house Officer Nelson is referring to, and although I'm grateful for the tip, I'm hesitant to automatically trust it when we have no idea who is behind this.

"Later, when he was driving past your house to go to the airport, he saw the police. That's when he thought to report the activity. We spoke with his wife as well, and we're not looking into either of them at this time. He was trying to help," Officer Nelson says.

Between me, Cynthia, and Harvey, no words are spoken. It doesn't feel like there's anything else to inquire about until they have more information, even though a million questions are flying around my brain. I sit back in my chair and bite my thumbnail.

"But that's not all. We found this on the floor of your living room." The officer holds up the evidence bag that's been in his hands this whole time. I was so focused on what he was saying that I didn't even consider what he was carrying. The bag contains the license of a redheaded woman who initially appears to be a stranger.

But when I stare at her photo harder, and then her name, I nearly let a gasp escape my lips.

The woman is Mary, who I met in the diner just last night.

"Are you trying to say a woman is behind this? And that's her?" Cynthia asks, unsure of what he's implying.

I'm equally puzzled. I didn't see it when I was looking for my cell phone to call 911, though I was rightfully panicked and far from clear-headed, earlier. But why would her license be in my house anyway?

Officer Nelson quiets his voice. "This is the ID of a woman we found murdered this morning a few minutes away from your house."

My hand is suddenly over my mouth, in complete disbelief at the development. Hours after I discussed Him with Mary, in a public space, she was murdered. She was the only person other than me to have ever seen Him.

It can't be a coincidence. No chance in hell.

My face must show one of astonishment, but Officer Nelson doesn't find it suspicious. He's just told me a murdered woman's ID was found in my house. But I don't tell him why I'm disturbed most of all. I can't help but think he'd start questioning me even further—for both attacks.

I look at Harvey, his head resting against the pillow. He seems somewhat checked out of the conversation. The poor guy has enough going on, his face sitting in a small grimace—though from pain or what the officer's saying, I can't tell.

Officer Nelson continues, "So, now we're thinking it's possible that whoever killed this woman came into your house afterward, knocked Mr. Stephens in the head for an undetermined reason, and fled, dropping the license in the process."

"Or planting it there," I offer in the most flippant voice I can muster through my nerves.

"You think a mass murderer hurt my son? And are you going to keep patrol on them to make sure they're safe?" Cynthia asks.

Officer Nelson puts his hand up. "Never said 'mass murderer.' And I'm not saying that's what occurred here. I'm just letting you know what we've got so far. We're doing everything we can to find them. You're safe here. We're working all angles of this."

Jack said something very similar yesterday and look where that got us. I refuse to sit back and take this anymore. Because more than before, I fear I'm next.

My phone buzzes in my pocket. I pull it out to see my local news app posting about the very thing we're speaking of: the murders.

The headline reads:

TWO NORTHWEST PORTLAND WOMEN FOUND MURDERED, POSSIBLE CONNECTION

I turn my phone toward Officer Nelson to show him. "Word's out," I mutter.

"Boy. Here we go," he says, checking his phone as a call comes in. "Duty calls. I'll have someone check in with you all later." Looking at Harvey, he states, "Hope you start feeling better soon, son."

I scroll through the article to learn that Felicity lived mere minutes from my house in an area I'm quite familiar with, and that police don't have any suspects thus far. Surprisingly, the article even mentions the questioning of Felicity's boyfriend. As I almost reach the part with the second victim's information—presumably Mary's—two recognizable words catch my eye in the last paragraph on Felicity: *Night Watch*. There's even an audio clip underneath it, and before I press Play, I know exactly what it is. As my thumb taps the screen, I hear my own voice speaking to Felicity last Friday night.

"How are you listening to that?" Harvey asks.

"It's in this article on the murders. Someone must have clipped it before we removed it from the podcast apps yesterday."

I pause the audio we've listened to more times than I'd like by now and read another shocking detail: Felicity's cause of death. Just like his original victims, she reportedly died by having her throat slit.

I rapidly fly down the article to see if Mary's cause of death has been released, and it hasn't yet. But considering she's been deceased for some handful of hours, I'm not surprised. With the murders being grouped together, I assume she died in the same horrific fashion.

I wince at the thought of it; the knife dragging across Mary's throat. The wonderful young woman who wanted to help get me more information dying at the hands of the very monster we discussed. Could it be?

Going through the details of both killings, it doesn't seem Felicity and Mary had anything in common. Felicity was forty-one years old, worked in mental health, and lived alone on a quiet street. On an equally quiet street nearby, Mary, who was almost ten years Felicity's junior, was murdered in her duplex.

How did both of these women draw the gaze of the same deranged character?

Seeing a photo of Felicity for the first time is difficult. Her eyes were kind. Her smile was winsome. Her fervor for life shone through her so visibly.

My phone buzzes in my hand as I stare at the screen. An incoming call pops down above the article.

It's Jack.

I answer as quickly as I can get my finger on the green Accept button.

"Hey," I say into the phone, standing up and walking across the room as Cynthia gives Harvey the Tylenol.

"I just got a call about Harvey. How's he holding up?" Jack asks.

I turn around briefly to look at him, as though that would give me the answer I'm searching for. "He's alive. Awake. I'm here with him at the hospital now."

"That was my next question, actually. I need to talk to you. Are you sticking around there for a little while longer?"

"I'm technically outside of visiting hours but the hospital said it's okay for me and his mom to stay and help keep him awake. So, I'll be here until they kick me out," I say.

I don't tell Jack that I need to talk to him about Mary, not wanting anyone else to hear me.

"Okay, I'll head over there now. Can you meet me in the parking lot when I get there?"

"Sure. Just call me when you're outside. And what's this about?" I ask, wondering if he's made the connection between Mary and Him all on his own.

A few seconds go by without him answering, making me think our call got disconnected.

"I can't get into it on the phone. I'll see you in fifteen minutes."

30

JACK

J ack pulls into the parking lot of the Archangel Portland Medical Center across town and sidles up behind the covered entry bay, not wanting to take up space meant for emergency vehicles or people in dire need of help.

He hasn't been here since his mother died nearly three years ago, withering away in one of the rooms upstairs. He pictures her paper-thin skin holding his hand as she faded away on that balmy, cloudless spring evening, her eyes locked on his. She had been suffering from dementia for three years, but on that final day, she was clearheaded and present. Jack was radiating with relief that her closing moments weren't thronged with confusion and hurt. For the last time she looked at her only child, she knew who he was. And she was happy.

Jack envisioned his mother's most positive memories playing in the space between their gazes. He had read a study in the newspaper the year prior which stated that, within thirty seconds after death, it's believed that the brain releases protective chemicals that cause a string of hallucinations as you die.

"Death is a process," the article said. He hoped her process was as dazzling as she had been throughout her seventy-six years.

He wishes the very same for Felicity and Mary: that instead of sensing the hot pain from their necks, or seeing the heinous mask of the person who stole the next sixty-odd years from them, they saw their loved ones' smiles, or memories of their favorite day.

These thoughts are the exact fuel he needs to mete out justice for those victims' loved ones. But their killer is steps ahead of him. Jack knows he needs to act quickly. Gleaning information from Nola could help him put these senseless murders to an end, two lives too late.

Although his heart tells him that his mother's death is the reason that he isn't going up to Harvey's room to meet Nola right now, his mind is focused on privacy. Harvey and his mother don't need to hear the news he has prepared for Nola. Not yet anyway.

Idling along a red-curbed sidewalk, Jack switches off his car's engine and sends a text to Nola.

I'm downstairs.

The rain is violently beating down on his windshield, with dreary views above. He considers stepping out of his car and standing in the hospital's entryway to await her emergence, but instead takes the little time he has to prepare himself for the words that are about to exit his mouth.

Jack picks at the stitching on his sedan's leather steering wheel as he plans the upcoming conversation in his head, nervously darting his eyes toward the entrance every few seconds. Suddenly, Nola walks out.

He hangs on to the moment longer than he needs to, watching her look around for his car as she shrugs a long, black duster onto her shoulders.

Jack gets out of the car and waves at her, before hopping back in and pulling his sedan up beside her so she doesn't have to step out in the rain.

"Get in," Jack yells through the loud droplets bouncing off the asphalt.

"Where are we going?" she asks before grabbing the door's handle.

"I'm just gonna pull into a spot over there," Jack says, pointing at the lines of cars taking up the lot. He finds a parking space a couple rows back, drives into it, and parks the car. For the first few moments they're parked, the only sounds are the low wave of the car's heater and the squeaking windshield wipers.

"I'm assuming you've either heard about or read about the second murder," Jack says, breaking the silence.

"Both," Nola replies softly.

"The second victim, as I'm sure you know, was a young woman named"—and in unison, Nola and Jack say—"Mary Clairemont."

He looks at Nola, and she spins a story about an internet post, Mary's sighting of the Hiding Man when he took his fourth victim, and a meeting with Mary at a local diner just last night.

When she's done, Jack sits in silence, puzzling the pieces together.

"I knew her name sounded familiar this morning," Jack says to himself. "I hadn't had a chance to look into it just yet."

"Did you know her?" Nola asks. "Back then?"

"I didn't speak with her that day Carrie Fenton was killed. But I read her statement. About what she saw through the window. Her statement helped confirm your sighting weeks later when Mia died."

"So, you believe that he's back now?" Nola inquires, relief in her tone. "What if I'm next? Can you make sure I'm protected?"

"I admit that it's a bizarre connection. And it may be more than that," Jack says carefully. "But I'm not sure you're being targeted."

She shakes her head in clear confusion. "What makes you say that?"

Jack slides his fingers along the top of his steering wheel, stalling a moment. "Do you think your dad could have possibly known Mary? Or did you tell him about this meeting by chance?"

"I mean, I don't see how he could know her. But I don't know everyone he knows," she admits. "I was at his house when Mary responded to me, but I didn't tell him about her. Just that I was headed to Moonie's for a bit."

Jack turns to look at Nola again, his face dropping lower than it was before. "We found your dad's wallet behind Mary's house this morning."

Nola's expression sits somewhere between distress and disbelief. She faintly shakes her head.

Jack continues, "You cannot share this information. I shouldn't even be telling you, but I'm hoping you can help. It was in the alleyway that led from the back of Mary's duplex to the street over—which feels like a pretty good exit point after committing a crime, if you ask me."

"My dad couldn't have done this. You know him. He's your friend."

Jack is equally upset. "I know, Nola," he says, a bit too aggressively. "But what am I supposed to do? No matter whose wallet it might have been, I would need to question that person—investigate it to the fullest extent of the law. Just because he is who he is to me doesn't mean I can blow it all away. I want nothing more than for there to be some magical explanation for what I found. But it's not looking good." He catches his breath.

"Okay, so ask him! He'll tell you exactly what he told me. That things have been going missing from his house lately."

"Doesn't that feel like a convenient answer to you?" Jack scoffs. Calming his tone, he asks, "I'm assuming he told you this when you went to his house yesterday."

"He wasn't answering my calls. He's been MIA a lot lately." She says that slowly, as if having some sort of revelation. Thinking Jack can read her mind, she quickly adds, "So I went over, and he'd just been sleeping and lounging all day. Nothing like what you're insinuating."

"We've been trying to contact him all morning and he hasn't answered us, either. I even went by his house, but he didn't come to the door. I have a guy trying to get a warrant for his phone right now."

"A warrant?" Nola slides honey-blond hair behind her left ear. "This is totally coming out of nowhere." She shifts her body toward Jack in her seat and says sternly, "Whoever is killing these women is the same person who killed all those people twenty years ago. I know you guys think something happened to the killer for him to have stopped for all this time, but unless it's an exact copycat, I believe it's the same person."

"Exactly," Jack replies. He takes a deep breath and continues, moving his hands a lot as he speaks. "The night Mia was killed, your dad didn't come to the scene right away. Do you remember that?"

"Kind of. Yeah," Nola scoffs.

"He told me and your mom that he went to the studio. We were able to verify that he did. But only for a short while. There's a pocket of time that's unaccounted for."

"Why would he kill Mia? He would never do something like that. He knows how much she meant to me," Nola says harshly. "And he doesn't even have a motive! He's not a killer!"

"He was fucking her!" Jack says loudly, a small drop of spit flying off his lip at the sharp *F*.

The tension thrummed in the car only moments ago, but now, everything is frozen; he could hear a pin drop.

Jack plunges his head into his hands, regretting his wording. "I'm sorry. I didn't mean for it to come out that way. I just need you to know why my head is where it is. I have known your dad for a very long time. And I agree that it doesn't feel like he would be capable of something like this. But there are some weird coincidences. You just have to trust me."

A delicate set of tears glass over Nola's eyes.

"He was cheating on my mom? With Mia?" Nola asks softly. "You're wrong. Why would you say that?"

"He told me that night. The same night he couldn't come up with a single solid alibi for the evenings that any of the other murders took place."

Jack didn't plan on sharing so many details with Nola. But he's hoping that explaining his reasoning behind possibly suspecting her father could give her a chance to correct all the doubts in his mind. Or maybe he just wanted someone to vent to—someone to tell him he's wrong, and mean it.

The rain beats down harder, matching the emotions taking up all the air inside Jack's car. As the wipers slowly clear away the falling water, someone walks across the front of his vehicle and briefly peers in. With the obvious strain inside, and being in a hospital parking lot, the person probably surmises that the two strangers just lost a loved one. In a way, it feels like they may just have.

"So, *he* was the boyfriend. The one that would take her to the coast and to lavish dinners. The one that was older," Nola says in a numb whisper, ignoring the latter portion of what Jack admitted. "She blatantly told me about her boyfriend, knowing he was my dad."

Jack silently gives her time to process what she's just learned.

"Is this why my parents split up? Does my mom know?"

"That was years later, of course. But I'm sure it played a part," Jack responds. "He never personally told me about any other women, though I'd imagine there could have been more." Jack attempts to meet Nola's eyes. "Look. I'm sorry to have been the one to tell you this. But this just adds to the reasons I would like to talk to him and get this squared away."

"Between this and his new book," Nola stops herself. "The book. Why do you think he would write a book on the killer if he *is* the killer?"

"I have no idea. But I need to act fast here. I can't let another person die," Jack says. "You said your dad has been hard to reach lately. Why did you go over there yesterday? And what was his excuse for not answering his phone?"

Nola explains to Jack in detail how he was hungover and in bed all day, even mentioning Chick's acknowledgment of having the evidence boxes. Reluctantly, she also explains that he was seemingly missing on Friday night—the night of Felicity's murder. And that she received a suspicious piece of mail from one of the very boxes that was in Chick's possession—which, since the attack on Harvey, is missing.

As far as motive goes, Jack can't think of a single one for any of the victims, besides Mia. He also can't figure out why Chick would go into his own daughter's house in the night and hurt her friend and his former colleague.

Jack wonders if Chick could have had an affair with any of the other women or if he at least had grown obsessed with some of the young women he couldn't have. It will be easier to determine if Chick had any contact with Felicity or Mary, but at this point it would be nearly impossible to track decades-old movements between him and the other victims.

Clearly, Chick has a baseline fascination with the Hiding Man murders—enough to write a book on the subject. Is it possible that after his years of research and digging, he has decided to take the Hiding Man out of hiding? The timing is rather odd; Jack almost wonders if this is some ridiculously excessive ploy to drive book sales.

"If you hear anything from your dad, you call me, okay? Believe it or not, I'm trying to help him. Everyone in my department has eyes out for him, and the last thing we want is his name getting out there before he has a chance to defend himself."

"Okay," Nola says hesitantly.

"And again, I've told you all of this in confidence. You cannot repeat a word of any of this to him. You promise?"

"I promise," Nola says more matter-of-factly this time.

Nola wipes some runaway tears from her chin and, as she exits Jack's car, he leans over and says, "I'll touch base soon."

Without responding, she closes the door firmly and walks back to the hospital entrance, not bothering to shield her head from the downpour.

Jack backs out of the parking spot and begins driving toward the exit, unsure of where he's even headed. Should he return to his office? Try Chick's house again? Drive off a cliff?

While he waits in the line of cars at the Stop sign, his phone rings. It's one of the officers helping him look for Chick.

Jack's heart drops at the possibility of news. It's like he didn't realize until this moment that maybe he didn't want them to find Chick after all.

"De Lacey," he snaps into the phone.

"We found Chick Strate. He's on his way down to the station."

31

NOLA

I storm across the hospital parking lot in a flurry of emotions. My father's hidden infidelities are a clear demonstration of his oblivious, ego-inflated nature. And unbeknownst to me, it tore our family apart. But is he a killer?

I'm overtaken with anger and uncertainty already; all before noon.

I look up at the beating sky above, ready to release a cathartic howl, deep from the caverns of my spirit. I could collapse on the asphalt, right here, and let the rain wash me away.

As I reach the hospital's covered entryway, I dial my dad—hoping to find him before Jack does. I intend on keeping my promise to Jack, but I want my dad to explain this to me on his own, without the sensation of being under a microscope.

I search his name in my phone and hit Call. But as I bring the speaker to my ear, I get his voicemail without a single ring.

"Hi. You've reached Chick. Sorry to have missed your call, but if you leave a message, I'll return it promptly."

I press End before the beep, curious as to why his phone is off. It's impossible not to wonder if he's in hiding.

I stumble through the hospital doors in an incredulous stupor, aimless and unsure. People in scrubs and civilian clothes pass me in the hallway as I pace back and forth, becoming an obstruction for all who stroll in this area. It's only a matter of time before someone in a pastel-toned hospital uniform tells me to get out of the way. I back myself against the wall in anticipation of this. Bathed in fluorescent light, feeling like a mouse in a maze, I practice deep breathing.

My phone buzzes again, and I find a flurry of texts from Amoli, asking about the article she read, and why I haven't told her about the call. Amoli knows all about what happened twenty years ago—she's one of my only friends who does—so she also asks if I'm doing okay, and if the murders are bringing up old memories.

I send her a reassuring response for now, hoping to buy more time until I have to confide in her about it—with, inevitably, more updates, as this surely isn't over yet.

The only person I want to vent to right now is my mom, who should be completing her anniversary cabin trip in the woods of Vermont by now.

I pull my phone up to my face again and dial her, begging I don't get her voicemail like I got my dad's.

"Hi, honey!" my mom's cheery voice says on the other end. "You caught me at the perfect time. We're just heading home and stopping for gas. Well, Bryan's grabbing some snacks inside."

Her voice rushes a calmness across me that I so desperately needed.

"Hey, Mom," I say, smiling. "I want to hear about your trip but there's a lot going on over here. It's not good," I add in a low voice as I try to find a quiet place to talk to her.

"What do you mean? What's not good?" she asks worriedly.

Uninterested in occupying the hectic waiting room among those standing by for loved ones, I head toward the exit again. As I walk through the waiting room and toward the front door, a man rushes in front of me holding what looks like the tip of his finger in a plastic bag on ice.

"Is it my turn yet? My finger is in a fucking bag here. I need help, now," the man pleads.

"You should be seen any minute now," the employee behind the counter says flatly. "Keep applying pressure and wait for your name to be called. And please, sit down, sir. You could faint."

"Would fainting get me in faster?" he replies angrily.

"Who was that? Where are you?" my mom asks into the phone, panic rising in her voice.

Wide-eyed, I skitter out through the automatic doors and slump against the front of the brick building. I'm under an awning in the porte cochere with the sounds of rain shielding my voice from any strangers that may pass. Though right now, I'm the only one out here besides a man smoking a cigarette on the other side.

"Did you ever think back in the day that Dad could have, you know—" I swallow, hesitant to say it aloud. "—that Dad could have been the Hiding Man."

There's silence on the other end, and I can picture my mom thinking in puzzlement.

"There's a killer in Portland again and I'm scared it's the same person from when I was a kid," I say, breathing heavily now. I'm on the brink of tears from the stress, but push them back and continue.

"The past few days have been horrible. I think the killer was in my house. He hurt Harvey. And Dad—"

"Honey, slow down," my mom says sternly, interrupting me. "Is Harvey okay? What do you mean there was a killer in your house?"

"Someone came into my house last night and hit Harvey while we were sleeping. I'm at the hospital right now, and he's okay. The police are looking into it, and I think they believe it could be Dad."

I tell her about the murders of Felicity and Mary, regurgitating part of my latest conversation with Jack, ignoring his request to keep it between us.

"I know that they questioned him all those years ago," I add. "And I know about the affair."

I'm met with silence.

"Mom, please answer me," I beg.

"I don't even know what to say," she replies. "Yes, the police thought for a moment he could have been behind it, but I think I remember him just being at home with us those nights. I never questioned his guilt in this because, well, why would he do something like that?" She takes a deep breath. "Until I learned about the cheating, things were good between us. He was there for us as much as he could be while he supported us, so I could raise you. When I found out about Mia, things changed. But he's not a killer."

I lean my head against the brick building and release a rooted huff, relieved she believes in his innocence.

"Except there were the scratches," she adds.

"What scratches?" I ask, relief dissipating.

"The night Mia was killed, the three of us stayed in a hotel—you might remember. I was taking a bath while you watched TV in bed and your dad came in. There were three long, red scratches on his back. I think there were a few on his chest, too, and they looked like fingernail markings. They looked like they were fresh," she said slowly. "And they weren't from me, because we hadn't had sex since—"

"God. Mom, please," I say, cutting her off.

"Oh, relax. Anyhow. They weren't from me. I just remember they looked like they had bled a little, so I asked him about it. All he said was he had scratched himself too hard and it was nothing. And I didn't think anything more of it."

Thinking back to my research yesterday, I had read that there wasn't physical evidence found at any of his crime scenes. Surely if those scratches were made during Mia's murder, I'd imagine they would have found his DNA under her fingernails. Right?

"Do you think anything more of it now?" I ask, skeptical about this confirming anything. If I was thought to be a murderer for every strange scratch on my body, they'd call me the Zodiac Killer.

"This is a big conversation to have over the phone, but now I'm worried about you. I'll get you out of there on the next flight," she adds.

"No, I can't leave. Harvey's in the hospital and I need to find Dad and I start my workweek tomorrow with the Tuesday show and—"

"Don't think about work right now. If Harvey's in the hospital, then I think it's best that everyone takes some time off with what's going on," she says sharply. "I need more details and I won't allow you to be there if there's a killer on the loose. I would have been all over this news if I hadn't been on this damn trip."

I almost regret calling her. Why did I think it would be a good idea to spring a horror story on her about a killer in my house and expect her not to wedge in and try to save me? There's nothing I'd love more than to get as far away from this city as I can, but I need to find the truth.

"I don't know a lot right now, Mom. But everything is being handled. If it makes you feel better, I'll stay with Dad this week, and fly out to you this month like we talked about," I offer. "I'm safe."

My mom moves the phone off her mouth and begins talking to someone else. I suspect Bryan has finished purchasing snacks from the gas station's convenience store and has returned to the car to find a fear-stricken version of his wife.

Most of what she's saying can only be discerned through the phone as mumbles, but certain words stand out. "Nola," "father," and "police" are a few I catch.

Mist caresses my cheeks as the rain splashes against the ground, creating a hazy scene in front of me. I pull my coat tighter around my neck when a breeze comes through, dotting my face with more moisture. My mom chatters away as though I'm not still on the line.

"Mom?" I ask, hoping to pull her back into the conversation.

"Sorry. Bryan agrees that you should get out and come visit us. We don't feel comfortable with you staying there with everything you say is happening."

"Really, I'm okay. Jack is all over it. The entire city's on alert, I'm sure," I say, trying to convince her just as much as myself. "I need to get back to Harvey, but I'll text you later and keep you updated. Please don't worry."

"Do you want us to come to you? Keep you company in the house?" Bryan chimes in.

"I'd love to see you both, but I'll be okay. I'll talk to Mom later this week about coming over there for Thanksgiving." Before either of them have a chance to protest, I say, "Hope you guys had a fun weekend! Love you and I'll call you later so you can tell me all about it."

Without trying to hang up on them, I wait until my mom says

the words "I love you" before pressing the red button on my screen and hoisting myself off the cold cement ground.

As I turn toward the hospital entrance, I notice the man who was previously smoking a cigarette now leaning against the wall with the hood of his black windbreaker up, shielding most of his face. His head is pointed down.

When I stare at him for a few seconds, he turns on his heels and quickly walks into the parking lot with purpose—sending a shock of anxiety through me.

I rush into the hospital and catch the elevator just before the doors close, joining an older woman and a little blond-haired boy who are already inside.

"What floor?" the boy asks me.

"Four, thanks." I rest my hands on the rail behind me and watch the numbers quickly change on the little black screen.

When I spring out of the elevator on the way back to Harvey's room, Officer Nelson stops me again.

"Hey, I thought you left," I say to him.

"I was going to, but I came back looking for you. I meant to ask you about your home cameras. Did you capture anything on them this morning? That will be a huge help."

I still need to call my security company to get my camera fixed after the storm tore them offline permanently. If I don't call, they won't magically go back up.

"No," I say, scrunching my face. "Believe it or not, they're both broken right now from the rain. I need to call the company today, actually."

"Bummer. Let me know if you hear anything or remember anything else." Officer Nelson hands me his business card before walking down the hall.

I open the Northwest Protect app to double-check that what I told the officer is true and see that for both my Front Door camera and Side House camera it says, THIS DEVICE IS OFFLINE.

Curious if anyone else is having the same issue, I click the Neighbors tab on the home screen of the app. It shows me a map of Northwest Portland and a little house emoji where I live. As I scroll down the posts that mostly include titles about missing or found pets and package thieves, I see one that catches my eye. The title reads CAMERA OUTAGES.

The post is from last night at 9:54 p.m. It must have gotten lost in the shuffle, because the post has zero comments.

It reads, "Has anyone else's camera been turning on and off? I'm sure it's weather-related but can't seem to get it to come back on at all. Has this happened to anyone else this weekend? Any help until I can call the company would be appreciated."

As I click to comment, ready to ask if she's been able to get it fixed, I notice the poster's username: maryc7. If Mary Clairemont's name wasn't fresh in my head from the article and my conversation with Jack, I would have looked right over that. I exit the app and reopen the article on Felicity's and Mary's murders, and scroll down until I find photos and information about Mary. The article doesn't list her exact address, but with the general location they provided and the photos of her home, I can surmise the precise location. Returning to the Northwest Protect app, I see a blue bubble over the area in which maryc7 posted. It's the same spot.

Pushing my phone back into my pocket, I head for Harvey's hospital room. I'll just run in, grab my things, and say goodbye to Harvey and his mom; promise to stop back in later.

Right now, my attention is needed elsewhere.

32

JACK

Three minutes after leaving Nola at the hospital, Jack got the call informing him that Chick Strate had been taken down to the station.

Originally imagining they had caught him during a high-speed chase down the I-5 or while performing a welfare check at his home, Jack was somewhat surprised to learn instead that he simply answered the door at the officer's second visit, expressly unaware that anyone had been looking for him.

Chick wasn't pleased with the inconvenience of disrupting his morning but was reportedly receptive to the officer's request to accompany him to the station for formal questioning.

Jack imagines the officer telling his years-long friend that they need to ask him some questions about the Hiding Man murders, and the investigation that took place in his past Goose Hollow home two decades earlier. Chick's undoubted alarm flashes across Jack's mind, either because he's completely unaware of the true reasoning for his questioning, or because he's petrified that he's been caught.

Having worked with zero serial killers face-to-face during his career, Jack has no personal experience here. With murders, he is very familiar. But serial murders are an entirely different ball game.

Jack was first enticed into an investigative career after following the Green River Killings as a teenager back in the 1980s. A case like the Hiding Man's is precisely what he signed up for all those years ago after his high school graduation. In the high-profile case he clung to, a man who would come to be identified as Gary Ridgway committed the murders that went unsolved in the Pacific Northwest for more than fifteen years. As the bodies of innocent women and girls littered forested areas one by one, each killed with the same modus operandi, gripping headlines collected on Jack's childhood desk.

POLICE ADD FOUR WOMEN TO LIST OF GREEN RIVER KILLER'S VICTIMS

GREEN RIVER KILLER BAFFLING THE EXPERTS

His mother almost worried about what she felt was becoming an obsession with her son discovering the identity of the man behind a long string of murders he wasn't connected to. But it was this very case that brought him to the Police Academy and the specific position he has now.

The years of conjuring supposed criminal profiles and dotting the crime scenes on a map tacked to his suburban bedroom wall lacked a crucial piece of the real thing: accountability.

He didn't have to hear from the victims' families, spend day and night sifting through countless tips that led nowhere, or feel the burden from a lack of arrests. That was a load solely handled by police—not teenage armchair sleuth Jack De Lacey. The Green River Killer's victims weren't real to Jack. They were just pawns in a thrilling game he played in between homework assignments and before cruising the streets in the back of his buddy's car, sucking down warm beer and thinking of nothing but his prettiest classmates.

When Jack began investigating the Hiding Man murders just a few years into his career, he realized the full weight of a serial killer investigation, and almost scoffed at his younger self for finding it so amusing. And now, all these years later, the sheer force of it has nearly broken him, leading Jack to the possibility of the killer being someone he has considered dear since before the slayings even occurred.

As he approaches the station to sit across from Chick and ask the questions he has yet to prepare, his hands itch to make a sudden U-turn and drive as far away as he can get. He bets the weather in Southern California is nice in November. A fifteen-hour drive down I-5 or twenty hours down the attractive, coastal 101 would be just the thing.

He pictures his rear end cemented to a chaise lounge under the Santa Monica sun, bottomless margaritas in his grip. He can almost feel the gritty sand in his toes and the glass's condensation in his palms.

It's moments like these that he wishes he considered his other childhood dream of opening a seafood shack on the beach, wearing tank tops and getting tanner than anyone needs to be.

But as he pulls into his reserved parking spot in the lot outside his sunless office, he sees the faces of Felicity, Mary, and all the women who came before them. The women who were plucked from the earth by a madman. He wants to finish this for them and everyone who has ever loved them. He just hopes he's getting it right.

Jack hardly knows how to greet Chick when he walks into the very same room they sat in twenty years earlier to discuss this same topic.

The room has gotten a bit of a facelift since Chick last visited. It used to be cold and drab, possibly designed to make those being questioned less comfortable. It almost looked like a morgue. But now, the previously gray walls are painted beige, the metal table is wooden, the plastic chairs are upholstered, the concrete floors topped with carpet. Considering the number of times in a month Jack is in rooms like this, he appreciates the sunnier tone. The conversations that take place within it are grim enough; the room doesn't need to be, too.

Jack doesn't have to greet Chick upon entry, because as soon as he walks into the room, Chick says, "Man, what the fuck is this?"

Jack immediately raises a brow, taking note that Chick is on the defense, versus calm and trying to help like he supposedly was when he was initially brought in with the officer. Is he upset because they had suspended his morning? Or because he feels a pang of guilt for the bad things he's done?

Knowing he has a chance to fix the mistakes he made in his last questioning with Chick, he decides to take off his friend cap for the time being.

"I've been with people all weekend. I didn't kill anybody!" Chick boasts.

"Friday night?" Jack asks.

"I was with my agent Clarence at the pub on Northwest 23rd

from seven until around ten thirty. Ask him. Or the bartender, John."

"And after that?"

Chick takes a beat. Suddenly remembering, he snaps his fingers. "My old colleague Craig's house for a nightcap until around one in the morning or so. He lives a few streets from me. Call him," he demands.

"I will. But other than Craig's potential word, do you have anything else to prove your whereabouts for later that night?"

Chick looks around the room with his eyes, thinking. "No. But I was there."

"Because your cell phone didn't leave your house all night. I thought it was interesting that you purposely left it behind."

Chick sighs loudly.

Jack tosses Chick's wallet on the table, and it lands perfectly in front of him. They had already collected evidence from it to see if they could lift a foreign print, or if Chick's DNA was the sole finding, but the results have yet to come back.

"We found your wallet at the scene of a murder this morning. Care to explain how it got there?"

He chooses not to tell Chick that the wallet was found in the alley behind the house. But it was technically still on Mary Clairemont's property, so it counts as being a part of the crime scene.

Part of this discovery is suspicious to Jack, knowing that, in the original Hiding Man murders, there wasn't a single piece of evidence pointing to any one person. In a way, it feels convenient that Chick's wallet was left behind. Though he can't see why someone would try to plant it there and frame him.

If Chick really is behind it all, Jack considers the idea that he's gotten sloppy.

"I haven't had my wallet since Friday. Things have been going missing in my house for days. And it's not just my wallet," Chick replies firmly.

"What else has gone missing?" Jack asks, finally taking a seat across from him.

Chick hesitates for a moment, as if trying to make sure the wrong thing doesn't spill out. "You know. Um, my reading glasses, my keys were displaced. Stuff like that."

"What else?" Jack asks, knowing there's more. He's waiting for the words "evidence" and "boxes" to come out of Chick's mouth.

"I don't think you want me to say it here."

"What else?" Jack asks, trying to keep a professional composure.

Chick tuts. "Two of the Hiding Man evidence boxes."

"The ones you stole?" Jack asks, heart thumping at the thought of them being gone.

"The ones you let me look at!" Chick hisses.

Jack's upper lip begins to sweat, knowing the surveillance camera in the corner of the room is rolling and picking up their conversation. He thinks about what could happen to his job if anyone found out that he let two of the evidence boxes in the biggest serial killer case in their city's history go missing.

"Why did you take those boxes out of this building? Was there evidence in them that you were trying to get rid of?"

"I came to you years ago wanting to write a book on the Hiding Man. You didn't have a problem with it. I wanted to look through the evidence to get some insider information. Something that could hook the readers," Chick explains. "You said yourself the case was dead."

"Speaking of your book. It's quite fitting timing to announce the release of the book just as other murders are occurring in town," Jack says, trying to steer this in a particular direction.

"You're saying they're connected?" Chick asks.

"Didn't say that. I'm more interested in knowing what you know about them."

"All I know about the murders is what my daughter told me, based on the call that came into the show. And what I read in the news this morning about the second one."

"For the record, please state what you mean by 'the show.'"

Chick sighs and shifts to a mocking tone. "My daughter, Nola Strate, hosts the radio show *Night Watch*. She received a phone call into *Night Watch* last week that included audio from one of your murder victims." He shifts back to his normal voice. "I-I don't know the woman's name."

"And how did you learn about this?"

"She came to my house hysterical about it on Friday night. She believed something had happened to the woman, and she was right."

"Her name was Felicity Morton," Jack says, leaning over the table now. "Did you kill her?"

"No, I did not."

"Did you have anything to do with the Hiding Man murders of Jamie York, Jasey Levy, Kendra Lloyd, Carrie Fenton, Mia Parsons, Jasmine Petri, or Doniesha Wilks?"

"No, I did not," Chick repeats.

"Did you have anything to do with the murder of Mary Claire-mont? The woman whose house *your* wallet was discovered at?"

"No. I did not. I don't know how my wallet got there. I'm just as concerned as you are about that," Chick says, the tension rising in his voice. He pockets his wallet.

"Where were you last night?" Jack presses.

"I was extremely hungover from my book release party the night before. I just laid in bed all day and watched movies and slept."

"Do you have anyone who can corroborate this story?"

"Nola. She stopped by the house yesterday to talk. That's also when I noticed the evidence boxes were gone. She'll tell you."

Chick gives every answer without hesitation. But this is one of the hardest parts of Jack's job: deciphering if something that's said during an interview is a rehearsed lie or the truth.

Without any other evidence tying Chick to the scene, all Jack can do is hope that, if Chick is the killer, he will confess. But that's not happening here. And the Oregon State Crime Lab won't have the evidence that was lifted from Mary's crime scene for at least a couple weeks—despite the rush he pressed for. Same goes for Felicity's. Meaning unless Chick says something self-incriminating or a big tip comes in that could put him at the scene, there's not much Jack can do here. A wallet being found behind the building is quite incriminating on its own, but it's not enough. Maybe enough to hold him and buy them some time to gather more evidence against him. But to ruin a man's reputation and lose the city's trust, it's inadequate.

"Why did you decide to write a book on the Hiding Man?" Jack attempts.

"He terrorized my daughter. Killed a woman I cared about. He scared the whole city, and beyond. Then, people just seemed to forget. I wanted to write the official account on what happened. Because, though not directly, I was a part of the story."

"What about Harvey Stephens? Did you have something to do with what happened to him this morning?"

Chick appears shocked. "What happened to Harvey?"

Jack watches Chick's face carefully here to attempt at determining if he knows his daughter was in danger this morning.

"He was attacked in Nola's house before sunrise. He's recovering at the hospital now. And he's talking."

Chick sits up from his chair suddenly. "Is my daughter all right? What happened?"

"A neighbor witnessed someone running out of her house after nearly bludgeoning Harvey to death. He's starting to remember things," Jack says, knowing that last detail was a partial lie.

"Look. I was sleeping since that officer came and knocked on my door this morning. I did not do this. Where's Nola right now?"

"Nola wasn't hurt," Jack begins, right as Officer Boris Keller knocks on the door and enters. He requests Jack follow him outside for a moment. Jack excuses himself, then steps out and into a private room with Officer Keller.

"Are you getting anything out of him?" he asks.

"He's not budging. He keeps saying he didn't commit any of the murders," Jack says flatly.

"What was his excuse for the wallet?" Officer Keller asks.

"He said he lost it."

"Well, we just got an anonymous phone tip from a guy that claims he saw Chick in Mary's neighborhood last night. Said he recognized him immediately because he's a fan."

"What did he say Chick was doing? And did he give a time?" Jack asks, agitation filling him.

"All he said was it was late at night before he went to bed, and that he was closing his blinds when Chick walked by. Said they made eye contact."

"We can't arrest him on an anonymous tip," Jack says.

"I'm just relaying the message," Officer Keller gently protests. "But if this guy's telling the truth *and* you found Chick's wallet at the scene, *and* he was dating one of the previous victims. I mean, what do *you* think?"

33

NOLA

Seafoam green is an interesting color for a house, I think as I step out of my Jeep and approach Felicity's home on Dover Street.

Caution tape pastes stripes of highlighter yellow against it, making the seafoam green color look even worse. The police cordoned off her country-style porch, probably to avoid peepers and break-ins, and to keep the crime scene secured. Lucky for them, I have no intention of crossing that barrier. Even if I'm morbidly curious as to what's inside, or what the killer's view was from the window, reliving the hellacious minutes of that phone call is not something that would benefit me. I can tell even from down here on the sidewalk that the house's curtains are closed, which gives me a sliver of relief. If they were open, my mind would be running rampant, wondering if her killer were inside, looking out at me.

Large trees cover Felicity's section of the street, but from where I'm standing, her porch is mostly visible. Much of her house is covered by an in-bloom cherry blossom tree, giving its encore for the autumn season before scrapping its flowers until spring. Staring at the house sends chills up my spine, knowing that someone very bad shared this exact view of Felicity's perfect little home, disguised by the black of night.

I wearily ascend the steps leading up to her property to get a better look. As I make my way up, I get the nauseating realization that the crime scene likely hasn't been cleaned up quite yet. Knowing her cause of death now, I hesitantly picture her lying in that same position in her closet until police arrived the next morning to haul her body down to the coroner's office.

Besides the caution tape surrounding her house, Felicity's home really does look normal—even cheery. The paint looks fresh, and the combination of the colors and the building style look like something on the sand of an East Coast hamlet. Certainly not what you'd imagine when you think of a grisly murder scene. Felicity kept her yard fresh, the grass trimmed, and the leaves from October's shedding have been swept and collected. Felicity's attentiveness to her home is obvious, even from the outside.

The weather has taken yet another turn for the worse, forcing residents inside and creating an eerier tone to the street. Clutching my coat to my chest, I study the windows of Felicity's house, then her view down onto the street. I can almost hear her screams in the wind.

I found my way here the exact same way I secured the address of Mary Clairemont's house: by being an expert of the Northwest section of the city. Well, that and my internet skills. One of the article's photos included a snapshot of Felicity's street, and in it, I noted the name of a coffee shop a few houses down from hers. With a quick search for Elders Coffee, the location was secured. It almost scared me how easily I found it, wondering if He discovered my address in a similar fashion.

Having seen enough of her house, I jog down the staircase back to the sidewalk, where I spot the hanging sign for the coffee shop, violently swinging in the wind. Hair whips past my face as I stroll over to it, hoping to get a better cup than the one from the hospital—and maybe even some inside information from a local.

As I make my way to the shop, a familiar, jarring ringing sound comes from my phone, despite being switched to vibrate. Thinking it's an Amber Alert that could possibly be related to the case, I yank my phone out of my coat pocket to find a different type of emergency alert instead. It reads:

National Weather Service: SEVERE RAINSTORM WARNING in effect for your area from 3:00 PM PST to 10:00 PM PST. FLOOD WATCH.

I shove my phone back into my pocket, already anticipating the jitters that an upcoming torrential downpour can bring.

Small teardrops escape from my eyes as the icy gust makes each passing step more challenging than the last. As I push into the wooden, sage-colored door of the shop, I nearly stumble inside at the change in air pressure.

Low-volume indie music plays to an empty shop, and whiffs of pastry and freshly roasted beans are evident in the air.

It seems slow, even for an early Monday afternoon, with the glass pastry case full of croissants and scones aplenty. The wind blowing the rustling hanging sign outside is equally audible from inside, reminding me that the upcoming storm is keeping as many people inside their homes today as possible. In a city that's used to forty or so inches of rain a year, you'd think it would be just another day. But the murders have altered the atmosphere, raising the question: Are the residents staying indoors for fear of the storm, or fear of the reaper?

A curly-haired brunette rounds the corner with a small smile, asking me what she can get for me. Peeking at the mirror over her head that lists the handwritten menu, I peruse the festive beverages. "How's the spiced butterscotch latte?" I ask.

"It's my favorite," she gleams. "We make the syrup in-house."

"Sounds good. I'll take one, please. Small, hot."

After the barista rings me up, she turns to make a shot of espresso.

"I've been wanting to come in here for a while," I say, coming up with the segue as I go. "My friend always talked about this place. Or she used to," I lie, referring to Felicity.

I'm not sure if she ever came in here. But if she did, I'm betting this barista would know.

Tamping the espresso, she says, "Well I'm glad you could finally make it in. You came at the right time, too. We're closing early today because of that storm."

She didn't take the bait. I hide a disappointed look.

"What a weird week it's been over here, huh?" I inquire. "The storm, that murder. I don't know how you're working here alone today."

The barista looks up at me and sighs. "It's so scary. Another girl was supposed to work with me today, but she called out. Ever since they found the body on Saturday, it's like everyone's avoiding this street."

"Did you ever see her come in here? She seemed like a nice person." I make a pout, attempting to come off as genuinely as I can.

The barista squirts golden syrup into a cup and tops it with fresh espresso. "She came in here a lot, actually. Well, everyone on the block does—which is how I started working here. I live a few houses down on the other side of Felicity's, in one of the apartments. She was sweet."

"I wonder if she knew the guy. God, I hope they catch him soon," I add.

Passing me the latte after topping it with steaming froth, I take a sip. Its hot liquid sends goosebumps up my back.

"I kind of have this idea that she did know them. The day before it happened, she was in here. She looked really tired. Barely said a word to me, which wasn't like her usual, friendly self." She shrugs. "Maybe she was just having a bad day, but I can't get it out of my head."

Knowing Felicity first called us that night, Thursday, I can guess why she was acting strange when she visited here. She'd been losing sleep and feeling unsettled at the idea that a spirit was in her house. Her final days were filled with disarray and terror.

"This just doesn't seem like the area where someone would lurk around or kill someone," I say, looking out the window over my shoulder. "Such a pretty street."

"I don't know. Now that I think about it, I have noticed some weird things lately."

I give her a concerned look, seeing if she'll offer more details on her own.

"It's a tale as old as time. The white creeper van," she says, scoffing a laugh. "We had an employee Halloween party the week before last, so I was here much later than usual. I walked home by myself like I always do, and I passed this white utility van with lights on inside. A few houses down from Felicity's." She leans over the counter. "But they weren't, like, the usual car overhead lights. It was a blue light, like from a screen." She glances out the window behind me. "It was too late for a work van to be out on a job, so it kind of freaked me out."

I see how a white van parked out on the street by your home could be seen as ominous, especially with vague signs of life inside, when you're walking home alone in the dark. But I was hoping she would have better insider information as someone who was on the block when it happened.

"Creepy. Did you ever see it again?" I take a sip of my coffee. Its sweet notes of buttery sugar bring me some small comfort.

"Yeah, actually. Because now that I think about it, I saw it again last week." She grabs a rag and starts wiping miscellaneous droplets of espresso off the white countertop. "It's probably nothing, though. I mean, I didn't see anyone inside it and, whoever it was, they didn't do anything sketchy that I saw, so..." She shrugs.

"Did you tell the police just in case?"

"No, I'm only just remembering. But I'm probably overstressing. Nothing has felt the same the past couple days. I think we're all a bit hysterical."

The door opens behind me as a woman stumbles in.

"Well. Thanks for the latte. Stay safe from the storm," I say, then walk out the door, back into the blustering wind.

With a final gaze to Felicity's house, I blow a sympathetic kiss and climb into my Jeep. Taking a big swig of coffee, I turn on the ignition and drive away.

Next stop: Mary's house.

34

JACK

Jack stares at Chick through the one-way mirror as he plays with his fingers, having nothing else to do while he sits alone.

Chick hasn't been arrested, so he is free to go if he pleases, and he knows it. Meaning Jack's time to ask him the right questions and squeeze out potentially critical information is running out. If such potentially critical information even exists within Chick's brain.

"What else do you need to nail him today?" Officer Keller asks him.

"Actual fucking evidence," Jack replies, leaning back in his chair.

Officer Keller sighs. "An anonymous tip put him at the scene before Mary's murder, he has a connection to and motive for one of the victims, and he has no solid alibis. You know he's the best we've got."

"He doesn't need to be the best we've got. He has to be the only person who could have committed all these murders. Or at least some of them. We have the weight of nine families and an entire city riding on this. We cannot get this wrong," Jack explains.

"What happens if he walks out of here today and somebody else dies? Are you willing to risk adding another family to the list?"

Jack tuts, rubbing his eyes. "We just need more."

"Then get him on possession of stolen property so we can hold him until we get some more evidence against him."

"It was my fault those evidence boxes left the room that day. I wasn't paying attention," Jack admits. "And unless we find them in his house, we can't prove he stole them."

They sit in silence for a minute, mulling over the options in their heads. Ruining Chick's reputation would somehow be the least worrisome aspect of the entire situation if Jack makes a mistake. The victims' surviving family members would be some of the first people to hear the news of an arrest. They would come down to the station themselves and gang up in Jack's office, demanding the evidence that put the bad man behind bars, twenty years too late for some. They would challenge Jack for answers to questions he can't yet comprehend himself. To make a life-altering decision on behalf of innumerable civilians without assurance is just irresponsible. With Jack's stack of detective-related mistakes in the past, there is no room for new error.

Another officer comes into the room and closes the door behind him. "Hey, Jack? We just received another anonymous phone tip about Chick."

Jack buries his face in his hands. This is not how he wanted any of this to go. Pressuring Chick in the interrogation room was his way of pushing to prove Chick's innocence. If he utilized this time with him now to ask the right questions and get the right answers, everyone would agree on his lack of guilt and Jack could let his friend go. He could get back to the investigation waiting at his desk, get to questioning Felicity's patients' parents, and find someone else to focus on: the real killer.

But as the minutes progress, things are looking worse and worse for the last person he wanted to be responsible for this madness. The puzzle pieces are slowly magnetizing into place, creating an image far too horrific to bear.

"What is it?" Jack asks, not truly wanting to be given an answer.

"The caller said to ask Chick Strate about his relationship with Jasmine Petri."

Jasmine Petri was the Hiding Man's sixth victim, murdered more than a month after Mia Parsons. Jack had interviewed Chick on the night of Mia's murder and the day after, but not again following that. Although he didn't have a strong alibi for the dates of the previous slayings, his wife, Donna, vouched for him, stating that he didn't go out much on his nights off work anymore, and was typically home with her and their daughter. She was confident that was the case for the nights in question. Despite the fact that he was absent from the holiday party during the time Mia was killed, and technically had a motive to want her dead, there wasn't physical evidence or witness accounts to place him at any of the crime scenes. That, and Jack being able to substantiate his character, was enough for him to be ruled out.

During the investigation into Jasmine Petri's murder, Jack did extensive research into her life. Knowing she had worked as a barista in Southeast Portland, Jack became a frequent visitor of the coffee shop himself, questioning her coworkers repeatedly. The only thing they had revealed that seemed to be any help was that Jasmine had mentioned an attractive man coming in during her shifts, sparking conversation that was more personal than the typical barista-customer dialogue. But the store didn't have cameras at the time, and none of her coworkers had seen this man or witnessed their encounters.

While reviewing her cell phone records, Jack uncovered sporadic phone calls from a number that he couldn't place. It wasn't registered to a person or an address, and it was associated with a prepaid phone plan. This led Jack to believe that the phone had likely been a burner, which are often used for illicit or even illegal activities. Jack worked hour after hour to determine the person's identity, but he fell flat every time. The phone number didn't show up in any of the other victims' call logs, so he eventually surmised that it might not be connected.

Jack now wonders if the technological advancements of the last twenty years since her murder would help reveal who that number belonged to. But he then remembers that Jasmine's evidence box is presently missing from the property room. And Chick was the last person to possess it.

"That's it? Did the caller mention why, or what they know about their supposed connection?" Jack asks.

"Nope. That's pretty much all they said," the officer says.

Jack is usually grateful for any tip that comes in, even when he's flooded with clues that mostly lead him right back to where he already was. But anonymous tips can be troublesome. Often times, the tipster doesn't give enough information, or says something baseless and unreliable that can't be followed up on because, well, it's anonymous. Sometimes tipsters mask their numbers on caller ID and they can't be traced. Jack wonders which is the case for this tip.

"Got a phone number?" Jack asks.

"Yeah. They called from a local pay phone."

In the adjacent room, Chick stands up and looks directly through the one-way mirror. "Come on, guys. I'm here as a courtesy. Send Jack back in here so we can wrap this up. I've told him everything there is to tell, and I'd love to go check in with my daughter now."

Not everything, it seems, Jack thinks.

Jack goes back into the interrogation room. He says, "Sorry about that," and takes a seat across from Chick.

Chick looks Jack in the eye. "This is a waste of both our time. I'm gonna go, all right?"

"First," Jack tries. "Tell me, is there a reason you stole Jasmine Petri's evidence box in particular?"

"Borrowed, not stole," Chick corrects. "It was one of the two boxes you showed me in your office. I figured whatever I could get would help my research for the book."

"No other reason?"

"Nope."

"That's interesting. Because I know that you and Jasmine had a connection. A relationship." A pit forms in Jack's stomach, like it always does when he lies to a suspect. Not that Chick is a suspect just yet, but the pit grows.

A few beats pass with nothing but a confused look coming from Chick. "What are you talking about?"

"You tell me. How is it that you had a relationship with two of the victims in a serial murder case that you claim you had nothing to do with?"

"I didn't. It was only Mia. We talked about this the night she died."

"We both know that's not true, Chick. She wasn't the only one. It's time to fess up."

The tension in the room is soaring. Jack almost wants to remove his jacket to vent the steam rising off his collar. He just hopes he isn't getting this all wrong.

He continues pressing. "Admit it. You bought a burner phone so you could discreetly communicate with Jasmine Petri, a twenty-five-year-old woman you were in yet another secret relationship with. When she threatened to expose you to your family, you killed her just like you killed Mia Parsons. Because you thought you could get away with it like you'd gotten away with Mia's murder." Jack is standing over the table now, piercing Chick's eyes with his. Chick's jaw is visibly clenched. "You preyed on all those young women until things got a little too sticky for you and it threatened life as you knew it. So you killed all seven of them before they could ruin you. And you realized you kind of liked the power you had over them. The act of killing. And after sliding under our noses, you stopped before we caught on. But now, with the hopes of pushing book sales and regaining that old feeling, you're at it again. And you're not getting away with it this time."

35

NOLA

Dark clouds rumble across the sky as I pull up to Mary's house, strikes of lightning and whipping thunder following me. Now *this* is weather that even Oregonians don't like being out in. After finishing up my sleuthing here, I'll be on my way to an indoor location—whether that's back to the hospital or to my dad's house. It certainly won't be my own.

Two vans are posted outside Mary's home, meaning there are still either law enforcement officers or forensics teams on the premises. Her front door is open, revealing numerous people in white coveralls crouched on the floor inspecting something inches inside her home.

The fact that I thought I could break into a woman's house who died hours ago inside said house is ridiculous. But I have no idea how long a crime scene is initially investigated. Hours? Days? Weeks? I can imagine it varies on a per-case basis. Either way, they're still here. With not much else to do, I park across the street and back three houses, facing toward her place, to keep watch until they finish up—or until I get restless enough to leave, whichever comes first. Cranking my seat back to lounge chair status, I close my eyes and wait.

The harsh splatter of raindrops against my windshield startles me awake to see a quiet street view ahead. The vans that were parked outside of Mary's house are gone now, with the front door closed and strung with caution tape.

I grab my phone off the passenger seat and check the time—3:45 p.m. I've been asleep for more than three hours.

With the short handful of time that I slept last night, I must have been more tired than I realized—the latte failing to do its job on me. With the sun just an hour and a half from setting, I still have time to sneak into Mary's house and gather whatever I can about her and what happened. At this point, it feels like it's the only way I can save myself. Because it doesn't seem like Jack is going to do that for me.

Suddenly the same level of fear I had while approaching Felicity's house vibrates inside of me. Surely her body is gone, but does the rest of the scene remain?

I flip the hood of my duster up over my head, jump out of my car, and sprint across the street. When I reach the front door, I pause, grazing my hand over the caution tape in acknowledgment. Having spotted the forensics team just past this door, I decide that there's something in that region I don't want to see or stumble into. Looking around the doorframe, I take note that there is no front camera—and I think back to Mary's post on the Northwest Protect app.

Must be in the back.

As the rain pounds the ground, I run around to the back of her duplex looking for another door until I see one. There's a covered porch area in the rear of her home, where I find a small bistro table. It's probably a spot where Mary enjoyed cups of tea or wine with a friend. Now, it's empty and covered in water. I look around the back door frame and the surrounding wall but still don't spot a security camera.

I know I'm at the right house. So could maryc7 be a different person?

Surprisingly, the blinds back here are open, revealing the inside of Mary's kitchen. Her outdated, white tile backsplash, creaky-looking cupboards, and vintage appliances are things that might have appeared charming even yesterday. But now, the life has been sucked out of it all.

I look down to find cardboard boxes of disposable shoe covers, blue latex gloves, and disposable face masks stacked against the brick building. Snapping gloves on my hands, I bypass the caution tape and try the doorknob. It pops right open. Before entering the threshold, I slip shoe covers on my wet boots and slowly walk inside.

The vans are gone out front, but the unlocked door makes me concerned that someone may still be working inside. To ensure I'm alone, I shout, "Hello? Anybody in here?"

Silence.

I tiptoe through the kitchen and into the dining room. The only light is coming from the windows around the small home. The storm outside is painting the entire place with an unsettling blue hue.

The style throughout is clean with a Parisian flair that would give off good vibrations on any other day. The living room is visible through the arched opening, so, in search of Mary's bedroom, I walk ahead until I'm suddenly in the middle of a crime scene. By the looks of it, one that is still in the process of being inspected.

On the pastel rug under the velvet, rust-colored sofa is a gigantic pool of blood, sunken into the fibers and probably the glossy hardwood beneath it.

My eyes brim with tears as my hand claps over my mouth, an unfamiliar feeling washing over me. I've never seen this much blood since Mia was killed. And it came from an innocent woman I sat with at a diner over French fries less than twenty-four hours ago.

The banging thunder makes this discovery more haunting than it already is—if that's even possible. My hands are trembling now, so I move my eyes off the puddle of literal death and jog up the staircase. Now that I know where she was killed, I feel confident that the upstairs is a safe zone. Or at least I hope it is.

To my left is a bedroom, the door wide open and exposing a tidy space. Unsure whether or not it's Mary's, I gently inch my way inside.

A gold, ornate mirror hanging on one wall hosts multiple photo strips and prints. I look closer and see countless images of Mary's smile, her beautiful red hair down along her face in each one—posing with friends, a dog, or outside of foreign monuments.

Moving over to her desk, I use my latex-gloved fingertips to wake her iMac.

Knowing I need a password to log in, I start sifting through her desk—flipping her keyboard, checking drawers, the whole lot. After opening a planner from the top drawer, I gently unfold a pink Post-it note on the first page to find a list of passwords for multiple websites. They mostly include the same one: FranklinBoy2018. I type it into her keyboard, and it unlocks on the first try.

Leaning over her desk, I stare at the open log of texts in the

Messages tab that was already fastened on her screen. Most of the texts are people desperately trying to reach her, others are postmortem messages as a sort of farewell to her after they heard the news of her death. The most recent is a long paragraph from someone named Mabel, telling Mary how great of a roommate and friend she was. A wave of guilt washes over me, like I shouldn't be in a deceased woman's room, reading her private exchanges. As I prepare to close the window, I notice the last sentence Mabel wrote:

We will find him.

The text above the paragraph was also from Mabel, coming in at 5:53 a.m. It reads,

Hey Mar you ok?? What ended up
happening last night? Text me so I know
you're alive or call when you wake up.

Before that, I see multiple texts from Mary to Mabel. They started at 9:08 p.m. last night and ended at 11:34 p.m.

Hey, you awake? I know it's late over there
but I'm really scared.

I wish you were home right now!!

Remember the other day when I heard that
tapping on the kitchen window? I keep
hearing it again around the house. But I also
just heard like a bang out back.

I wish you could come look outside with me.

Call me when you wake up. I'm still kinda
scared but going to sleep soon. Lol hoping
Franklin keeps me safe. Talk tomorrow.

These texts line up with everything I know about Him. This proves that what I've been positing is correct. It wasn't just Felicity who was afraid of something she couldn't see. It was Mary too. She didn't mention being afraid to me or hearing anything. She even admitted hardly knowing about Felicity's death. But maybe she was in denial or didn't make the correlation until it was too late.

I find the Northwest Protect app on the desktop's dock and open it up. She's already logged in. On the homepage is a single camera screen that is blocked out with the exact message as the one on mine: THIS DEVICE IS OFFLINE. The name of the camera is Franklin Cam, but it doesn't indicate where the camera is located. Opening the notifications tab, I see alert after alert about her camera outages. The last one was the night before last at 2:44 a.m., and after that, it didn't come back on. The final notification was the one indicating the outage.

I scroll through her camera history to find the last recording. It was at 12:09 a.m., a couple hours before the storm took it offline for good. The room is in black-and-white night vision, so it's hard to see where in the house it is. As I look across the video, I see Mary patting her dog on his head before crossing the room and getting into her bed. Looking around the room, I see the dog bed right behind me on the floor. Slowly turning my head to the right, I look for a visible camera.

On a shelf above her distressed, cream dresser, I see a vintage trinket box with something behind it. Getting closer, I notice a doorbell camera hidden behind the box, with just the top, black lens portion exposed.

With the camera being called Franklin Cam, I imagine its purpose was to check in on her dog when she was out of the house, and possibly for general bedroom security.

I click out of the video just as the sound of a door closing outside draws my attention to the window.

It's another forensics van. Panicked, I quit out of the app and put her computer to sleep before dashing down the staircase and out the back door faster than if I were being chased.

36

HIM

One Night Earlier

Mary is his first redhead. Lucious and banged, like Ginger from *Gilligan's Island*. A childhood fantasy come to life. Only Mary isn't egomaniacal with Hollywood sex appeal. She's seductive in her own bookish, sensible way. And tonight, she's all his.

Mary lies on her bed, dressed in a peach-colored silk robe and white sweatpants. A soft-toned outfit to match her natural copper locks and milky skin. The ideal shades to highlight and sop up the blood that will soon be spilling out above her décolletage.

Her persistent visits to her bedroom and living room windows, face full of fear, are a mating call to the man. Each rustle in the roses by her front door, each light tap on her dining room window, slowly suck the air out of her lungs, readying her for him. Not nearly enough to call the authorities, but more than enough to frighten her. It's only a matter of time until she comes outside to check on all the noise, puffing out her chest in an attempt at cosplaying bravery.

Months after he started to stealthily observe her, and years after she saw him for the first time through her neighbor's window, they'll finally meet face-to-face. Tonight. He hadn't known at the time that she was watching him from her bedroom window. But when he read about it in the paper when Carrie's murder broke, he yearned to give her a taste of her own medicine by watching her in return. Lucky for him, she's sprouted into an attractive, appealing examinee.

For days now, the man has been waiting to get Mary alone. He wasn't aware that her roommate left town until hearing Mary talk about it last night on the phone with her mother. She paced around the kitchen as he observed from the other side of the window, hidden in the darkness behind the glass. If she looked hard out of the pane above the sink, their eyes would have met. But her focus remained on making her usual nighttime snack and telling her mom that she would be all right by herself.

How wrong Mary was.

She hasn't approached her bedroom window in a spell of time that the man would consider satisfactory. His only option is to speed the situation up a notch. Covertly making his way back to the front door—camouflaged by the black clouds above and lack of nearby streetlamps—he does something he didn't for the other eight. Nor the girls in Washington. The man knocks on the door.

It's nearly midnight now, so it's unlikely she'll be expecting a guest. But she'll come down and check who it is anyway.

The man's heart beats in his throat, aroused at what's to come.

For too long, he's sustained himself on the memories of all the other kills. It's as though he's been locked in a basement during the longest imaginable nuclear war, eating years-old soggy peas straight from the can or stale crackers from an emergency stockpile. Surviving, not prospering. But now, there's no one standing in his way. He can run back up the dingy basement stairs and feast on real, fresh food from the kitchen, no longer dining on echoes of the past.

The man looks up at Mary's bedroom to see her shadowed movements shrinking, affirming her descent down the stairs. Her final act is about to commence.

He conceals himself at the building's side. Roughly thirty seconds pass before the lock clicks and the door sweeps off its resting spot.

"Hello?" Mary utters, assumedly looking around for the knocker. Her feet shuffle against the Welcome mat as she exits her home. *Good girl*, the man thinks.

"What the hell," she whispers under her shuddered breath. And then, another shuffle against the mat and the thump of her foot back on the hardwood inside her home.

Before Mary can shut the door, the man quietly leaps from his hiding place and grabs her from behind, slamming the door closed with his foot. Holding her mouth shut in one hand, he drags a knife against her throat with the other.

As she's laid down, Mary gasps for air that will never come, staring into the eyes behind his mask. Blood rushes out beneath her neck, soaking into the floor and narrowly missing him.

For these moments, the man feels inexplicably normal. The mask he's wearing feels more like his real face than the one beneath it. The skin that makes up his own is simply part of a disguise he must preserve, hiding his authentic self from society.

Under the mask, he smiles.

37

JACK

Jack conjured this theory of Chick's guilt only as the words came out of his mouth like scorching lava, unable to reverse the damage he'd done. The confidence in his voice as he stated Chick's motive for killing all nine women, and why he started it up again, sounded rehearsed, as though he'd found every last piece of evidence to support his claims just before walking back into the room. He's even surprised at himself for spewing it so seamlessly.

It was nothing but a big, fat guess, meant to stir Chick up so Jack could gauge his reaction and response. So far, he's just sitting in his chair, blinking at Jack, unmoving. It's not the broiled, explosive riposte that Jack was anticipating. But he can tell Chick is having an internal battle, unsure if he should leak his thoughts into the room or keep them locked inside his head.

They're no longer two friends across a table from each other. They are person of interest and investigator. Stranger and stranger, not buddy and buddy. And they may never be again. If he's guilty of anything Jack just said he was, the years of dive bars and joint family holidays are a thing of the cloudy past. And even if he's not, Chick will never forgive him for implicating that he was capable of such violent, unthinkable acts.

Chick sighs across the table. Which, unofficially, feels like a sign of defeat.

"I'm not going to get out of this, am I?" he asks.

Jack is speechless but trying not to show it. He must proceed with caution. If he remains too aggressive, Chick might leave. If Jack appears meek, or insecure, Chick might think they have nothing on him, and then again, leave. The words are so close from exiting his mouth that Jack can almost taste it.

"Tell me what you did, Chick," Jack says in a soft yet firm tone.

"You seem like you have it all figured out, Jack. Except you don't."

Jack feels close, like every word he chooses to use will make or break this entire conversation. And right now, he hasn't a single guess as to where it's headed.

"I do have it all figured out. You, Chick Strate, are the Hiding Man. You've been caught. It's done."

"So why aren't I in cuffs?" Chick asks calmly. "It's because you're lying. You have nothing. We both know I can walk out of here right now. Yet here I sit."

"And why's that?" Jack asks, genuinely curious.

"Because I'm going to tell you something I should have told you in 2004."

He stops at that with a dramatic pause. Nothing else follows it but a slight hand movement to suggest Jack sit down, as he's been standing over the table since he walked in the room just a minute ago. Not wanting to lose the possibility of a confession, he obliges, swiftly sitting in his chair and crossing one leg over the other. With clasped hands on his knee, Jack awaits what's to follow.

"The night of Mia's murder—" Chick swallows. "—I told my wife and you that I went to the studio and stayed there, even after Thomas left and went back to the party. And that was true. But I didn't tell you the whole truth."

Jack remembers Chick telling him that he stayed at the studio to check some emails. The time slipped away from him, and he didn't see Donna calling him about what was happening at the house and *that* was why he was late, arriving over half an hour after Donna and the police did.

Chick takes his time, biting his thumbnail and staring at the table before continuing. It's like he knows whatever is coming next will shoot him in the foot.

"I met Jasmine Petri at the coffee shop she worked at. I thought she was cute. I was a married asshole. I went after her. It wasn't just Mia I was seeing behind my wife's back. It was Jasmine, too. And she was who I was with on the night of Mia's murder."

If he's telling the truth, then *Chick* was the man Jasmine's coworkers told him about—the customer she met at work, who she was smitten with. That would mean...

"She called me while I was at the party. Told me she needed to see me, that she missed me. I thought showing Thomas the studio would be a good opportunity for me to get out of there to see her before she left to be with family for the holiday," Chick continues. "Donna knew some wives at the party, so I figured she wouldn't miss me if I was gone for just a little while. When Thomas left the studio, Jasmine was already waiting outside. That's why I wasn't on my phone to see the incoming calls. I was with someone else."

In his imagination, Jack is throwing the table across the room, asking Chick why he didn't tell him this before. And when he's finished getting mad, Jack pictures sitting down and laughing hysterically—so hard that he falls out of his chair.

I'm just supposed to believe that out of the three hundred thousand females who live in this city, you "happened" to be having an affair with two of the women who were murdered in the same serial killing case? That's what Jack wants to ask him, but he doesn't.

Keeping his cards close to his chest, he says, "You're the guy with the untraceable phone that started showing up on Jasmine's call log months before she went missing."

"Probably. I had a prepaid phone."

"Why didn't you talk to Mia on it?" Jack inquires.

"Because she was my kid's babysitter. Talking to her wouldn't have looked too weird to my wife if she happened to see a call coming in, or a text."

"So, you just got a burner phone for Jasmine Petri and Jasmine Petri only? Did you have a burner for each of the other five victims? What about for Felicity? Mary?"

"I didn't kill anybody," Chick insists.

"You had affairs with two of the seven past victims, Chick. That isn't just a coincidence. You killed Mia and then you killed Jasmine because they were going to ruin your perfect, happy outward image of being a successful, married father. You wanted to have it all."

"I was devastated when they died," Chick says through his teeth. "They were wonderful, innocent women."

"So why didn't you talk to me? If you were really innocent, I could have helped you. But now I don't believe a word you say."

"I was worried about my family's safety," Chick shouts. "Because I felt like I knew who did it. Or at least I thought I did back then."

Jack can't believe what he's hearing. All of a sudden, Chick is claiming he has known who the killer is? For the first time, Jack is convinced of Chick's responsibility.

"Right. And who would that be?" Jack asks, dumbfounded, almost ready to arrest him.

"I don't know his name," Chick replies.

Jack throws his arms into the air with a laugh.

Chick raises his voice. "This fan came into a bar one night and I fucked him off and he got pissed. He had this look on his face. It made me instantly regret giving him a hard time. Like there was a darkness in him." He softens his tone. "He said I'd be sorry. For treating him badly. There was something about him, something in his eyes. I couldn't get it out of my mind after that." Chick shakes his head. "When Mia died weeks later, and then Jasmine, his words repeated in my head. 'You'll be sorry.' I didn't want him to hurt my family. So, I didn't say anything just in case."

"You're telling me that you believe a total stranger somehow found out you were having two affairs and then killed both women? What about the others, then? And why not just come after someone closer to you, like your family? It feels a bit odd that he wouldn't kill your own daughter when he had the chance."

"Maybe it gave him a reason to pin this all on me. Killing only the mistresses. Like a warning message. I don't know."

Jack considers what he's saying for a moment. But this is all coming out so suddenly and randomly that it's impossible to believe. Chick knows Jack is getting to him, so he's inventing anything that will get him out of it.

"Cut the crap, Chick," Jack says, leaning forward again. "What about Doniesha Wilks? She died right after Jasmine, as I know you know well. How'd you meet her?"

"Enough!" Chick shouts, standing from his chair. "I'm going home." Without hesitation, he leaves.

Jack isn't convinced of Chick's innocence, feeling like there's another piece at play here. He just needs to figure out what that is. But there's no time to waste. Between the tips and the new information that Chick has confessed to, he thinks he'll be able to get a judge to sign off on a warrant to search his house. And due to the severity of the case—with this rapidly becoming the biggest story in the state—he thinks he can get that warrant in the next few hours. Abrupt affairs with at least two of the victims, his wallet being found at a crime scene, witnesses placing Chick near the scene of a murder, and lying to a law enforcement officer during an interrogation and then admitting to it should be enough probable cause to get this done in a timely manner.

Noticing on the wall clock that it's well into the afternoon now, he knows he'd better get moving. It's only a matter of time before patrol cars are swarming Chick Strate's house.

38

NOLA

The reflection of my headlights on the rain-drenched roads makes it look like I'm driving on mirrors on the way to my dad's house. He still hasn't answered any of my calls, and my mind is racing more than ever. Still reeling from what Jack told me this morning about my dad and Mia dating, I need to get answers from him. But the constant chasing via telephone and showing up at his house is getting old. Alas, up the hill I go, further into the storm.

In the lane to my right, a car pulls up to me, speakers blaring loud enough that the bass shakes my car. "Semi-Charmed Life" by Third Eye Blind bellows out the open windows as rain-spotted youths sing the most sunny-day song on the planet, undoubtedly drenching the inside of their car. Even in this storm, they're embracing the day with song and togetherness. I envy their carefree attitudes, free of the horrors of recent events. I can't help but send them a small smile as they hurl past. Meanwhile, I sit in silence, nothing but the sounds of bad weather around me.

Looking back at the road ahead, I yelp when my ringing phone pierces through my car's speakers. Looking at my Jeep's touch screen, I see that the call is coming from a number I don't recognize.

Is it the police trying to find and charge me with unlawful entry? Or is my dad using me as his one phone call from jail because he's been arrested?

I answer the phone with a weary "Hello?" before a joyful-voiced woman squeals on the other line.

"You are on fire, kid!" she shouts. "It's Nicole. Only your favorite sales director at Telegraph One."

"What number are you calling from? And what's up?"

I can't even fake a temperate tone with her at a time like this, nor can I tell her what's wrong if she even asks. I just wish I hadn't answered the phone.

"This is my new office line, so save it. And sorry for the cold call, but I wanted to follow up after our texts yesterday. Your podcast download numbers are still skyrocketing, and I imagine the live listens will do the same when you get back in the studio tomorrow. Whatever that call was on Friday night, it helped. The clip is all over that Reddit website."

It makes sense that people are talking about the call. It was alarming. Instant-internet-sensation worthy. Some probably don't even know that it's real, nor that it was taken out by Harvey yesterday since it's linked to a real-life murder case where the woman died within minutes of the call dropping. Nicole still seems oblivious to this fact, meaning she probably hasn't read the article.

"I saw an article about the caller's murder in the *Oregonian*," she adds. "It's only a matter of time before her call to the show hits major news stations across the country."

That answers that. How is she still so happy?

"Yeah, it's pretty terrible, don't you think? It's been a difficult weekend to say the least," I say, choosing not to tell Nicole just yet that we made the moral decision to remove it from the podcast episode. She doesn't have any say on the matter anyway.

"Nola. Did you hear me? Your numbers are going crazy. If this woman were alive, we'd thank her. It's horrible, for sure. But it's bringing a ton of new listeners in. We're getting bombarded with advertising requests already and it's only Monday."

My windshield wipers work their asses off to keep my vision clear of water, but it's hardly doing the job because of how hard it's raining. All I have to do is jerk the wheel to the left and I'll get myself into a head-on collision. Probably die on impact. Nicole's heartless comments are tempting the joints in my wrist to spazz but one, tiny flick.

Flick, and I'm gone. Flick, and I don't have to worry about my dad or my neighbor or anyone else I know or don't know being a horrific masked killer. Flick, and the guilt I've carried for so many years about Mia's murder being *my* fault because she was only at my house to babysit *me* would vanish into the fog.

On the other hand: Flick, I break my mother's heart. Flick, I never see Harvey again and he grows old with someone else. Flick, I don't find out the truth about who is behind all of this madness and why. Flick, the earth keeps spinning on its axis and life carries on without me. Flick, Nola Strate ceases to exist.

No. I don't want that. I deserve to finish this and come out on the other side.

"Nola? Am I losing you?" Nicole asks. "I'm trying to tell you that big things are happening for you and the show." Her voice remains upbeat. The sunshine in her tone is blinding.

Although I long for one week ago when good news from Telegraph One would have made me dizzy with thrill, it seems meaningless today. Falsifying excitement is an impossible feat, even just for this phone call. So, I don't do it.

"I hear you. I think it's great that people are finding the show, but this just isn't a good time. I'm so sorry," I say, bearing down on the gas pedal.

"No problem. Want to call me in a bit when you're free?" she asks, sounding sincere for a fleeting moment. Then, her subject change drags her back down to "cold-blooded" on the callousness scale. "Oh wait—last thing. So, I've been trying to reach your dad today so we can have him do a guest spot on an upcoming episode. Because not only is there major buzz surrounding *Night Watch* but also your dad's new book. I think this woman's murder is helping you both. Well, you know what I mean." She giggles. "But having him back on for a highlight sounds great, doesn't it? I really think you guys should consider it. And soon."

If I hear one more remark, I'm chucking my phone out the window.

"Nicole? I can't hear you, I'm driving into a dead zone," I lie. "Let's try again tomorrow, okay?"

I end the call.

As I inch my face closer to my windshield with eyes wide open so I can see out in front of me, the sky darkens further as the invisible sun falls closer to the mountains. It's getting harder to see—and steer—as the wind pushes against my tires. I grip my fingers around the wheel and keep my eyes locked on the vanishing glimpses of clear road so that I don't miss my dad's turn.

When I reach it, I nearly hydroplane during the too-sharp right turn I make going up the hill toward his house, causing my whole body to tremble. The storm is getting ferocious. And it's only going to get more so as the day turns into night.

Before I see my dad's house, I notice the glow of police lights against the thick, murky air. The red and blue flashes cease as I pull up to find three police cruisers canvassing my dad's house.

Furrowing my brows, I can only wonder: What did Jack uncover?

39

NOLA

The police must have arrived minutes before I did, as some of the officers are still prepping and getting things out of their patrol vehicles. It seems like a relatively relaxed scene: no shouting, no gunshots, no handcuff slinging. But where is my dad?

I roll my car by ever so slowly to get a glimpse into his front door, which is wide open and showing two officers inside. My dad isn't holding the door open for them, nor is he sitting in any of the vehicles that are haphazardly parked in his driveway. He's nowhere. I bring my wheels to a halt and peer around to gather as much as I can, wondering if I should get out of the car or not.

"Move along," an officer says outside my passenger window, loud enough to spook me. I didn't even see him approach my car. He's dressed in a long, HiVis raincoat with the hood up, and he knocks his index finger against the glass.

I roll down the passenger window. "This is my dad's house. What's going on?"

"We have a warrant to search the premises."

"On what grounds?"

"I can't tell you that, ma'am. You're going to have to leave, please." He gestures up the street. "Move it. We gotta keep the road open."

Without another word, I drive down my dad's street and call him again. No answer. It goes straight to voicemail, just like it has been. Does that mean he's on the phone already, or have they confiscated it as evidence? What. Is. Happening.

As I hang up, an incoming call pops up on my screen. It's Cynthia.

"Hey, is everything all right? How's Harvey feeling?"

I try to disguise my distress as much as possible, knowing Harvey was the one who was physically attacked today, while everything I'm experiencing is purely mental.

"Hey, it's Harvey. My phone's still somewhere at your house. I'm using my mom's."

That's right...

I drive up the windy, hillside neighborhood road until I'm out of the police officer's sight and park my car. The rain is deafening, so I turn up the volume on my speakers while Harvey continues talking.

"But I'm feeling much better now that I'm on pain meds," he adds. "They kicked in a few hours ago, so I'm like a whole new guy. But anyway, that's not important right now. I had my mom run down and get my other laptop from my house earlier when she was grabbing lunch and I've been reviewing some work calls."

That is just like Harvey. This man will work until he's dead.

"I thought you're not supposed to look at screens right now because of your concussion. You should rest," I say delicately.

"Well, I probably shouldn't be, but—"

"Just take a break. We honestly should call tomorrow night's show off anyway. I think we could all use it, especially you," I add. "I can make a social media post today."

"Nola, listen," he says anxiously. "Something really weird came up on the hotline. I'm sending it to you now."

The *Night Watch* "hotline" is essentially an online voicemail system for people who don't want to call in live for one reason or another. It's not used very frequently, because most people like to call their stories in when they can talk to us. But sometimes, there are interesting messages that come in, and we play them on the show sporadically and discuss.

"What is it?" I ask. "What do you mean by weird?"

"It's us."

"What do you mean it's us?"

"Someone sent in a recording of you and me talking. It's from last night when we were on your balcony reading about the Hiding Man. I don't know how, or why, but someone recorded us."

My entire body slows, yet my heart rate quickens. Since I was so paranoid last night, I looked over my balcony railing constantly, watching the street for anyone walking down below, or unfamiliar cars parked or driving by. I didn't see anything that seemed off.

An email from Harvey's laptop hosting an audio file pops up on my phone. I should hang up with him so I can listen to it, but I'm too afraid to hear it alone—even while in the safety of my car, before sunset, parked around the corner from multiple police officers. I sit in silence for a few moments, still thinking back to last night.

"What if it was your neighbor? The one in the hammock on their balcony?" Harvey asks.

That was the only strange thing I noticed outside last night. But

I determined it was probably nothing because I can't help but feel like if they were in the hammock the entire time we were outside, we would have seen them earlier. I can't be sure.

"Listen to the call. I'll stay on the phone and mute myself," Harvey offers.

Hesitant, I click the forty-six-second audio file and press Play. At first, I hear only the *woosh* of the wind. After a few seconds, I hear my own voice.

"Do you want him to know where you live?" I hear myself ask.

"I absolutely do not," I distantly hear Harvey say with a laugh. "But I don't like that this person seems to know where you live."

"Tell me about it," I say to Harvey. "I'm sure everything will be okay. I wouldn't willingly put you in harm's way by being here if I really thought someone was coming."

"That's so thoughtful of you," Harvey joked.

More wind, and the sound of movement for a few seconds. Neither of us speaks.

"'The creak, the squeak, from in the night / Is quite enough to cause a fright.'" That's Harvey.

"What's that?" I hear myself ask him.

"'But when you see his wielding knife / It's far too late, he'll take your life.' Have you read this?"

"I don't even know what that is," I say, but again it sounds distant.

"'He lurks from deep beyond the gray / He thrives as loose among the prey / Like a fox, to his hen / This "He" is called the Hiding Man.'"

Click.

That's the end of the recording. I can't tell what direction it came from or how far away the person was. But considering you can still hear our voices fairly well, they must have been close.

Tears of fear form in my eyes. "Screw this. I'm going over there," I say, pushing my gearshift into Drive.

"Going over where? To your neighbor's?"

"Yes. I'm done with all the not knowing. If that son of a bitch recorded us to torment me, I need to talk to him. I'm going to get some answers."

I drive down the street, making my way through my dad's neighborhood on a route I don't usually take. Adrenaline releases into my bloodstream, fast. I'm not even scared anymore, I'm just mad. Big, fucking mad.

"Nola, please don't go alone. They won't let me leave yet, but maybe Jack will come with you if you play him the recording. You cannot go alone." It's more of a demand than a request, but I know he's trying to help and make sure I don't get myself killed.

I mull it over for a second, knowing that if I tell him I'm going over there anyway, he'll continue to fight it in every way possible. I know Jack won't help me. I've already tried that. He wants me to stay in my lane and mind my business. But this is officially my business, and it has been ever since Felicity called into my job three nights ago. Or maybe it's been my business for twenty years.

"Just come to the hospital," Harvey continues. "It's safe here, there's people all around. Doctors, police, me. I know you can keep yourself safe, but I want to. So, please, let me."

"Okay," I sigh. "I'll be right over."

I hang up the phone and continue driving down the hill. But not toward the hospital—toward my next-door neighbor's house.

40

NOLA

My neighbor's house has a storybook-like style that's similar to mine. But instead of boasting an all-white paint job, their exterior walls are the color of stone with black trim. I stare at the charming, paned windows and arched doors looking for any sign of life.

The slate driveway is empty, but the porch light and a single interior light are on. Both of our driveways face a hill of greenery, meaning there are no across-the-street neighbors watching after me as I venture to the front porch by myself at sunset. The house on the other side of this neighbor's is protected by cypress trees, tall enough to enclose it.

Would anyone even hear my screams? I think.

The sky is littered with clouds; there's been no sight of the sun all day. But I can tell by how dark the sky is getting—and by the time—that darkness will fall upon the city within fifteen minutes or so.

I don't even bother throwing my hood over my head. The rain is coming down so hard that it's practically hitting me in the face with each step I take along the road. When my feet cross the threshold onto my neighbor's driveway, the garage floodlights flash on, enveloping me in light.

No turning back now.

I walk straight up to the door and pound three times on the wood. I don't even know what I'm going to say, but I hope it comes to me if or when someone answers. The wall of windows where I saw a person peeping out at Harvey's ambulance this morning sits directly to my right. But the room beyond the windows is pitch-black, curtains closed. The front door hosts a large, circular-paned window, allowing me to peek into the house. The only light on is coming from the living room to the right, but I don't see anyone lounging or moving. All is still.

I wipe raindrops off my forehead and knock again. "It's your neighbor," I shout. "I just want to talk."

I continue to look into the front door's window, noticing the dark dining room straight ahead. To the left is the kitchen, facing toward my house, also dark.

"Is anybody home?" I shout, knocking again.

Suddenly considering the doorbell, I ring it twice.

As I think about the recording and the spying from their balcony, anger floods through me once again. I knock harder and ring the bell once more. "I know you're home," I lie. "Get out here and show yourself, you coward."

But still, nothing. I wipe more water off my face and wring my hair out before knocking again.

Just then, I notice slight movement to my right. As I look directly into the wall of windows that sit two feet from me, I make eye contact with a face.

I shriek and stumble backward, falling off the two porch steps and onto my back. Hot pain sears from my left hip as I roll around on the slate. I grip my back with my hands and let out another cry. I'm helpless, lying in my neighbor's driveway.

All I can do is wail in pain and rotate into the fetal position, holding and rubbing the back of my hip bone. That's when the front door swings open, but I can't bother to look. Too much pain.

"Are you all right, miss?" a man's voice calls out from inside.

I stretch my back out on the ground like a helpless, upside-down beetle and turn my head over to the source of the question.

An elderly man—face full of worry—sits in his wheelchair in the home's entryway. He's dressed in a red sweater, khaki pants, and house slippers.

"I'd help you up, but I can't get down the steps myself. Do you need me to call someone?" His voice is kind and gentle, his face pale, brows furrowed. Not at all the person I pictured to reside in this house.

Now spread-eagled on the ground, I twist my back to crack it and continue to stretch, assessing the damage. As with most of my clumsy spills, the pain has largely subsided already. I imagine it'll turn into a bruise and be sore for a few days, but I think I can get myself out of the rain.

I roll onto my knees and slowly position myself to standing again, still holding my backside. "I'm so sorry, sir. I must be mistaken."

"Would you like to come in for a minute? I can't get down the stairs, but I can make you a cup of tea."

Knowing I can make my own tea just a hop, skip, and jump from here, I open my mouth to decline. But having the opportunity to sit down and ask him some questions would be a good idea.

"Sure, thanks. I'm Nola. I actually live right there," I say, pointing at my house.

He closes the door behind me. "I'm Luther Crow. Sorry we've never met. I don't get out of the house much."

Luther wheels into the kitchen and reaches over the counter to snap his electric kettle on from his seat. "Chamomile?" he asks.

"That's perfect, thanks." My entire body is dripping rainwater all over his entryway. "Are you sure? I'm getting your house soaking wet. I can just go."

"Oh, hell with it," he says with a chuckle. "My caretaker Susan will be back in the morning. She keeps the house clean for me. Come sit." He gestures to the breakfast table inside the kitchen.

Somehow, this is just how I thought the kitchen would look. From my view, I can only see through the casement window—the one that usually has a candle sitting in it. From my house, part of the walnut cabinets and stainless steel appliances are visible. But still, everything else is where I imagined it'd be.

"What is it that you were hollering about outside? Did something happen?" Luther asks as the water begins to boil, joining me at the table.

"Um, I guess I thought—I…" I struggle to speak, releasing a sigh instead. "Were you on your balcony last night? Someone has been watching me. And I noticed you."

"Yes, I was out there last night," Luther says with a small chuckle. "The rain had settled, so Susan let me go out in the hammock for a while. It's such a beautiful view we have up here."

"It's just strange because I've never seen you before. Not even out on the balcony."

"Now it sounds like you're watching *me*," he says with another laugh. "But no, I don't make it out there much. Susan's here once a day, and I usually keep to the living room or my bedroom." He points behind me down the hall. His bedroom and living room are on the side of the house away from mine. And his bedroom, I guess, is the one I saw him peeking out of tonight and this morning.

I nod, thinking on it.

Luther couldn't have been the one to hurt Harvey. He's in a wheelchair, for God's sake. And I doubt he was the one who recorded us. Luther doesn't even look like the kind of guy that has a smartphone.

"Was everything okay this morning? I saw an ambulance."

"Actually, we had a break-in. Did you happen to hear or see anything?"

As the kettle starts to screech, Luther returns to his previous spot at the counter and grabs a mug off the drying rack, then a packet of tea out of a drawer. From my positioning, I can't see what he's doing with the tea.

"Honey?"

I almost offer to help, but he seems to be comfortable using his wheelchair. I stop myself from asking how long he's needed it.

"No, thanks."

He turns around, mug in hand. "That's terrible about the break-in. And someone was hurt?"

"Yeah, my friend was. But he's recovering," I say cautiously. "So, you really didn't hear or see anything? And you haven't noticed anything strange here at your house?"

Luther shrugs. "Not a thing. I wish I would have been keeping watch. You said someone's been following you?" He hands me my tea and joins me at the breakfast table again, scooting his wheelchair under the glass top.

"Yes. I've been seeing someone out on the street below ours," I say, sipping my tea.

"And then there's those murders. What is going on these days?" he says lightly. Too lightly.

Something about the way he said *those murders* sends a chill down my spine. So nonchalant, almost mocking. "It's awful," he continues. "That's why I never leave the house. But it's nice to have some unique company for a change."

I take larger gulps of my tea, just wanting to finish it, even if it singes my throat in the process. Serves me right for coming in here at all.

"Well then, I'm so sorry to say, but I really have to get going. I need to grab something from my house before I head back to the hospital to see my friend. He's waiting for me." I rise from my chair and nearly topple over from the surging pain in my hip. "Thanks for the tea. I'll have to stop by another time," I add, wincing through it.

"That's a shame, but I understand. I hope your friend gets better."

I send him a wave and head for the door.

"Don't be a stranger, now!" he shouts across the foyer while I walk out.

As I cross Luther's driveway on the way to mine, I can't help but kick myself. I came here with rage and a score to settle. Now I'm leaving minutes later with a deflated ego and a sore back.

I fish my keys out of my duster's pocket and march toward my pitch-black house. The sun is almost set, so if I hurry, I can get out of these wet clothes, grab Harvey's phone, and be back to the hospital in no time.

41

NOLA

As I enter my house, I'm plagued with questions. If it wasn't Luther, my supposed non-peeping neighbor, then who recorded Harvey and me talking on my balcony? Who has been watching me? And lastly, if I were Harvey's phone, where would I be hiding?

The first thing I do is turn on every light in the living room, dining room, and kitchen so that no one can creep up in the dark, and so I can see every inch of space to find his damn phone as fast as possible. I call his phone with mine, pleading it hasn't run out of battery, and immediately hear the harsh vibrations of it.

It's somewhere in the living room.

My living room blinds are open from this morning, giving me a view into Luther's house. This was probably done by the paramedics to achieve all the natural light they could get while they were rescuing Harvey. But as always, his home is dark, sans a single candle burning in his window.

I continue to look for Harvey's phone before I reach his voice-mail. Walking slowly to focus my earshot on its location, I narrow my range to the sectional sofa. Placing my palm on a cushion, I feel the quavers within the sofa and find his phone lodged between two cushions.

Gotcha.

I text Cynthia from my phone saying,

> Found Harvey's cell! On my way to the
> hospital now.

Even if Harvey reads it and gets mad that I came into my house by myself instead of heading straight to the hospital to be around him and other people, he'll surely have a smile on his face when I safely arrive in fifteen minutes with his iPhone in hand.

I remove my duster and hang it on the rack by my front door. In the back of my brain, those two questions regarding Harvey's attack still scratch away. Who, and how?

Before jogging up to my bedroom to change out of my sweater and soaked pants, I first open my balcony door just as the sun sets beyond the mountains.

Get out of here, fast, I tell myself.

I don't want to be here alone, especially at night, but I need to peek around before I go, still wondering about that audio clip of us. The balcony door remains unlocked from this morning as I scan my surroundings looking for an answer to my questions. My eyes meet Luther's empty balcony, and my heart drops when I notice him sit-ting in his wheelchair at the dining room's double French doors that lead out to his deck. He's just sitting there, in the dark, on the other side of the glass, staring at my balcony. I send a flat smile and wave his way, and he sends an even bigger one of both before wheeling out of the room.

It appears he was watching out for me in a small way, knowing I'm in here by myself.

The slanted rain hits me in the face as I turn back toward the rest of the street to observe a perfectly peaceful neighborhood, sans the minor flooding.

Clang. Clang. Clang.

The sound of repeated metal on metal comes from the other side of my balcony, around the corner where the wooden staircase is that leads down to my garage and carport. It sounds like my gate at the bottom of the stairs is opening and shutting rapidly.

Must be from the wind.

I move across the deck and around the corner to find my suspicions to be correct; it's just the gate. I jog down the steps, slam the gate into place, and turn around to climb them again when something catches my eye.

The side security camera.

A red dot in the corner is visible, indicating the camera is in working order.

Previous questions of how our voices were recorded circle around my head in dizzying fashion as I realize something. My camera is on right now, even though yesterday and this morning, my cameras were both down. How, during the worst storm of the year, is my camera popping back on? Something about that isn't right to me.

I can't shake the sense that someone is watching me now, the red dot glaring at me. I wonder, too, if my front-door camera is suddenly working as well.

My chest begins to tighten and restrict, and my body gets covered in goosebumps. My stomach is knotted, and my head continues to whir. I sprint up the stairs, still holding my stinging hip, and run into my house as fast as possible, then slam and lock the door behind me. With my back against the glass, I struggle to open my Northwest Protect app, my hands trembling harder than a megaquake on the Richter scale.

When the home screen pops up, the first thing I see is that both of my cameras are on, showcasing my front porch and driveway on one, and my side staircase and carport on the other. No one is outside or in front of either of them.

I click the Notifications button to see the history.

On, Off, On, Off.

My cameras have been fluctuating for days. They were off yesterday when I arrived home and grabbed the mail, but unbeknownst to me, they turned back on last night. I run through my side camera's recorded history from yesterday evening, only to find exactly what I worried I would. I can't see myself or Harvey, as the camera is located on the side of the house, but I can hear us. I can hear the exact audio that Harvey texted me in a clip.

This is how he's been doing it.

I go back into my notifications to see that the cameras turned off again at 4:48 a.m. That must have been just before someone entered my house and hurt Harvey.

He's had the upper hand this entire time. He knows every move I make. When I'm home and when I'm out. When I'm alone, and when I'm not.

Like right now.

The utility van, my mind rings.

I saw a utility van under the streetlamp that night. The night I saw that figure waving at me. And the barista at the coffee shop mentioned seeing a white van parked on her street with a blue light coming from inside. Blue lights—like from a screen. Like monitors. Does this man work for the security company that I've trusted to protect me all this time? One step ahead all along.

As my mind scrambles at the thought of utility vans and security company vehicles, I think about what Mary said to me last night.

At the diner, Mary told me that there was a security patrol vehicle driving around on her street shortly before Carrie was murdered back in 2004. Was that Him? Has He been camouflaging as a security patrolman all these years?

I want to message her about my revelation to see what she thinks, but I can't. She's dead.

And then I remember that I must be next.

If I had just checked my notification history this morning at the hospital when Officer Nelson asked me if my cameras caught anything, I would have uncovered this then. I would have been in the safety of daylight and people, not alone just as the sun sets.

There's no time to run upstairs and change. He could be on his way to my house, seeing on the cameras that I'm home. I need to get out of here. Now.

But just as I start running toward the front door, the power goes out.

42

HIM

The man has been hiding in Nola's guest room for nearly an hour awaiting her eventual arrival. When he moved her and Harvey's phones early this morning before fleeing, he anticipated this exact moment, when she would need to retrieve one or both of them. She'd have to come back home, likely alone. And he timed it almost perfectly.

Knowing she'd be upset about what happened to Harvey in the night, she'd be rushing out of the house, not giving herself enough time to get everything she needed. Either way, he had the pronounced impression that she'd be back.

When he whacked Harvey over the head with a candlestick, even he was aghast at the action. He had crept in quietly enough through the deck's door, certainly not expecting anyone to catch him. After all the alcohol they'd drunken hours before, he'd presumed they'd be near comatose. But as he approached them by the fireplace, admiring Nola in her stillness, Harvey began to toss and turn. Killing him wouldn't have pleased the man, as he wasn't the intended target. He simply needed to incapacitate Harvey to make a swift exit, unseen. Not before sending Nola a grim, prominent message to say, *I'll be back*, with the use of Harvey's calf.

By controlling her cameras he gave her a sense of nakedness—like she wasn't safe even in her own home. A feeling he's relished giving all the girls.

Last week, after the semitruck took the only two people that the man truly loved—his beloved wife and son—he threw all caution to the wind. He had half a mind to find the driver and brutally kill him. But that would have led police directly to him, as his motive would have been too obvious.

When Benji was born, the man could no longer seek such risky pleasures. He could only watch, and from afar. Having a wife and son will do that to you. Keep you busy, accounted for. He couldn't show up at home covered in blood, or chance having either of them see the mask—which had been stored away in a box for more than fifteen years to ensure his growing son wouldn't stumble upon it.

Getting a job at Northwest Protect helped keep his urges at bay, and provided him with the ability to watch the girls, unbeknownst to them. He could still show up at their homes and frighten them in person, by moving their things, or scratching at the window in the early hours. Sometimes he'd sit in his work van outside their houses and gaze up as they looked out into the street in panic, wondering where the noises originated.

Now that his family is gone, the man has nothing left to lose. Nobody watching *him*.

When he learned Jolene and Benji were dead, hours after they fled the house to Jolene's parents, there was one person even more to blame than the semi driver: Felicity Morton.

He had been observing Felicity already for weeks, taking more pleasure out of terrifying her than some of the others. It was payback for her filling twelve-year-old Benji's head with nonsense about him.

That nonsense was looping in their minds as they sped away from home, trying to escape him, and they died on the highway. He blamed Felicity, and he made sure she suffered for it.

Mary was easy to watch through the intimacy of her bedroom camera lens. And with his plans to move back up to Washington this week, whose life better to take before Nola's than the only other girl who ever saw him?

Nola is one he's been especially holding out for, all thanks to her father. He's grown particularly close to her since she took over *Night Watch*, feeling an intimate connection from years of following the show. He always knew that some way, somehow, they'd meet again.

After her father drunkenly humiliated the man in front of everyone in the bar that night back in 2004, he's ached to torture him.

"M-Mr. Strate," the man had stuttered after approaching Chick at the bar. "S-sorry to bother you, but I'm a huge fan. *Night Watch* keeps me awake during my graveyard shifts. I tune in every night that I can." He stood there, hands clasped.

Maybe it was his meek stutter or gentle demeanor that caused Chick to laugh. Chuckling at the soft exterior of a privately vicious man. For a moment, he thought he'd walked in on a hilarious conversation, Chick's laughter a delayed response to something someone else said. But when his friends joined in, the man knew it was at his own expense. His hands and eyes began to twitch as soon as another burst rumbled from Chick's diaphragm.

"You know what, little guy?" he mocked, slurring and spitting in a pathetically drunken stupor from his seat. "You *are* bothering me."

Chick stood up from his bar stool, stumbled, and grabbed the man's shoulder. As he did, the man shoved his hand off in a rage, which the friends seemed to enjoy. But it didn't give the man power. They were still on Chick's side.

"Oh!" they all cackled.

"Little guy's got some fight in him," Chick sneered, trying to widen his eyes. "Get lost," he said slowly to the man. Another laugh.

There was nothing little about the man. Chick was just a high school bully in the flesh, assuming that the man's gentle demeanor meant he was weak and undersized. Even though he towered over Chick in stature, and had more strength than Chick could know, the words made him feel like the small boy he once was. Chick Strate thrust him back to a version of himself to which he had hoped never to return.

The man narrowed his eyes and calmly spoke to Chick's twisted, sweaty face. "You have no idea what these hands have done," he said quietly with a smile, nearly spilling tales of the four women's lives he'd taken thus far.

"What was that?" Chick asked, quickly leaning in. As he did, beer flung from his glass and splashed across the man's pants and shoes.

"Oh, you'll be sorry for this," he whispered confidently into Chick's ear, jaw tightened.

He was pitifully belligerent, and his friends continued to roar while Chick's expression shifted to a disturbed look. It seemed the threat had struck a chord.

Underneath the man's provoking, vindictive outer shell, he was thinking back to those nights at home as a child, his own father chastising him across the dinner table. His father, wasted, would slap, mock, shame him. Sometimes even in front of his friends. Much like this instance with Chick, his father and posse would have their laughs at his expense, intoxicated and cruel.

He considered pulling the buck knife out of his pocket in that moment and dicing Chick up right in front of his buddies. But he refrained, and stormed out of the bar like a feeble mouse, hatching the perfect plan to get back at him. To make the pompous, handsome, wealthy fuck—someone he once looked up to—pay.

"Pussy!" Chick called, laugher erupting once again from his puppets.

As the man turned the corner outside, his eyes fell to his pants, still covered in beer. It looked like he pissed himself. Two young women even snickered at him as they walked past, eyes glued to his crotch. Not in admiration, but in pity.

That pushed him over an edge he thought he'd already catapulted off. The rage was overwhelming. He knew what he needed to do.

After that night, he plotted against Chick Strate, a man pathetically easy to frame. Especially after taking the lives of both of his girlfriends.

For a married man who had affairs with two different young women, one would think he would have been more discreet. Merely following him from the radio station after work led the man to witness his erotic adventures firsthand. He had hoped back then that taking Mia's and Jasmine's lives would punish Chick, even set him up as a suspect. But the simpleminded officers and investigators leading the task force at the time didn't seem to know left from right.

It was a mistake not to leave behind any physical evidence pointing to his enemy in the original murders. But the man would be damned if he would make the same mistake twice.

Although aware that two decades is more than sufficient time to move on from such a grudge, the only way to stop police from narrowing in on him as their prime suspect is to place another one right into their lap. And with Chick already on their radar as a person of interest, it'd be silly not to utilize him. But this time, the man has taken steps to point the killings in Chick's direction once again: dropping his license near the scene of Mary's murder, planting two of his hairs—taken from his own bathroom—at Felicity's, and calling in with anonymous tips from a phone booth to drop the blame directly in his lap.

To keep the ruse alive, he'll need to make Nola's murder look like a suicide so police don't question why Chick would kill his own child. That could give them reason to believe he didn't do any of it. A suicide will ensure his entire plan goes off without a single hitch.

The weight of finding out her father was a vicious serial killer will have been too much for her to bear. He plans to compose an email and send it around, making certain that everyone knows exactly why she took her own life. It'll be the perfect cherry on top of the Hiding Man case.

The man hears Nola's back door open and slam shut. Then the lock clicks into place.

She's come back inside the house.

As he grips the butcher's knife taken from her kitchen, he quietly makes his way into the hall to give her one final scare. But just as he does, all the lights go out.

This time, he didn't shut the power off himself.

43

NOLA

A crack of thunder echoes against the air outside as power lines swing from excessive wind and rainfall. The storm knocked out the lights just as the sun said its final goodbyes for the day behind the black clouds, creating pure darkness across most of the city.

As the lights flashed off, I froze in place. I could have kept running, made it to the door even in the blackness. But when everything went dark, I was so taken aback by it that I stopped in my tracks. I still can't move. I can see the outline of the front door from here as my eyes slowly adjust to the lack of light, yet somehow it feels so far away.

The moon is stuck behind the clouds, promising a dingy evening, which makes this whole power-outage situation even more difficult.

I picture the figure down at the streetlight again, standing under the now-unlit post—watching me, waiting for me to come outside so He can get me. But with the front door unlocked, He can easily run up the hill and come right in all on His own. He doesn't have to wait for me anymore.

As I stand in the middle of the room, numb and unmoving, I try hard not to let this moment trigger an identical memory. Just like before, I'm confident that He knows where I am. But I don't know where He is.

Running to the front door is risky. If He's outside, He's probably going toward the front. But that's where my car is, so that's where I need to get to. If I go back onto the balcony, I'll have a larger view of the area and a better escape route, and maybe I can even flag Luther to call for help. But I won't be next to my vehicle.

There's no room whatsoever for error here, but I don't know what the right choice is. Hence, frozen in place. Thinking as fast as my brain will allow, I land on the balcony plan. As I turn around to bolt back toward the balcony door, the power suddenly flashes back on, filling the room with light. I let out a small sigh of relief, as though power will somehow save me from a deranged masked killer.

I look forward at the glass door in front of me, ready to swing it open and rush outside. But before I can, I notice something in the reflection behind my back. A tall person, clad in black clothes and a soulless white mask.

The Hiding Man is standing right behind me.

44

JACK

After getting held up at his desk with work on Felicity's and Mary's cases, Jack pulls up to Chick's house twenty minutes after the other officers do to search his home for the stolen evidence boxes.

With what they have against Chick already—and the possibility of more evidence being tied to him after the crime lab tests the samples—Jack believes the judge will approve an arrest warrant for Chick Strate for the murders of Mia Parsons and Jasmine Petri, to start. Once they retrieve his DNA swab, the lab will test it against everything they have from all nine Portland murders in question and see what comes of it. Jack isn't putting too much weight into that path proving anything in the '04 and '05 cases, as the killer never left behind notable evidence. He was always exceptionally careful to leave no trace of himself. But it's worth a try.

If Chick had confessed to Jack that he had been with another woman on the night of Mia's murder—instead of lying that he was simply at the office sending emails—Jack could have investigated it back then. He could have interviewed Jasmine before her murder to see if Chick was telling the truth. But now that she's dead and so much time has passed, he can't confirm or deny Chick's claims. But the concept that two women he was dating were both murdered in the same manner is too great to ignore.

After Jack wrote up the search warrant application earlier this afternoon, he looked deeper into Mary's murder. He checked her text messages and calls, discovered she had a security camera, and looked for any trace of a connection in her phone records that could indicate her ever meeting Chick. But unless Jack and the other officers find a collection of burner phones during the execution of this warrant tonight, nothing seems to connect them beyond Chick's license being at the scene.

Like with anyone, there was a collection of phone calls in Mary's records from unknown numbers, which Minnie is working on now. But otherwise, nothing seems unusual. Similar to the other victims, Mary was clearly afraid of something before she died. She texted her roommate and another friend that she kept hearing strange noises outside, and that they were frightening her. But no one else on her street reported any suspicious activity or unfamiliar cars parked outside that night. Most admitted to staying indoors much of the previous week with the incoming storms, so none of them had been walking outside or staying out late. This meant that suspicious activity and unfamiliar cars weren't things they were naturally on the lookout for anyway.

Jack still needs to put more hours into Felicity's murder, as he's contacted and interviewed only some of the parents of Felicity's adolescent clients, to no avail. His workload continues to stack up, but if he can nail Chick Strate for the murders, it'll all be behind him.

Felicity Morton and Mary Clairemont have virtually no connections, zero mutual contacts. The only similar aspect about them is the area they lived in, just a few streets away from each other. But even that isn't spectacular. So why did Chick target them? Jack needs to find out, and quickly.

Jack steps out of his car and jogs to Chick's covered porch to check in with the other officers on their findings. He steps into the familiar, contemporary home and spots Chick at his dining table. Staring at the warrant in front of him, he remains silent as officers raid every personal corner of his house.

A pang of guilt radiates through Jack's body. What if he's getting this all wrong? It's a difficult possibility to believe considering there are a variety of clues that specifically point to Chick—and always have. Jack figures that the feeling is coming from their lengthy, positive history. But once again, he needs to stuff those feelings away and focus on the job at hand: finding a killer.

Jack makes his way into the garage to begin upending every corner, just as an officer yells his name across the house and comes barreling into the room.

"All on-duty officers in the area have been called to a house up the street for a possible murder," the officer tells him.

How could this be? Jack thinks, looking back across the room at Chick. Chick has been with him most of the day. Did he do something in the hours between leaving the station and letting the officers in to serve the search warrant?

Jack gets the address from the officer and demands that two of them stay back to keep an eye on Chick and continue their search.

He hasn't been personally called to the scene, but if this is connected, he needs to see it for himself. As he rushes back to his car outside, he looks at the address again and only now recognizes it.

It's Nola Strate's house.

45

NOLA

I'd recognize that reflection anywhere. Even from the partially blurred image in front of me in the glass, the lights shining down on his face make it clear that it's the mask I saw when I was only eight years old.

Before I can even process what's happening, the man behind me lunges straight toward me. But as he does, I crouch and whirl around to face him. I don't think he anticipated the lights coming on and me catching a glimpse of him in the glass. If the power hadn't returned just seconds after going out, he probably would have killed me like he did the others, seamlessly and quietly. But now, we're in a full-on brawl.

I don't even have time to be scared because I'm fighting for my life. As soon as I turn around to face him, I want to go limp. I want to fall into the fetal position again and cry and make him disappear. I don't want to look at his hideous mask. But I need to defeat him, no matter the cost.

As my eyes meet his black, beady ones, his arm is already swinging toward me. He had been reaching for my arm with one hand and holding a large knife in the other, but when I turned around the way I did, his knife unintentionally plunged into my side. It was a quick mistake that he immediately corrected by pulling the blade out and tackling me onto the floor. I dropped my phone somewhere in the process.

Blood spurts out of me. It's not until I see it that I register the flaming pain radiating from my side. I grab my belly as I squirm on the floor.

His face is suddenly in front of mine. Instead of reaching for the knife in his hand, I reach for his head, attempting to pull the mask off so I can see his real face. I refuse to die before seeing it.

Inches away from him, I notice just how handmade the mask is. It's distressed rubber with old, black string threaded around the slits for the mouth, nose, and two eyes. There's not enough space to see skin underneath it, making him appear more like a monster than ever before. But I know underneath it is a real, human face. And if I can just rip the mask off, some of my fear might dissipate.

His knife is against my throat as I move my free hand up to the back of his head, trying to find the base of the mask. His entire weight is on top of me, but the knife is unmoving. It's like he's calibrating his next step.

Registering what I'm trying to do, he puts more pressure on the knife and uses his other hand to press into my body. He pushes my back harder into the hardwood floors, making me screech from the pain of my already bruised hip and my fresh, gaping wound. If I can just get him off the floor, maybe Luther or another neighbor will spot our struggle and call the police. But I can't move at all. I can't even reach the back of his head.

Instead, I push my hand into his face, grab the mask at his nose, and poke my fingers through the holes. I use all my might to snap it forward, causing the man to inch backward.

The mask is still on his face.

I successfully turn over and start crawling toward my dining table. Just as I begin to lift off the ground into a standing position, he yanks my foot and drags me back toward him. I'm screaming at this point, hoping my cries will be heard over the booming storm outside.

I flip on my back to be met mask-to-face once again. Only this time, he's pinning both of my arms to the floor, straddling me.

"Get off me, you sick fuck," I spit through my teeth. "You pathetic, weak excuse for a man. You think hurting girls makes you tough? Makes you powerful?" My tone is mocking and condescending. "It just makes you a coward," I hiss.

I wrestle as hard as I can against his grip, but it's strong. Like swimming against a vigorous current, I thrash and struggle but get nowhere. I can't even find my phone to call for help.

Getting closer to my left ear, he whispers something to me, as pacific and hushed as though he were saying something peaceful.

"I told you I'd be watching. But this time, I'm going to get you."

Chills rattle my body as my eyes fill with tears. They're blurring my vision completely, but I can't help it. Between the pain in my hip and my bleeding side, the stark fact that I'm about to die at the hands of this unknown, merciless psycho is overwhelming.

I scream louder than ever before, a rough wail bellowing out of the depths of my being.

Pulling vigor from those depths, I use all my strength to drive my knee into his groin—the force of which causes him to release one of my hands—and I tear the stupid mask right off his head.

Rapidly blinking to clear my vision, I gasp when I finally expose him for the person he is. Especially because I recognize him.

46

HIM

The man's plan already isn't going the way it was supposed to. Before the lights came back on, he began edging toward the living room, ready to take Nola by surprise. Her suicide method of choice was going to be a long, vertical slice up her arm. He even borrowed a knife from the block in her kitchen so it could remain lying next to her as she bled out. He'd hold her down to stop her from fleeing until she died, then stage the scene just right.

But as he emerged from the hallway, the lights turned back on, and she saw him standing behind her. The man wanted to yell, angry that she ruined the plan. That she spotted him when she wasn't supposed to. And even worse, as she turned around to face him, the butcher knife sank into her body in a place it wasn't meant to. Nevertheless, even when she spewed silly nonsense in his face, he knew he had power over her. He knew she was afraid. And it felt glorious.

His new plan would be to stick her any way he'd like. He'd take his time killing her, feeding off her fear. And then, he'd make her disappear. He'd haul her body out of the house, clean the scene spotless, and leave a note all the same.

He'd write that she left Oregon—ran away. She couldn't handle her dad being a vicious killer. She refused to continue a career on a show that such a horrific person created. She wanted to start over, in a new place with new people. It's only natural.

And then, no one would ever hear from her again.

After all, adults are allowed to vanish if they so choose. It's their God-given right.

As the plan forms in his head, he mounts her on the floor again, ready to plunge the knife back into her supple skin. But as he does, she howls, kicks the man's crotch, and wrestles his mask off in one fell swoop. And suddenly, his face is bare.

47

NOLA

I chuck his mask a few feet away so he can't take it back.

Hanging over me now is a man. A man who immediately looks familiar to me. At first, I can't quite place his face. But considering I saw it just two nights ago, it doesn't take long to remember exactly where I saw him. The first and only time I have.

It's the man from my dad's book signing. The one I ran into outside of the elevator on the ground floor. The one who was looking for the correct room so he could get his book signed. The one who wouldn't let me go without a conversation.

My heart drops at the realization that this must mean I really did see Him that night, masked in the stairwell outside my dad's book signing. I ran around the entire store looking for Him, and I can only guess that He scrambled outside, ditched his disguise, and snaked his way back into the building just in time to run into me as I tried to get to my Uber.

Now, he's unmasked, hovering over me, with the bangs of his scraggly salt-and-pepper hair dangling down. His eyes are still black and beady. His skin is pale, his lips quivering into a small grin.

"Recognize me?" he asks in a low, growly voice.

He's back to pinning me down, holding my arms on either side of my body. The weight of his palms above my wrists aches. I take a deep breath and harness every cell of fight I have left.

"Yes," I grunt. "You're just as annoying as I remember." I swing my upper body off the floor and smack his chin with the top of my head.

He recoils in pain, loosening his grip enough for me to break free. Hopping off the ground, I kick his hand with the tip of my boot, knocking the butcher knife out of his grip. I give him another kick, screaming at the top of my lungs, still hoping to draw attention from the outside world.

My holler is primal, like I'm purging every ounce of distress this man has ever caused me, and every other woman in his wake.

Blood is spilling off his lips as he stumbles on his side, proving my headbutt caused some damage.

I lift my foot up to kick him down and finish him, but he grabs my leg again and tugs me down onto my left side.

"Fuck!" I shout in pain. I can't take another blow to the side. I already feel like I'm seconds away from passing out with the injuries I've sustained.

The man crawls on top of me, his blood drooling onto my face in slow, long droplets. He smiles with crimson teeth, sitting on top of me and pressing his groin on my belly. I turn my head, blood dripping into my hair now, and spot the knife about two feet away.

"I'm going to enjoy watching you die, Nola. It's twenty years in the making," the man gently hisses.

"No," I grunt. "This is."

I thrust my right arm out of his clutch and lunge for the knife, just barely grabbing it. As his hand tries to find mine, I slash the blade horizontally across the top of his neck, at the bit of space between his jaw and his black turtleneck. I'm suddenly being bathed in his blood as he fails to keep it all in with his hands. He collapses beside me.

Over the silence of my bated breath, the sound of his choking rings loud. And after all this time, it's better than my favorite song. It's the sound of justice for all his victims' families, the defeat of fear, and peace at last.

I lie next to him, unable to do anything but. I cough hard, my throat dry from the screaming and loss of breath. I lose it all over again when my front door busts open, Jack and multiple officers running inside the house, guns drawn.

"Nola, are you okay?" Jack shouts. And somehow, it comes out in slow motion, like a cloudy dream.

The next thing I know, I'm lying in the back of an ambulance. I don't know if I passed out or if the traumatic nature of what unfolded inside my house caught up with me. All that matters is that I'm alive.

A paramedic is putting pressure on my knife wound, while another is preparing to close the back doors and send me off to the same hospital that Harvey's at.

Before he does, I see Luther, sitting in his wheelchair outside his front door, sending me a thumbs-up.

I send an appreciative smile, knowing he must have kept an eye out for me exactly when I needed him to.

48

NOLA

A dull memory of arriving at the hospital last night sweeps into my head, slipping into a morphine trance shortly after being wheeled in.

I roll my eyes open, with blurry vision at first, to find myself in a hospital bed. The overcast skies glow through the wall of windows, telling me it's daytime. I'm safe.

Get Well Soon balloons are fastened in the corner by the windows, accompanied by a bouquet of orange roses and a pink donut box. Suddenly I realize that the seat next to the table hosts a person, snoozing silently in an upholstered chair.

It's Harvey.

I adjust into an upright position and am quickly reminded of the wound in my side. I unintentionally let out a small cry from pain as I drop my back against the bed again. When I do, Harvey's eyes pop open, and he rushes over to me.

"You're awake," he says, beaming. "How are you feeling?"

"I can't tell yet," I say honestly, flooded with memories of last night's events.

I killed a man. In my own home. I watched him die as he wrestled against his fate on the floor beside me.

Imagining his blood spilling onto my chest, I touch my collarbone to find curiously clean skin. I close my eyes, terror taking over. But then Harvey takes my hand in his.

"You're a legend," he says, grinning. "Everyone here is talking about how incredible you are."

"I don't feel incredible," I admit. "It was awful, Harvey. But he's gone forever. We got him."

"*You* got him," he says, sweeping strands of hair off my cheeks. "You spearheaded this entire thing all on your own. It's impressive."

I smirk up at Harvey, feeling true solace for the first time in days.

"I can't believe you're willingly still in this place. When did you get discharged?"

"A few hours ago," he says. "But I had to come back. I mean, I know firsthand how terrible their breakfast is." Harvey gestures to the pink box.

I release a laugh small enough that I don't feel the pain. "And now I'm the one in the assless gown."

"And you've never looked hotter."

A small knock on the door draws both of our attention. Standing there is my dad, holding a beautiful bouquet of flowers.

"I'll give you guys some time," Harvey says, squeezing my hand. As he passes my dad, they share a hug, and I hear my dad thank him before he leaves the room.

"Hey, fighter," my dad says with a pouty grin. He pulls a chair to my bedside and sets the flowers among Harvey's gifts.

Just the sight of him after my kiss with death brings tears to my eyes, and his. Without saying anything, he leans over and hugs me, holding me tightly while we both weep silently.

When he pulls away, wiping the droplets from my face, he says, "I thought I'd lost you, Nol." He takes a heavy breath. "And when I found out this morning that it was my fault, that you were targeted because of my actions…" He shakes his head. "I almost got you killed."

I sniffle, biting the corner of my mouth. "I know you didn't want any of this to happen. But you could have ruined Jack's career. You tore our family apart," I say, words spilling out. This is the first time I've spoken to him since learning what he did, and I can't ignore it. "Why wasn't Mom good enough? You had a wonderful life. Why'd you have to go and destroy it? None of us deserved that."

He's just shaking his head, shame reddening his face, cheeks glistening wet. His mouth shudders, but nothing comes out.

"Do you know how much of my childhood I spent waiting around for you?" I continue in a sincere whisper. "It hurt so much when you weren't there. It still hurts. All I ever wanted was my dad."

"I should have been there more," he admits, wiping his face dry. I haven't seen my dad cry since the first time I almost died.

As much as it hurts to kick him while he's down, these are things I've wanted to say to him for ages. It never felt like the right time until now.

"You made me feel like I didn't matter. Or wasn't important. You hurt a lot of people."

"You're right. About all of it. And I hate myself for who I've been," he says finally, looking down at our clasped hands. "For the way I've acted for so long. I was bad to your mother, I was unfaithful. I was absent. I was a jerk. I've *been* a jerk." He looks me in the eyes. "I'm sorry I've never been the father you needed. But I'm so proud to be your dad."

Satisfaction envelops me, finally hearing him say those words. It won't take away years of disappointment, but it's a great start to a new way forward.

"You promise to act like it from now on?" I ask.

"I promise, baby."

Something in the corner of the room catches my eye. When I look toward the door of my hospital room, I see my favorite person standing there.

"Mom," I say, a warmth spreading through me at the sight of her.

The next thing I know she's embracing me, holding me tighter than ever before.

"Your dad called me last night. I got on the first plane I could," she says. "I'm just so glad you're alive. Do you need anything? Are you hurting?"

I try to adjust again, pain vibrating into my toes. Lightly touching my belly wound, I say, "My side."

"I'm on it," my mom says, standing to look at my dad. "Hey, Chick." Her tone is light, even though she hasn't been in the same room as my dad in years.

"Hey, D," he says sympathetically, wrapping her in a tight hug.

It's a beautiful sight to see them embrace; something I've wanted to witness for a long while. Getting to a time when my parents could be cordial—friendly even—has always been on my wish list. We may never be one happy family again, but if we can have something like it, in our own, hodgepodge way, I'll take it.

"Can I join you to find the nurse? I'd love a chance to talk—if you're open. Things I should have said a long time ago," my dad offers, devoted to this path of vindication.

"I'd like that," my mom says with a soft smile.

Suddenly, as I look at them, the stab wound to my torso doesn't sting quite as bad.

49

JACK

Under the Hiding Man's pseudonym and mask is a disturbed man named Eddie Moor. He's around Jack's age, and his son was just a few years younger than Jack's own. Only Eddie's son, Benji Moor, much like Eddie himself, is dead.

Jack ponders now if he could have drawn the connection between Eddie and the slayings himself, knowing he was planning to investigate Benji's family, along with Felicity's other clients, as soon as he dealt with Chick.

After Eddie was caught, Jack learned as much as he could about the man who'd spent his life between Oregon and Washington. He pored over every progress note Felicity wrote after her sessions with Benji, uncovering the ins and outs of Eddie's abuse. Jack spoke to coworkers and neighbors on Eddie's Southeast Portland street to learn who Eddie was in the real world: a misfit, a loner, a manipulator. And although he was unable to speak to Eddie himself, or his now-deceased wife, Jolene, Jack developed as clear a picture of him as he could. Each one of Eddie's victims was a cog in an obsession machine; obsession with revenge, or power, depending on the victim. An obsession with tracking and terrorizing.

At his home, police found the unmarked work van that he used to stalk Mary and Nola, and evidence of their connected security cameras was still in his vehicle. He might have also utilized the van to watch Felicity, but since she didn't have security cameras, he would have watched her the old-fashioned way—from the comfort of his van, perched outside her home. On his computer are hundreds of saved files of the women he watched for years under his security position. Jack also discovered that his *first* security position was as a patrolman in Carrie Fenton's neighborhood, getting the job months before her murder and quitting months afterward. Although he hadn't been working on the night of her death, to Jack's horror, they had interviewed him briefly back then alongside his colleagues.

Inside his house, Jack also helped uncover the candlestick Eddie Moor used to attack Harvey, whose blood was still etched in its crevices; the evidence boxes he stole from Chick's house; and Nola's childhood drawing of him. In a locked box in his closet, Jack's team found newspaper clippings from the original Hiding Man murders, alongside a typewriter that is currently being processed for a match against the letter they received after Jamie York's slaying.

Jack's team even uncovered security camera footage around the area of the pay phone used to call in the recent tips against Chick. The footage showed a man who bore a striking resemblance to Eddie Moor, and this confirmed Jack's newfound belief in Chick's framing.

Jack sits back in his office and reviews the evidence. He wishes they'd found more convincing proof that Eddie was behind the original murders. Though, based on what they *have* found, Jack and the department are confident that he was responsible, and they will continue to look for connections between him and the other victims. Today, he'll contact the rest of the victims' families to break the news, revealing the circumstantial evidence he has found to back up their beliefs. It's been four days since Eddie Moor died, and Jack has successfully been able to keep his name out of the media while he finished investigating the mountain of evidence in Eddie's home.

A knock sounds on Jack's office door, then Minnie slowly pushes it open with a white box in hand.

"Chick Strate just dropped this off for you. I told him you were on a call."

Jack releases a sigh from his dry lips. He's lost count of how many times Chick has called this week, and how many times he's hit the Ignore button. Well aware of his own mistakes in the investigation—he nearly pinned a heinous string of crimes on an innocent man—he's found it hard to apologize. Especially since the killer's masterful framing job should, in a sense, absolve Jack from any guilt of nearly sticking the wrong person. It would have happened to anyone else in his position.

He promised himself after Eddie was found that, once he closed the Hiding Man case, he would talk to Chick. Though part of him feels like he deserves an apology as well, for the lies Chick told him during the investigation, and for stealing crucial evidence boxes from Jack's lawful place of work.

With all the calls and texts, it seems Chick is ready to forgive him and likely express regret of his own, wanting to put it behind them. And Jack is almost ready to do the same.

Minnie places the box on Jack's desk and exits the room.

He strokes it with his thumb before opening it, deep in thought, and then pries off the lid of the cardboard box. Inside is a ceramic mug, attractively wrapped in emerald tissue paper. It reads Worst Detective Ever, in stark contrast to his Best Detective Ever mug from his son. Underneath it is a card, which Jack gently picks up and opens.

"I'm sorry for everything. Let's go back to being friends—for good. PS I got myself the Biggest Asshole mug."

Jack can't help but let out a soft chuckle. Pouring the coffee from his other mug into his new one, he sits back and takes a thoughtful sip.

50

NOLA

We have a special guest in the studio tonight for the twenty-fifth anniversary of our show," I say halfway through the episode. "My father, your old host and the creator of *Night Watch*: Chick Strate."

I quietly applaud his entrance alongside Harvey and Josiah, giving Harvey a wink.

It's been four weeks since I killed a man in my house, yet it feels like eons. It was hard to settle back into my home originally, knowing death had touched it. But with Harvey staying with me most nights now, and the source of my biggest fear defeated and gone for good, I don't allow anxiety to control me any longer.

"Thank you, thank you. Happy to be here. Happy to be back. Especially for such a massive milestone. I can't believe we're still going, and I couldn't be happier that my daughter has taken over as skillfully as she has," my dad says, squeezing my shoulder.

I blush at the sentiment. "Jeez. You're gonna make me cry over here." We share a chuckle.

It's a chuckle that transcends time and hurt. One we likely couldn't have shared in the same way if we didn't travel the most disturbing healing journey one could. This terrible near-death experience brought so much into the light for us. It spotlighted long-buried traumas and six-foot secrets. It let us have the tearful heart-to-heart we should have had long ago.

"Before we take some calls today, why don't you tell us about your book. I know a lot of people want to hear about it—particularly now with everything that's come out on the subject," I say.

With my permission, my dad added to his Hiding Man book. I told him it was all fair game. I'd explained everything I remember about my first encounter with him, all the way to our standoff in my house. What once was a touchy subject suddenly feels cathartic to discuss, now that I can officially put that experience behind me. Because he's never coming back. I made sure of it.

My dad describes his book and also tells listeners when they can expect a physical copy, which won't be until next year, as it goes. He ends his spiel by saying, "I couldn't have brought the book to where it is now without the help of my daughter, and the victims' loved ones. So, all proceeds will be donated to the families of Jamie, Jasey, Kendra, Carrie, Mia, Jasmine, Doniesha, Felicity, and Mary. As well as the women from Washington: Abigail, Jennifer, and Alex—which we can now confirm, thanks to new evidence, were killed by the same person."

"Let's share a moment of silence for them all," I suggest, and we do.

"Well, what do you say, Chick? Ready to take some live calls?" Harvey asks from the control room.

"You just have to promise to be nice, this time around," I whisper to him away from the microphone. "You never know who's calling." I'm painfully aware that his offending the wrong person came back to bite him—us—in the past.

"Let's do it," my dad says excitedly.

"All right, Riley from Washington, welcome to *Night Watch*," Harvey introduces.

The woman on the other end is panting, yelping. It sounds like she's running. A coldness creeps up my neck as I experience déjà vu.

"Come back here!" she hisses, breathless.

I slowly make eye contact with my dad, and then Harvey, unsure of what to say.

"Riley, what's going on?" my dad asks.

More panting. And then silence.

"Hello?" Riley says curiously, her frustration calmed. "Shoot. Am I live?"

"Yup, you're on the air," Harvey confirms.

Unexpectedly, Riley bursts into laughter. "I was chasing my dog. I didn't realize I was put through!" she says. "Man, that's embarrassing. But I have a cool UFO sighting I want to share with you guys."

I drop my head in my hands.

Although the call was initially startling, bringing me back to the terrors of last month, I can't help but laugh along with her. Maybe it's coming from a place of relief, but I'm done being scared.

I watch my dad's face flatten, post-worry. When he notices I'm laughing, he joins. And so does Harvey and Josiah, bursting into a collective, head-shaking titter.

After all I've been through, a thin coat of armor wraps around every bit of my skin. I embrace paranoia and fear, knowing those are the things that liberated me in the wake of evil, and saved countless other young women from falling victim to a sick excuse of a man who now rots below the earth.

But I will stay diligent, always keeping an eye out for the greater good. Because, just like my listeners, I am a Night Watcher.

ACKNOWLEDGMENTS

In writing *Night Watcher*, along with creating a fictional and "entertaining" tale, I longed to express the true pain experienced by loved ones and investigators as they pursue justice for the victims, the countless number of people who have wrongfully been killed by monsters. For many, there are years of uncertainty and suffering associated with unanswered questions regarding their beloved's fate. Whether they have been confirmed murdered, or are somewhere lost out there, deceased or hurting, the pain persists. In my own family, the disappearance—and presumed murder—of my aunt, Carol Woolsoncroft, my mother's sister, was a profoundly impactful loss. Though I wasn't alive when she was taken—senselessly by one of those monsters, we are confident—I recognize the unhealing scar her sudden absence has left, for those immediately involved and those of us who came after. Carol, like the fictional women in this book and the other real people who have been plucked from the earth long before anyone should be (in a way no one should be), deserved a happy and long life. And it will never be fair that she, and the others, didn't get that. In my years of researching and studying similar stories for my true crime podcast *Going West*, I've become acutely aware of the unwavering anguish—and the dogged fight to hold accountable those who have perpetrated these heinous crimes—that the ones left behind have to bear. I wanted to acknowledge that in these pages.

I love you, Mom. Your strength and sunshine through the darkness help make you so special. You and Grandma both. You're a couple of silly ladies, forever ready to brighten anyone and everyone's day. Thank you for being you, and (alongside Dad) raising me on Nancy Drew, Alfred Hitchcock, *The Twilight Zone*, and Universal Monster movies. This book wouldn't exist if you hadn't created a love of mysteries in me, along with a passion to search for truth.

Thank you to my agent, Dan Milaschewski, with UTA. You cheered me on from our very first meeting and gave me such encouragement to pursue this dream of penning a horror story. You have made me feel seen and good enough throughout this entire process, and in you, I have found not only a wonderful literary agent, but also a friend. Now, let's do it again!

Many thanks to my editor, Lyssa Keusch, with Grand Central Publishing, for fighting for this book and proving to me in your beautiful initial letter that you cared about the story. Choosing to work with you and GCP the day after my wedding, during exchanged phone calls while I sat alongside family at the Cat & Fiddle pub for a post-wedding brunch, was an exciting and emotional afternoon that I will never forget. Thank you for giving me that, and for your expertly pointed suggestions and notes that made this book what it's become. This story was greatly improved by your masterful lens.

Thank you to the team at GCP for your help along the way: Ben Sevier, Beth deGuzman, Karen Kosztolnyik, Matthew Ballast, Albert Tang, Alexander Lozano, Liz Connor, Rebecca Holland, Stacey Sharp, Taylor Navis, Laura Essex, and Danielle Thomas.

ACKNOWLEDGMENTS

Thank you to the amazing Alden Whittemore for illustrating Nola's drawing of the Hiding Man exactly as I believe she would have as a child. And to her mom, my friend, Jessie Pray, for being so supportive when I asked her, "Would you be comfortable asking Alden if she'd want to draw this scary man for me?" To which Jessie said, "She would be SO DOWN."

Finally, thank you to anyone who has listened to my podcast, *Going West*, old and new—but especially those who have championed my co-host (and husband) Heath and I for so many years (since 2018!) with your kind words and eternal weekly support; for listening to every episode, for helping give victims their voices back in a small (but mighty) way, and for calling the monsters a "piece of shit" alongside Heath to show how much we all want justice and peace for the suffering.

As I (and now Luther) would say... Don't be a stranger.

I sure won't be because there's more books (and *Going West* true crime episodes) on the way.

ABOUT THE AUTHOR

Daphne Woolsoncroft, a Los Angeles native, is the host and producer of the hit true-crime podcast *Going West*. When she's not writing or researching true-crime cases, you can find her traveling to gloomy destinations, catching the newest horror films in theaters, or reading on the couch with her plump English bulldog, Dewey.

For more information you can visit:
TikTok @daphnewool
Instagram @daphne.woolsoncroft
Facebook.com/goingwestpodcast